W9-BYG-141

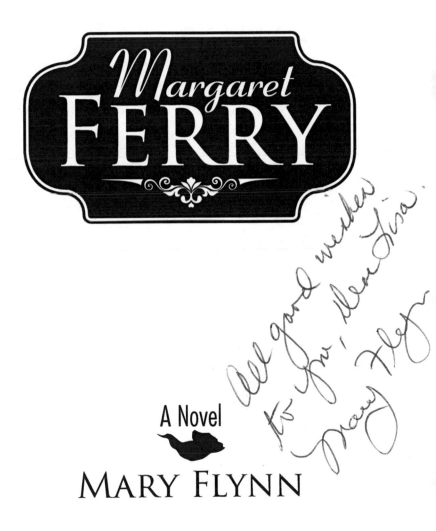

Margaret FERRY

A Novel

MARY FLYNN

All good wishes to you, dear Lisa.
Mary Flynn

To Philipp—for all the years

Acknowledgments

I would like to thank the people who helped me bring this little enterprise to fruition. My dear and very, very long-time friend, Charlotte Kane, who was the first to hear my idea and listened over time with her typical bright encouragement and support. Jhon Usmanov, the historian and genealogist at Greenwood Cemetery in Brooklyn, who was so generous with his time and knowledge. My patient and astute editor, Marsha Butler, who (patiently, I say again) led me through all the bumps and dings. Kerry Fastenau, poet, author and friend, who came to the rescue with her knowledge of Massapequa Park. My wonderful colleagues at the Mount Dora, Florida Writers Group, who just so happen to know a lot and made me the beneficiary of their great wisdom—Claudia Caporale, Linda Barbosa, Bettie Nebergall, Steve Leitschuh, Dallas Gorham, Lisa Anders, Jake Beahan, Joanne Jacquart, Kate Maier and Vickey Cheney. My truly extraordinary graphic designer, Michael Butler. And to all the friends who showed interest for a very long time, and will be happy to realize there really is a book.

"How far that little candle throws his beams!
So shines a good deed in a weary world."

—Shakespeare, *The Merchant of Venice*

PROLOGUE

Bursa, Turkey—June 1920

When at last it was her turn, she stepped toward the platform, her heart drumming in her ears. In the growing darkness, beneath the sprawling canopy of sycamore and chestnut, she saw ahead the scattered stream of those who had gone before her moving slowly toward the open field and the large gray tent lit by flickering votives.

Her legs were less steady now—she had come so far, traveled so arduously. Against the wishes and pleas of family, she had journeyed with more than a dozen others on this month-long pilgrimage—the painfully crowded, days-long train ride from Milan through Venice, Trieste and Belgrade to arrive, finally, in Istanbul. Then the grueling ragtag caravan of rickety Turkish wagons, clumsy and halting, skirting east along the Marmara, the air thick with the mixed sweetness and acidity of olive, salt-cedar, Greek strawberry and mastic resin and the pungent miasma of people too long in close contact. None of it mattered in this mystical setting where the last shimmer of sunlight caught for a moment the gold of a ring, a metal button, a dark eye glistening tearful. Only the plaintive sobs and murmured prayers broke the sacred silence of the balmy Anatolian twilight.

Those in line behind her stood back one from the other, heads bowed, a trail of dark-clothed figures appearing like uneven fence posts in the meadow long trampled flat.

The young seminarian reached toward her to guide her up the wooden steps and to remind her of the instructions that she and the others in her group had received from the Bishop's office prior to the pilgrimage: she must not touch the statue; she could leave only an appropriate small object such as a medal or a flower at the foot of the statue; no photographic devices were allowed; if she chose to speak, she must do so only in a whisper; she would have three minutes.

Time meant nothing now. She followed like an expectant but wary child being dressed for the first day of school. As he had done with the others, the seminarian helped her with the stethoscope-like apparatus, having cleansed the earpieces with alcohol. Then he made sure they were properly in place. He touched her arm and gave her a look as if to ask if she were comfortable and ready, their glances intersecting at innocence and desolation. Could this young man possibly have any idea of the burdens borne by the hearts of those who passed here, his warm, youthful eyes still shining with noble purpose, unaware? What had he lost, sheltered from the scorched reality of war? Had anyone been taken from him forever? Forever. Pray Lord, not forever.

She made the sign of the cross, stiffened her shoulders, and took a deep breath, her nostrils filling with the rich night air. Then, with delicacy and reverence, she lifted the fine white lace shawl to cover her head in this holiest of holy places.

She dipped her head respectfully to the seminarian, who placed his hand under her elbow and with measured footing walked her around to the simple stone alcove that housed the statue. Her heartbeat quickened as she approached the large marble sculpture, seeing at first only the smooth white feet of "The Lady" whose miracle had defied the logic and scrutiny of scholars, theologians and archaeologists the world over.

The seminarian took the end of the listening device and

gently placed it against the cold, ancient marble breast. Slowly, the woman lifted her face to the full beauty of what stood before her at this, the Shrine of the Most Sorrowful Heart of Mary. She trembled at what she was hearing at last for herself…a heart…beating…as surely as her own. *Oh, most blessed wonder of wonders.*

Using the end of the shawl, she caressed the hard, fixed, outstretched hands before her as she silently prayed, *Ave Maria, piena di grazia, il Signore è con te. Tu sei benedetta fra le donne e benedetto è il frutto del tuo seno, Gesù. Santa Maria, Madre di Dio, prega per noi peccatori, adesso e nell'ora della nostra morte. Amen.*

Since the war in Europe ended, she had asked…pleaded… for a miracle a thousand times, ten times a thousand. Could it be denied her now before the mother who knew herself what it was like to lose her precious child? What would this blessed woman have given to have her son returned to her? Surely, she understood Libera Pascone's inconsolable suffering.

Muffling her sobs in the lace of her shawl, she whispered her prayers for intercession. She had nothing to leave but her petition. Here in this faraway land, in this fleeting moment so utterly astonishing and powerful and unfathomable, she would at last surrender in prayer, the return of her beloved Giovanna.

Book One

CHAPTER ONE

Brooklyn—Spring 1953

Margaret Ferry fidgeted in her chair outside the principal's office, fearing the worst. Her geography book lay unopened in her lap—who cared about the lava fields of Iceland, when so much was happening right here at St. Aloysius. All day long, she had worried about Peter, Stanny and Mikhail. What if they were sent away like the others? She laid the book on the chair beside her and glanced across the mint green plaster walls at the American flag on its brass pole midway down the hall. Pictures of saints. President Eisenhower. Pope Pius XII. Somebody could help, couldn't they?

She stood, then sat again, restless. The aromas of peanut butter sandwiches and vegetable soup lingered in the air from the basement lunchroom. She drew a deep breath. What was taking so long? Sister would remind her to practice patience, but that was harder than memorizing the dates of wars and treaties.

When the door finally opened, Margaret sat taller, smoothing the pleats of her plaid skirt—a rumpled uniform would never get her off to a good start with Sister. Two children came out, followed by a plump, round-faced woman wearing a flowery dress and a blue print kerchief tied in a knot under her chin. Margaret knew the little Russian boy from one of the lower grades; she had seen him in the lunchroom and playing in the schoolyard. His family had not been there even a year. They must have been so happy when they first arrived in America and at St. Aloysius. Now they all looked sad, including Sister Bernadine, who followed close behind with that tight, thin smile of hers, like a line you could draw in play dough with the tip of a pencil—the kind of smile you put on when there is really nothing at all to smile about.

Margaret felt sorry for the woman and her children, and for Sister, knowing how hard her job must be now that Monsignor Carnavan had taken over as pastor. She didn't believe Sister could be happy about any of it. Sister often looked stern, but that was just to scare everybody into behaving, mostly the boys. She only had to give Billy Orr that stern side-glance of hers and you could tell he wouldn't even think about blowing spitballs at the ceiling lamps in the hall.

Sister had always been especially kind to the Russian children. They didn't have as much as other kids. When there was milk left over, she let them take it home along with extra treats, but once Monsignor arrived after Christmas, things started changing in the worst possible way. Why did he have to come in the first place; weren't they doing just fine without him?

Margaret waited as Sister, hands clasped in front of her, watched the woman and her children make their way along the polished grey linoleum toward the outside doors of the school, the sound of their footsteps like a slow drumbeat. When they were gone, she waved Margaret in.

"How were your studies today, Margaret?"

"Fine, thank you, Sister." Margaret knew she had to pick just the right moment for her protest.

The room's usual smell of damp wood and kerosene had faded in the warm spring air coming through the ceiling-high windows. Sister Bernadine went to the corner of her large wood desk, picked up a sheet of paper, and handed it to Margaret.

"Here is a list of names. I need you to pull out the file for each one. Since you're very good at alphabetizing, you shouldn't have any problem finding them and keeping them in order. I'd like all of the remaining files, please, moved from the old file cabinet to the new."

Margaret nodded, noticing that the cabinet wasn't new at all, just new to Sister's office. Nothing in the school was new. Sister glanced up at the black-rimmed wall clock with its swift-moving second hand. "You won't have time to do it all today. Just be sure to give me the first eight folders for my meeting with Monsignor at 3:30. That's only ten minutes, Margaret, so focus. You can finish the rest tomorrow."

Margaret couldn't help noticing the dust particles floating in the sunlight above Sister's head. "Yes, Sister." She paused for a moment, then asked, "Are you and Monsignor going to talk about the Russian families? They're not all going to be sent away, are they, Sister?"

Sister Bernadine looked up from her papers without changing expression. "That is not a question for an eleven-year-old."

"I'll be twelve soon. I'm almost in high school."

"High school is more than a year away, Margaret. Just mind your task. And I do wish you would see to it that your hair is combed. What must your aunt think when you arrive home each day with your hair a tangled mess? God may have given you looks, child, but he does expect a little cooperation."

"Yes, Sister. Can you put in a word for Peter and Stanny? Mikhail too?"

"Margaret, I'll hear no more of this." The wimple of Sister's headpiece cut tight around her smooth, plain face, forcing out a knob of pale flesh under her chin. Some of the boys said that nuns shaved their heads and wore funny underwear. One year on Holy Saturday, when Margaret and Junie had brought their little bottles to the churchyard to get the newly blessed holy water, they went farther than they should have and saw a clothesline full of light gray undershirts and bloomers, like cut-down long johns. The caretaker chased them off.

Margaret took the stack of files to the small wooden worktable in the corner. When she was younger, she would wobble in her Aunt Etta's sling-back high heels, pretending to be a secretary in a big company in the City, stopping now and then to smoke a crayon cigarette. But she wasn't a child anymore and this wasn't pretending. Sister Bernadine had come to trust her with her office and her papers, a very grown-up thing to Margaret's way of thinking, and it made her feel proud.

She had Uncle Mike to thank for it. He had always corrected her grammar and made her look up any word she asked the meaning of. He read all her book reports and had her redo the ones he could tell she'd hurried through. She didn't like the extra work, but she did like all the A's she got for doing it. "Struggle early and you'll struggle less later on," he'd said more than once.

As Margaret looked over Sister's list, she noticed that once again all of the names were Russian—Aksakov, Andreyushkin, Avdeyev, Biryukov—and knew these must be the families Monsignor had already sent away or maybe was about to.

She was pulling the last file when she heard Monsignor's voice. She had thought Sister would meet with him at the rectory office across the street. Even without hearing him speak, she would have known him by the heaviness of his walk, which made her imagine he might knock over everything in his path. Sister went out to meet him in the hallway, but Margaret couldn't help hearing their conversation.

"Did you make it clear to them?" Monsignor asked. "Granted, you need to be polite, dear Sister Bernadine, but you must be firm."

As they entered the office, Margaret saw Sister motion to Monsignor that someone else was present. She had even cleared her throat, but Margaret realized that since he wasn't looking at Sister, and probably had no intention of listening to her, he didn't even notice. She knew it must be wrong to think of a monsignor as a bully, but she couldn't help thinking that's exactly what he was.

"St. Vincent's will gratefully welcome them," he was saying, "and I don't want to have to explain things to the Bishop, as last time. Please, Sister, do not put me in that position again."

She finally had to touch his sleeve. "Excuse me, Monsignor. That will be all, Margaret. Just leave the files."

Monsignor Carnavan turned sharply, a surprised look on his face. Margaret had not been this close to him before. He had a thick face and neck, and a bulky body in his black priest's suit with just that bit of white at the collar that reminded her of a penguin—maybe that was why he shifted from side to side as he walked. The very last thing she wanted to do right now was laugh.

She handed Sister the files and curtsied. Without smiling, Monsignor gave a slight nod. She paused when she reached the door. *Did she dare say anything to him about the Russians?* She could get into terrible trouble. But this might be her only chance. Her stomach flipped just like the first time she jumped off the high board at Sunset Pool. Uncle Mike would say, "Stay out of it—this is grown-up business." Aunt Etta would tell her it was sometimes better just to hold our tongues. Aunt Lolly believed we should find the good in things. Margaret turned and faced them. "The Russian families are very nice, Monsignor. Really. They're just like everybody else. I wish you would let them stay. They haven't done anything wrong." As soon as the words were out of her mouth, she knew she was in for it.

Sister Bernadine stepped forward, wide-eyed and tight-lipped, as if by squeezing her own mouth shut, Margaret would squeeze hers shut as well. "Margaret, please run along."

"It's all right, Sister. Margaret seems to be a bright, respectful young lady. Tell me, Margaret, what do you know about Russian immigrants?"

"I know that they are kind and polite, Monsignor, and the ones in my class seem shy, but they're fun to play with and they're good at geography and arithmetic." She spoke quickly to get in as much as she could. "Peter and Mikhail's mother is very nice. She baked a special Russian cake I can't pronounce for the whole class at Easter time. Their father is very nice too. I met him once. He's a carpenter. And Stanny..."

"A carpenter who can't find work." Monsignor tilted his head and smiled. Margaret had seen a movie where a man had the same kind of smile, but he had his men shoot the horse anyway.

"And do you notice," he went on, "that they wear the same clothing much of the time? And that their shoes are quite worn? And what you cannot notice, of course, dear girl, is that they are late with their tuition. Did you know that? Do you know that poor people who have difficulty speaking English and keeping a job and paying their bills cause an entire parish community to suffer? You're about to make your confirmation, are you not?

"Yes, Monsignor."

"Well, then, you're a big enough girl to understand certain realities of life."

Margaret could see Sister Bernadine standing silent behind Monsignor, head bowed, her hands clasped so rigidly in front of her that she had squeezed her fingers pink. Margaret would definitely be scrubbing desktops and clapping erasers for a week. But from the look on Sister's face, it might be even worse. Still, she'd had to take the chance. Maybe no one ever bothered telling Monsignor how nice the Russian families were.

"But if that's true, Monsignor," she said, without changing expression, "why are they okay for St. Vincent's?"

"Enough now, Margaret." Sister's tone was still sharp, but

Monsignor put his hand up and calmly responded in a voice as heavy as his footsteps.

"The Russians will fit in very nicely at our beloved St. Vincent's—just not here. It's a very poor match. You can see that."

No, she couldn't see that. She would never see that. "I think God would want us to help them and be nice to them." Maybe she wouldn't be in as much trouble now that she'd mentioned God.

Monsignor took a step forward, his fake smile gone. "Perhaps you would agree that as a Monsignor of the Church, I might have a better idea of what God wants than a sixth-grader."

Margaret was silent for a moment. There were times when even she knew when to stop. "Good afternoon, Monsignor, Sister." She turned to leave. She did not curtsy for fear they might take it as a sign that she was agreeing with him. She would never agree with him about this. She thought of what her Aunt Lolly once had told her, "Knowing *about* God is not the same as *knowing* God." Margaret had not understood it at the time, but now she thought this must be exactly what Lolly meant.

All the way home, she felt torn between being angry at Monsignor and feeling excited that he had spoken to her as if she were all grown-up, almost like a real conversation. The very idea of it gave her butterflies, making her forget for a moment that she was in big trouble with Sister Bernadine, and maybe in even bigger trouble with Aunt Etta and Uncle Mike, if they found out.

CHAPTER TWO

Monsignor had asked her a question, and let her speak, even when Sister didn't want her to. She had no idea what her punishment was going to be, but she was sure Sister would start out first thing in the morning with a serious talk about being impudent—one of Sister's favorite words. Still, she couldn't wait to stop by Junie's house so they could go around the corner to the candy store for a chocolate soda or a two-cent plain. Margaret had lots to tell her.

The candy store occupied a single storefront on a busy avenue of three-story apartment buildings that housed cold-water flats with stores below and fire escapes facing the street. Its entrance was marked by a red and white Coca-Cola ice chest, a great metal box larger than a steamer trunk that could be seen nearly two blocks away.

Mr. and Mrs. Wortman owned the store, but no one ever called it Wortman's the way they called the bread store Fiorenza's or the fabric store Meyer's. It was just "the candy store." Along with a section for penny candy, and a fancy glass case filled with two-cent French crèmes, the candy store carried cigarettes, magazines, racing forms and six different daily newspapers that had both a morning and evening edition. The worn wooden and glass door opened and closed constantly with the flow of regulars who rarely stayed longer than it took to pay and go or use one of the two phone booths at the back. But Margaret liked to stay a while when she could.

The store smelled of cream soda, newsprint and fresh sweet cigar tobacco, along with what she liked to call the mellow aroma of age. She had read those words once and thought they fit the candy store perfectly. What Margaret liked most were the ornate painted tin ceiling and the eight counter stools that ran from the front of the store to the back and were covered in worn green leather. She liked sitting up front, especially when Mr. Wortman wasn't around. He always hurried her along to finish, the way he hurried all the kids who liked to sit outside on top of the Coca-Cola chest. Mrs. Wortman would rush outside with her broom as if to sweep them away. She was calmer than her husband and about as cranky. Margaret had always thought it was nice that people got along with Mr. and Mrs. Wortman, crankiness and all.

"Tell me everything," Junie said. They had decided it was too close to suppertime for a soda, settling instead for a few little jelly watermelon slices covered in sugar.

Margaret told Junie about her conversation with Monsignor Carnavan and how angry Sister Bernadine looked.

"Oh, Mar." Junie laughed. "You are going to be doing trash baskets and erasers for a month. And do you know why? Because you were..." They looked at each other, laughing.

"Impudent!" they shouted.

Mr. Wortman was on them instantly, calling to them from behind the counter. "That's all now," he said, waving the damp, gray counter rag in front of them. "Out please. Always the silly girls, disrupting everything."

"We're sorry, Mr. Wortman," Junie said. "We'll be more quiet."

"You're always sorry, but never more quiet," Mrs. Wortman said, raising an eyebrow. Her Jewish accent was as thick as her husband's. "You know he's right—silliness. And why candy before supper? Your mother will blame us for selling it to you."

Margaret and Junie said goodbye pleasantly enough. They

knew better than to be disrespectful. Word would get home before they did. Besides, Margaret always felt a little sorry for Mr. and Mrs. Wortman, believing the stories that something terrible had happened to them a long time ago. No one seemed to know exactly what it was or, at least, no one ever talked about it.

The afternoon was cooler now and they were grateful for the sweaters that had been too bulky earlier in the day when the springtime sun had felt so good and at times even too hot, an almost impossible thought after such a long cold winter.

"We're going to get my confirmation dress tonight," Junie said. "I want one that goes to here." She pointed to the middle of her calf. "But I don't think my mother will let me get that kind."

"Mine is only a little bit below my knees. Aunt Etta says I'm not allowed to have a longer one till graduation."

Junie shook her head slowly. "I'm scared I won't be ready for the bishop's questions. It's less than two weeks away, but I'm still afraid I won't give him the right answers."

"I'm doubly scared, knowing how hard Peter and Mikhail and Stanny practiced with us. They might not even be here if Monsignor sends them away."

They turned the corner into a light wind and never heard him coming up behind them, speeding past them on his bike, close enough to tear the purse from Junie's shoulder and send it slapping into a puddle at the curb. They shrieked as Margaret's books tumbled from her arms and scattered across the sidewalk.

"Johnny Herring, I'm telling on you," Margaret yelled, but the boy just rode on, looking back only to laugh and stick out his tongue.

Mr. Piro, who had been sweeping around the wooden bins outside his produce store, hurried over. "That boy again," he said, shaking his fist in the air. "If I ever see his father, I'll tell him something. I wish I knew where he lived. I would go right now."

Mr. Piro helped Margaret collect her books, and handed Junie her purse, brushing away the dirt and wetness with the back of his apron. "This is a nice one, Junie. It's okay. Your mama will be able to clean it better. Don't worry."

"I could scream," Junie said, her tears building.

"Well," Mr. Piro said, "you already did that. So, now you'll just have your mama clean the purse and you'll be happy again. Yes?"

"I guess so," Junie said, wiping her eyes. And off they went.

———◄◆►———

"Tell me you didn't have a soda," Aunt Etta said, as she set the kitchen table. "Your uncle got home early and made your favorite."

"White stew!" Margaret nearly sang the words. She headed straight for the stove. "I smelled it coming up the steps."

"Dangling participle," came Uncle Mike's full round voice from the parlor. "The stew did not come up the stairs."

"Just a taste." Margaret called, although she knew he wouldn't let her off that easy. Sometimes she was happy Uncle Mike was a newspaper writer, sometimes not.

"First, the right way," he said, coming into the kitchen.

"I could smell it as I came up the steps."

Uncle Mike gave the smallest hint of a smile, lifted a china teacup off a hook in the cupboard above the stove and scooped out some of the stew.

"It doesn't matter how good you look..." he started.

Margaret and Aunt Etta turned to each other, laughing. "... an open mouth is an open book."

"And speaking of looks," Etta said, "could you not for once comb your hair? Did you even touch a comb to it since leaving the house this morning?"

Margaret knew she hadn't; there were just too many other things to think about. She gave her aunt a hug. "You're always so beautiful, Aunt Etta. I want to be just like you someday."

"Not at this rate." Etta looked into Margaret's eyes as she stroked the girl's hair. "You have such nice brown hair, Margaret. If only you'd comb it. Promise you'll try harder."

Bits of too-hot vegetables danced around the inside of her mouth. "I'll try," Margaret said awkwardly.

They lived one flight up in a neat Park Slope brownstone that housed an apartment on the first floor, which was temporarily unoccupied. Their front door opened into an oversized kitchen, with windows overlooking neatly trimmed backyards, most of which had fruit trees and vegetable gardens through summer.

They spent their evenings in the parlor, a large square room with creamy beige walls, mahogany furniture polished to a gleam, floral slipcovers, and a thick burgundy patterned rug. A Motorola television set in a dark wood cabinet stood against one wall and on the other, positioned between two windows that overlooked the street, a burl wood floor model Emerson radio. Uncle Mike had surprised them with the television the Christmas before; the Emerson radio had been there for as long as Margaret could remember, the family's gathering spot for favorite shows like *The Shadow* and *Fibber McGee and Molly*, Walter Winchell's newscasts, and, of course, Aunt Etta's favorite, the low background strains of *Martin Block and The Make Believe Ballroom*.

After she had finished her homework, Margaret went into the parlor. *The Million Dollar Movie* would be coming on soon and they would all watch it together—*Mrs. Miniver*, one of her favorites. But right now, Uncle Mike sat in his wing-backed chair, half listening to the news on WOR while focused on the latest issue of *Life* magazine with Lucille Ball, Desi Arnaz and their two children on the cover.

Aunt Etta occupied one end of the sofa, crocheting lace

edges on another of the white cotton handkerchief squares she liked to tuck away in her dresser to give as gifts throughout the year.

Margaret sat down on the rug in front of the radio to cut brown paper bags into new book covers. It was her favorite place, whether in winter when the house was warm and cozy or now with the curtains fluttering in the open windows.

They talked so much over supper that it was too late to go for a walk. Their conversations were always special to Margaret. Sometimes Mike talked about one of the stories he was working on for the paper, not the secret ones, of course, but the ones he was free to tell, like the series they were planning to run about the good job the animal shelters had done rescuing stray dogs from the freezing winter cold.

Sometimes Etta told about her day volunteering over at the 8th Street Armory. Following the war, it was used mostly for tours and day programs for the National Guard, along with school concerts and fairs.

This evening, Margaret had told them everything—well, nearly everything. She told them about Johnny Herring and Junie's purse and Mr. Piro's kindness. She didn't mention Mr. and Mrs. Wortman making them leave the candy store or that she was in trouble for challenging Monsignor—she would find herself in even bigger trouble.

"Uncle Mike, do you think it's fair to make all the Russian children leave school?"

"It doesn't matter what I think. Monsignor is making room for all the kids moving into those big fancy apartment buildings two blocks up from the school. There's money there."

"I don't understand," Margaret said, "why everybody going to St. Aloysius has to be rich?"

Mike and Etta laughed.

"Well, we hope that part isn't true," Etta said, "because three-quarters of St. Aloysius would be going to St. Vincent's, you included."

Margaret knew, of course, that they weren't rich. She just never thought of her life in terms of what anyone had. She had enough of everything she wanted. Not a bike, though, but that wasn't because of money—Aunt Etta worried about the traffic along the avenue, which was why they'd never had a dog either. "So why can't the Russian people go to St. Aloysius if they're no different?"

"But they are different, in their way." Mike closed the magazine and set it on the lamp table beside him. "A lot of them have less than most of us and there are more and more of them coming into the country right now, so it's hard for them to get work. Monsignor Carnavan wants them to be able to carry their load."

"What do you mean?"

"He means pay their full tuition." Etta rested her crochet hook in her lap. "We're not saying it's right, Mar, or that we agree."

"Can't somebody at church help them? Maybe one of the other priests."

"Monsignor Carnavan is in charge," Mike said, "so he can do as he pleases. He can have whatever kind of parish he wants. Running a parish is like running a business, and Monsignor has to make sure business is good. We can disagree with how he goes about things, but he's in charge." He leaned forward in his chair. "And I don't want you bringing this up all the time at school. You'll get a bad name for yourself and that can only bring trouble. Understood?"

"It's hard sometimes," Margaret said, fully aware that his advice was a little bit late.

"Understood?"

She put her head down, reluctant. "Understood," she said, realizing she had just been forced to make Uncle Mike a promise she had already broken.

CHAPTER THREE

Margaret lay there, restless, unable to sleep, the curtains fluttering from the breeze coming through the bedroom window. She thought about everything that had happened that day. She thought about her confirmation and the idea of being more grown-up than she had ever been in her life. There would be a party with her aunts and uncles and cousins. Aunt Lolly would be there, a visit Margaret eagerly awaited, but one that always made Aunt Etta nervous. Margaret was sure it was because of Lolly's handicap, which sometimes caused her to be unpredictable.

Everyone loved Lolly, but it did seem true that, whenever she was around, things somehow went wrong, like the time she was visiting and went to the park for a few hours in the afternoon. When she returned to their house, she had a bag lady with her whom she had invited to dinner. Even Lolly had to admit that the woman had "the mightiest aroma," which was the worst kind of remark Lolly would ever think of making about a person.

The woman stayed through dinner, never removing the shabby wool wrap that covered her oversized man's wool coat. The only two teeth in her mouth that touched had a small piece of silver foil sticking out from between them. Later, before leaving, the woman used the bathroom. Aunt Etta discreetly managed to check before the woman got out of the house and was gratified to see that not a thing was out of place. She had not thought to check the laundry hamper and later discovered that all of their dirty clothes were gone.

Margaret had never known Lolly any other way but with her slight limp and bit of weakness in her right arm, caused by a stroke years before. However handicapped she was, there was no limit to her bright spirit and her joy for life and for others. Margaret saw a certain beauty in Lolly's slightly crooked smile, a certain confidence in the way she held her head up with that glint in her eye that anyone could see came right from a good and merry heart. Lolly, the youngest of Etta's three sisters, had an oddness that endeared her to others but caused Etta anxiety. Etta was never comfortable with Margaret spending a lot of time in Lolly's company.

As she sometimes did before falling asleep, Margaret opened the middle drawer of her nightstand and glanced at the picture of her parents—Uncle Mike's brother, Ensign Daniel Ferry, there in his uniform, his arm around the shoulder of Margaret's mother, her beautiful large brim hat shading her smile from the afternoon sun near Lake Skancateles in upstate New York.

It was the only photo she had of them, taken on their wedding day, just before her dad went off to his first tour of duty. They looked so happy. Just like Aunt Etta and Uncle Mike. Just like Aunt Jo and Aunt Rae and their husbands. Thinking about it made her feel bad for Lolly. She wondered if Lolly had ever had a boyfriend, if she had ever been in love. She often wanted to ask Aunt Etta about that, and so many other things, but never found a time when it seemed like a good idea. There were certain things Etta did not like to talk about. One was the death of Margaret's parents, whom Margaret had never known. The other was Lolly.

There were always so many people to pray for. Tonight, she said a prayer for Mr. and Mrs. Wortman, who were too cranky most of the time but maybe for good reason, and for Mr. Piro and even Johnny Herring, the neighborhood bad boy, who had once tipped over an entire bin of Mr. Piro's apples.

She thought about the sad look on the face of the Russian woman turned away from school with her children. She didn't know what to pray for Sister Bernadine and Monsignor. It occurred to her that maybe no one prayed for them, and so they ended up needing it the most. She smiled, thinking again about Lolly, who always prayed for dead movie stars because she couldn't imagine that anyone else did. "And a special prayer," Lolly had once said during Thanksgiving grace, "for Rudolph Valentino and Jean Harlow." She said it with such sincerity that no one even thought of laughing.

She thought especially about Monsignor Carnavan, and had to fight the idea that he was such a big silly man, being so stern and formal and pompous. And mean. She supposed it might be a sin not to like him. "Find the good," Lolly always said. But that wasn't an easy thing to do when it came to Monsignor. He wasn't anything like their old pastor, such a friendly priest, who had played basketball in the schoolyard with the kids, coaching the boys and telling the girls how pretty they looked. He was the only pastor she had ever known before Monsignor showed up. He'd been there all through her years at St. Aloysius. Like Sister Bernadine and the other nuns, he treated the Russian children with kindness and had even learned a little of their language. "Dosvedanya," he would call out to them at the end of the school day, making them smile. Well, if pastors got to leave, maybe Monsignor himself would go before very long—that would make a good prayer. She really did have to ask for forgiveness for upsetting Sister Bernadine and for talking back to Monsignor, especially for thinking of him as a penguin. She would try very hard to be truly sorry about that.

Margaret turned over in the dark, and with Aunt Lolly, Monsignor Carnavan and the poor sad Russian woman tumbling through her restless thoughts, offered up one final prayer for it seemed to her that so much more could go wrong.

——◆·——

When the bell sounded, Margaret stayed in her seat as her classmates left for the day. Sister Bernadine had given her a week-long detention—*For the demonstration of impudent behavior in the presence of a Monsignor of the Holy Catholic Church* was the wording on the slip of paper that Sister only mildly threatened to put in Margaret's file if she continued to misbehave.

As it turned out, detention was the least of it. Mikhail and Peter and Stanny were gone. Just like that. There had not been a chance for anyone to say goodbye or to let them know how sorry everyone was. Mrs. Dorokhov and Mrs. Gachev had come by at lunchtime to pick up their things, and Margaret couldn't help overhearing some of their conversation with Sister Angelus in the schoolyard. She'd been out clapping erasers at the time, another weeklong assignment from Sister Bernadine.

"I am so very sorry," she had heard Sister Angelus say, as the two mothers, in tears, talked about the money they could hardly afford to pay for round trip bus fare every day to St. Vincent's—public school was not a consideration. Margaret thought how awful to come to America with such high hopes and then be treated so badly.

She looked up from her workbook to see Sister Bernadine standing in the doorway of the classroom. *Did Sister expect her to say something?* Margaret believed she had probably said enough already. Sister approached and stood in front of Margaret's desk, her hands tucked into the opposite sleeves of her habit.

"Are you satisfied?" she asked in a quiet voice.

So, detention wasn't going to be enough. Sister would lecture her, the part that Margaret would hate the most because it proved how disappointed Sister was in her.

"I was only trying to tell the Monsignor how nice the Russian people are. He doesn't want them to stay here and it isn't fair. Is it, Sister? Do you think it's fair? You like Mikhail and Peter and Stanny. They've been my friends and Junie's too for such a long time. Look at how many others have already left."

"Lots of things in life aren't fair, Margaret, but they go on just the same, no matter how we feel about them. At your age there is no point getting into trouble over this."

Margaret kept her eyes down as she made short mindless pencil strokes on the work page. Why did everything always end up being about age? Too young for this, too old for that, always the wrong age for doing the things she wanted to do the most.

"You mustn't do anything like that again." Sister's voice was steady and soft, but in the back of her mind Margaret heard Monsignor's words: *You must be firm, dear Sister.* "Monsignor was polite with you, but he may not be in the future if you bother him again with this."

Margaret felt her heart skip, thinking of how Uncle Mike had warned her about bringing this up to Monsignor. Wasn't there one thing that was fair anymore?

"And you put *me* in a very difficult situation."

Margaret looked up. She had never intended to do anything that would hurt Sister. "I'm sorry." Her face was hot; she felt the pressure in her eyes that comes before tears.

"Do you understand that sometimes being sorry is not enough?"

Like some of the other nuns, Sister Bernadine's plain look had a loveliness about it, but lately it appeared to hold more sadness. Margaret couldn't remember the last time she had seen Sister with a truly happy smile.

"I understand," was all Margaret could say.

There was a long silence.

Margaret watched Sister walk slowly to the front of the room, head bowed in thought, then circle back and half-sit against one of the desks. "I remember feeling about the same as you when I was a girl."

This took Margaret by surprise. She had never heard Sister talk about her own life.

Sister went on. "The problem was quite different, but I believe my feelings were probably as strong as yours."

Margaret put down her pencil. "What about?"

"Well, in the school that I went to, girls were not allowed to participate in sports. You might find this hard to believe, Margaret, but some people had the idea that it was inappropriate for young ladies to jump around and sweat in public."

Margaret's eyes grew wide; she could hardly fathom the idea. She knew it had to be a long time ago—Sister was older than Aunt Etta. She was sure of it.

"I know that may sound ridiculous, Margaret, but…well… there you are? Of course, I just couldn't stand still for anything so unfair, so I decided to write a proclamation." Sister's mouth curled up in a half smile. "That was a word we learned in History class. So, I decided to proclaim how unfair it was that girls could not do athletic activities or sweat in public, as boys could, and I wrote it up as a petition for all the girls to sign. Some of the boys even signed it. They thought it was great fun, but it was very important to me, and I believe I might have been as serious about it as you are about your Russian friends. Mrs. Hanneman, our principal, said I was clever and industrious and showed excellent initiative. She actually apologized for the fact that it would not change the school's position." Sister shrugged. "We can give it our all, Margaret, and still not get the outcome that we're so sure is the right one."

Margaret nodded her understanding. She liked Sister's way of explaining things. Uncle Mike was the same way. Whenever they finished talking, things were always clearer.

"Monsignor's in charge, Margaret. He doesn't do things the way we're used to, but he is pastor now, and he has his own ideas and he's entitled to them. We must remember that."

"Even if they're bad ideas?"

"I am not in a position to judge Monsignor's actions, Margaret. Nor are you."

Margaret fingered the corners of her work page. "But what if you talked with him? He might listen to you, and change his mind."

"Why is this so important to you, Margaret? What do you think it is that makes you care so much about it?"

Margaret shrugged. She had never thought about it. "I guess it's because people should be treated the same way. They shouldn't feel that nobody likes or wants them because they're different or poor or have more troubles than somebody else. Everyone has goodness in them. That's what my Aunt Lolly always says."

Sister Bernadine stepped forward and put her hand on Margaret's shoulder. "I truly agree with your Aunt Lolly about that, Margaret. Keep those wonderful ideas," she said, looking squarely into Margaret's eyes, "you of the golden heart."

"Then you'll talk to Monsignor?"

Sister shook her head. "I'm afraid not. You'll just have to trust that talking to Monsignor would not have the outcome you want. I can promise you that. Sometimes when there are people with great authority and strong intentions for what they want to accomplish, it can be…well…at the least, foolish to try to stand in their way. This is a challenging time for others beside you, Margaret. You had one conversation with Monsignor, but he is someone I have to work with every day. I am bound to follow his policies for the school, so please think twice before you add to the burden."

Margaret put her head down, ashamed.

"You're young and haven't had much experience with the ways of people. Go easy, child. Remember that prayer can be your greatest weapon." Sister looked at her watch. "You have only fifteen minutes left. Do some homework." She paused in the doorway. "Trust and pray."

After Sister left, Margaret looked around to see where the odd hissing sound was coming from. She saw Junie peeking around the inside doorway from the next classroom. She could always count on Junie to be nearby. They had started school on the same day and had been friends all the years since. Junie was fun to be with even if she sometimes had trouble knowing when not to be silly. She too had had a Russian friend, Liliana, who was sent over to St. Vincent's a few weeks earlier, but Junie didn't think you lose a friend just because they go to another school. Margaret knew better. Stanny, Peter and Mikhail lived in a different neighborhood; she would probably never see them again.

"I told you Sister was going to punish you," Junie said in a loud whisper. "How many days did you get?"

"Five." Margaret slowly traced a wider and wider circle on a blank notebook page with her pencil.

"Well, you want to hear some good news? I got my dress last night. It's really pretty."

Margaret kept her eyes and her pencil on the workbook page without responding. Her circles grew wider and darker.

"What's the matter?" Junie asked. "Did Sister really scare you? I couldn't hear everything she said."

"I want to stop by Panyi's on the way home. Can you come with me?"

Panyi owned the penny candy store on Tenth Street. Unlike Wortman's store, Panyi's had no counter, soda fountain, stools, phones, newspapers, cigarettes or cold drinks. What it had, in addition to the biggest selection of penny candy, was the biggest selection of school supplies, including shelf upon shelf of Skrip indelible blue, black and blue/black ink.

The Polish woman had a wonderful way with all the kids who came into her store, but Margaret and Junie knew that they were two of her favorites. They often helped her shovel the sidewalk after a heavy snowfall, and watered the potted flowers outside her door in spring.

Panyi gave them extra Mary Janes and jelly bars, and once even a whole Bonamo's Turkish Taffy each. Today, Margaret had a favor to ask—would Panyi please let her have four sheets of fine white bond paper and one envelope, well, two...just in case she made a mistake? She wanted this to be perfect. She would not be able to pay Panyi for two more days, when she received her allowance. Panyi would smile and nod her agreement.

"Why are we going to Panyi's?" Junie asked.

"I'll tell you on the way." Margaret walked over to the bookstand at the front of the classroom. She removed the large Webster's dictionary and brought it back to her desk. Tonight she would say a prayer for Mikhail and Peter and Stanny, along with an extra prayer for Panyi and Sister Bernadine, but right now all she wanted to do was look up the proper spelling of "proclamation."

CHAPTER FOUR

Mike Ferry pushed open the creaky iron gate and headed up the walkway to the three-story brownstone that served as both rectory and parish office for St. Aloysius. This was the closest he had ever been to the stately old place, and although it had some of the normal rumblings of age around the edges, its otherwise pristine condition impressed him.

At the top of the wide concrete staircase, Mike removed his hat, smoothed his black hair, and checked his tall, crackled reflection in the stained glass of the entry door. A stocky woman answered the buzzer and introduced herself soberly as Mrs. Hughes. She took his hat and led him to the large, darkly furnished study down the hall.

"Please have a seat," she said, gesturing to one of the two burgundy leather chairs opposite the massive mahogany desk. She was precise and gracious and wore a fixed smile as she straightened a few papers on the desk. "The Monsignor will be in shortly," she said with a polite bow.

The room was washed in a heavy amber light from the ornate iron desk lamp. The weighty maroon brocade that draped two tall windows was a somber contrast to the sycamores beyond, whose leaves waved tirelessly like children wanting someone to come out and play. The room felt close and stuffy with the faint mixed smells of furniture polish and kerosene heat.

Mike unbuttoned his suit jacket and leaned forward, resting his elbows on his knees. He felt uncomfortable not knowing why the Monsignor wanted to speak with him, but the gnawing in his gut suggested he already had a clue. When Mar told him and Etta about her conversation with the Monsignor regarding the Russian immigrants, Mike had suspected there might be consequences, but on this of all days, he might have little patience with Monsignor. Murphy's Law.

The call from the school had come around lunchtime. As sometimes happens in the busy copy room, it rang in on a phone at another desk. When they said it was the school calling, he allowed an unguarded moment that could cost him dearly. It couldn't have taken him longer than five minutes to learn from Monsignor's secretary, Mrs. Hughes, that the meeting was urgent and he should set the appointment for that afternoon. Mike returned to his desk to find that his briefcase was gone. His journal, all his research notes and contact information for the exposé he'd been working on for weeks were nowhere to be found. Now this.

Mike eyed the titles on one of the nearby shelves and was surprised to see *The Spirit of Medieval Philosophy* by Étienne Gilson, a somewhat obscure book that nonetheless had been responsible for opening Thomas Merton's mind to Catholicism. The more familiar *The Life of St. Augustine* brought back memories of Father Paul, a favorite of all the Jesuit teachers he'd had at St. Simeon's. Before Father Paul, Mike had never met someone with a harelip. He chuckled wryly to himself remembering his great surprise that a priest could have such a flaw. Mike heard the floorboards creak under the Monsignor's leaden step. He had met him only once at a parents' night social in the school auditorium not long after Monsignor arrived as pastor, and had found him to be formal and standoffish.

"Mr. Ferry," he said, immediately on entering the room, and shook Mike's hand.

"Nice to see you again, Monsignor."

"Yes," was all he said, circling around to the leather chair behind the desk, then turning momentarily to face the window. "Lovely time of year, isn't it? To be free again of overcoat and rubbers. A blessing." He turned back to face Mike. "School will be ending soon, Mr. Ferry, and soon again after that we'll start another year. I'm sure you and Mrs. Ferry will be eager for Margaret to return to us. Lovely girl, Margaret."

"Yes, she loves St. Aloysius."

"As do we all, Mr. Ferry. We do the Lord's work here and I am humbled to have been chosen to lead in that effort." He sat down at his desk.

"Well, we all wish you the greatest success, Monsignor."

"Not all, Mr. Ferry." For a moment, he rested his chin in the cup of his hand, then looked up directly at Mike. "Not your lovely Margaret."

So there it was, right off the bat. Mike had warned Margaret. He had warned her. "I'm not sure I follow, Monsignor."

"I'm certain that you are a busy man, Mr. Ferry. I trust that you would appreciate my getting right to the point." He put his pale thick hand on the small stack of papers that Mrs. Hughes had so carefully placed there for him, then slid them across the desk toward Mike.

"Did you have any knowledge of this, Mr. Ferry?"

As Mike reached for the papers, he saw the word "Proclamation" at the top of what was clearly several pages of names and signatures. He felt the knot in his stomach tighten.

"No. I don't know what this is...or what it has to do with Margaret."

"This is your niece's work. It's her petition, circulated for signatures throughout the school, students and staff alike, and then sent to, of all people, the Bishop."

Mike's mouth felt dry as sawdust.

"As a consequence, I spent a good part of my morning on the phone with Bishop Harriot. Have you any idea what an absolute embarrassment this has been to...St. Aloysius?"

"What is the petition for?" Mike asked, pretty certain he already knew.

"The immigrants." The Monsignor took a deep breath and leaned back in his chair, resting his laced fingers on his mid-section. "Keeping the Russian immigrants at St. Aloysius. That's all your niece seems to be concerned with these days, Mr. Ferry, regardless of whatever chaos might ensue. I can only assume this is a line of thinking that is being generated at home."

"With all due respect, Monsignor, that would be an incorrect assumption." Mike felt the artery in his neck thicken. With all else that had happened at work earlier in the day, this was the last thing…and the last person…Mike wanted to deal with. "Margaret has gotten this into her head on her own, although I can't say it's a bad thing. It's the fifties. A kid these days could be involved in a lot worse."

"Worse for whom, Mr. Ferry?"

"I'm sure Margaret had the best intentions. My niece is a sensible and sensitive girl. I'm sorry for whatever trouble this has caused you or the school."

"Mr. Ferry, you are a professional, one who is aware of things, I trust. Surely you know that there are four high-rise apartment buildings that have just passed occupancy not three blocks from here. More than two hundred children are taking up residency there, and an estimated two-thirds of those are of the Catholic faith. Very shortly, they will be registering for school. It is vital to their young souls that they choose a Catholic education, and it is vital to our parish that they choose St. Aloysius."

Mike sat back and nodded thoughtfully, as if considering this argument for the first time. *Hmm.* Priest or not, he'd like to reach across and choke this guy. "Wouldn't St. Catherine's figure into all of this? It's only a few blocks in the other direction from where those apartments will be located."

"Father Gregory is a fine pastor, but St. Catherine's is simply not able to offer what St. Aloysius can."

"What exactly do you believe our parish can offer that is better than the others, Monsignor? I'm not challenging you. I'm just curious as to how you see things."

Monsignor Carnavan stood and went to the window. "A bright future. Promise. Possibilities." He turned to Mike. "I have plans for this parish, Mr. Ferry. You will not recognize our beloved St. Aloysius in even the next two years let alone five or ten."

"And our good Russian neighbors have no place in your plan?"

"Let's just say they are better suited to another plan—at St. Vincent's, for example. Father Raymond is quite satisfied with the ordinary run of things."

"Everyone says Father Raymond is a good man. He's well-liked and respected." Mike could understand how Mar found herself in a disagreeable discussion with Carnavan—he was vexing at best, an authoritarian brute. Still, what Margaret had done was unacceptable. She was playing with fire; Mike could see that now. He would have to rein her in. Lord only knew what Carnavan had in mind.

"Popularity has its virtue, Mr. Ferry," said the Monsignor, "but it doesn't necessarily speak to progress or achievement. Father Raymond welcomes people who can offer little to the parish, who cannot pull their own weight. Here, where there are so many opportunities, we need people, perhaps like you, who will contribute to a bright future to benefit the carrying out of the Lord's work. Would you argue with that?"

"I wouldn't exactly disagree with that, Monsignor, except to say that the way I see things the future should also be bright for those who are not yet fully ready or able to pull their own weight." He leaned closer to the desk. "Every family in our parish came from somewhere else, or their parents did—Italy,

Ireland, Germany, Poland, even Russia. Our families all started the same way. Maybe yours did too. They struggled. I think if we took the time, we'd recognize that this new wave of Russian immigrants also has something to contribute. And I guess that probably lines up with how Margaret sees it, and how many others in our parish see it too."

"But that's just it, Mr. Ferry. What you and the others fail to see is that we don't have the kind of time required to shepherd these people along…"

"Shepherd is an interesting word, Monsignor."

Monsignor Carnavan faced Mike squarely from behind his desk. Mike could imagine that in earlier years Carnavan, now likely in his late fifties without paunch or sag, might have been a formidable figure on a college football field. "Mr. Ferry, you will have a decision to make. Margaret will fit into our parish plans or she will not. I will let you and her decide that. Now if you will excuse me, I must be over to the church for five o'clock mass."

———◆———

Etta pulled the clothes from the line that stretched from the second-story kitchen window to the tall wooden pole at the end of the yard, and breathed in the sweetness of the cotton. Only weeks earlier, everything had been frozen stiff in the winter cold when she stood Mar's dresses like great doll cut-outs on the kitchen floor before spraying them damp for the ironing basket. On the stove, a pot lid clanked. "Come drain the potatoes," she called out. "Your uncle will be coming through the door any minute. If we finish early we can all go for a walk."

Margaret hurried from the parlor. She loved their springtime evening walks. Often, she went ahead as Aunt Etta and Uncle Mike strolled along holding hands and talking their private talk. Sometimes Junie came along and she and Margaret had their own private talks about the boys they liked and the clothes they loved and their favorite movie stars.

Usually, it was just Margaret daydreaming her way past the wrought iron fences and brownstone airy ways with their yellow daffodils, low forsythia hedges and freshly potted zinnias. It was a time when the ice cream truck, new to the season, sounded its bells and calliope, signaling the last round of the day and the children straggled out in twos and threes up and down the block clamoring for toasted almond and coconut pops.

They hardly heard Mike come in without his customary lighthearted chatter. It took them by surprise. He nodded, then washed his hands in silence in the kitchen sink, his head down.

Etta handed him a towel. "What's wrong?"

He dried his hands without looking up. "Sit down, Margaret." He tossed the towel onto the counter.

"What's happened?" Etta asked again.

He went to the kitchen table and sat down, pointing to the seat opposite. "Here, please." He looked at Margaret. "Sit."

His tone was stern. Margaret didn't say a word.

"Do you have any idea where I've been for the past hour?"

Margaret blinked with the look of one whose mind is racing. She had come straight home after school without even seeing Junie or stopping at the candy store. Sister Bernadine had had a meeting to attend and said she didn't need her for office work. Margaret shook her head.

"I got a call at work today from Monsignor Carnavan."

Margaret swallowed.

"I've just come from the rectory." He turned to Etta. "Did you know she was running all over school with a damned petition for the Bishop? The Bishop—for God's sake!—so the Russian immigrants wouldn't have to leave St. Aloysius? Did you know that?"

Etta looked at Margaret. "What in God's name were you thinking?"

"I only…"

"I warned you, Margaret," Mike said, cutting her off. "Monsignor is fuming. I'm fuming. He's not someone you want to go head-to-head with. Not only because he's a Monsignor. Not only because he's an ambitious son-of-a…"

"Mike!"

"but because I said so. Didn't I? Didn't I say you would be seen as a troublemaker? That's exactly what he thinks you are and he's right. You are a troublemaker. You've made trouble for everybody, and believe me, you didn't help your Russian friends either. It's only for the grace of God that he didn't pitch you out on your ear right along with them. That would be nice, wouldn't it? We don't have enough problems right now."

Etta shot Mike a look.

"What problems?"

Mike went on without acknowledging the question. "When I tell you something, I expect you to listen."

"What problems?" Margaret asked again, looking nervously from Etta's face to Mike's.

"Pay attention, damn it! Do you realize what you've done? You are this close to hiking over to St. Vincent's. Is that what you want?"

Margaret put her head down.

"Is it?" he snapped.

"No," she whispered.

"I promise you, Margaret Ferry, if you pull something like this again, you'll go to St. Vincent's all right—Monsignor Carnavan will see to that—but I will see to it that you don't go out for a year."

She knew he was exaggerating, but he would most definitely punish her. It didn't happen often, but she remembered very clearly the time she disobeyed Aunt Etta about not going into the empty house around the corner. She and Junie had thought it would make a nice clubhouse, and climbed in through a back transom. What harm was there anyway? No one even had to know, except that nosey body Viola Steich saw them and told. Aunt Etta was furious. Uncle Mike wouldn't let her go to the movies for two weeks. She missed an Esther Williams movie and the Three Stooges one she had been waiting forever to see.

"I've said the last I'm going to say about this." It was. Mike didn't speak a word all through supper. When he was finished, he got up from the table and took his newspaper into the parlor. After a few minutes, Etta joined him, leaving Margaret at the kitchen table.

The house seemed filled with an angry silence and the spring breeze felt suddenly cold against her back. What if she really was next on Monsignor's list?

CHAPTER FIVE

Etta brought a cup of tea into the living room and placed it on the table beside Mike. "You all right?"

"I don't know what goes on in that kid's head. She has to learn you don't butt heads with somebody like that, making him look bad in front of the Bishop. A petition, for God's sake. Now, she just looks the wrong way and she's out."

"Honestly, I had no idea what she was up to." Etta came around to sit on the arm of the chair. These days in the lamplight, she could notice those first threads of silver in his black hair. She stroked the back of his head. "Sometimes her compassion goes to extremes. I'll have a talk with her. She can be so strong-willed. You know that and you also must know where she gets it."

Mike took Etta's hand. "I'm not that bad, am I?" His tone was softer now.

She loved his mix of strength and gentleness, his confidence and humility. "I'd never call it bad. You're a man of principle and determination and you've somehow managed to pass it on to your niece." She pressed his hand to her cheek. "Don't forget, your brother Dan is in there too."

"And…" Mike took a deep breath. "She's certainly got her mother's sensitive heart for others."

Etta nodded. "Every bit. Still, she's going to need a few lessons in temperance."

He hadn't touched the tea, but looked straight ahead, off

somewhere. She saw his jaw flex.

"What else?" she asked. "I can tell there's more."

Mike leaned forward and shook his head, "Well…this was a day of days, Et."

"Oh?"

"My journal's gone."

"What do you mean *gone?*"

"Stolen. Along with my briefcase, notes, contacts. That's the only way I can account for it. I know exactly where I left it. And I know who took it."

"But why? Who?"

Mike got up and went to the window. "I'll give you three guesses."

"I can't imagine. Maybe it's a mistake."

"Wallace Loughlin. No mistake."

Etta went over to him. "Are you serious? He'd be crazy to do something like that. Anyone would be." But she knew it really wasn't so crazy at all. Loughlin had been a thorn in Mike's side ever since he started at the paper. Mike said he was lazy and he had caught him in a couple of lies.

"For a cool, smooth-talking snake, this is just the next plateau, Et."

"How did it happen? Did anyone see him?"

"He's way too slick. And the timing was perfect with everyone in deadline mode. You could walk an elephant through the copy room and the typewriters wouldn't miss a beat."

"Is it possible that…

"I'd bet my eye teeth. I know just how and when it happened. I let my guard down." Mike turned and sat against the arm of the chair. "Carnavan's secretary called. But the call came in at Jim Gordon's desk. It threw me when Jim said it was the school—they never call me. I thought…well…anyway… my briefcase was under the desk. I just tossed the journal in and slid the briefcase back a little with my foot. I couldn't have been on the phone five minutes, and that's all the time Loughlin needed."

"Oh, Mike."

Mike ran his fingers through his hair. "When I got back to my desk the briefcase was gone. A bunch of us combed the place. No book. And, by the way, no Loughlin."

"All your work. Weeks and weeks of it."

"Names, dates. Every contact. Every bit of information I had for the Central Commerce story. It's all in Loughlin's hands now. But I swear to you, Et, he's not going to get away with it."

"Get away with what?" Margaret stood in the doorway, holding a dishtowel. "Who's Loughlin?"

They looked up. "Just someone your uncle works with," Etta said. "Have you finished the dishes?"

"Has he done something bad?"

"Nothing to be concerned about, Mar." Mike's tone with Margaret was mellower now. "Go finish your homework."

When Margaret was out of earshot, Etta leaned closer to Mike. Such a delicate balance now that Margaret was getting older, uncertain as to what was appropriate to share with her. Etta knew the girl's sensitivities. The last thing she wanted was to plant an idea in her head that might cause her to worry. "Do you think Loughlin will destroy the journal? All your research?"

"Not a chance." Mike went back and stood at the window, his hands crammed deep into his trouser pockets. "Central Commerce Trust. The exposé of the decade. No, he's going to work it."

She could see his frustration, his restlessness. He was a fair-minded man accustomed to being in control. This would eat him up, and she had no idea how to help.

"He's going to use every bit of that research to write the series—there's almost enough there. He'll just claim it for his own. Who's going to question it?"

"But what about the people you spoke with? Can't you go back to them?"

"Those people are bank insiders. They put their jobs and a lot more on the line to expose shady dealings, account fraud, money laundering, embezzlement, you name it. They step up once. You get one shot. There's no going back so they can tell the world it was really me they blew the whistle to and not this guy named Wallace Loughlin. So, if there's a Pulitzer in this, Et, it won't go to me, that's for sure. And we can kiss that promotion goodbye along with it."

"What does Bill think? He's bound to suspect something when Loughlin shows up with the story."

"I'll talk to Bill in the morning. But without that journal, I have nothing but my word and, technically, I have no proof it was Loughlin."

"Mike, look at me." She faced him square on and reached up to put her hands on his shoulders. "Your word is worth more than all the documentation in the world and they know it. Bill Fulton surely knows it; you've worked for him and with him how many years? All through the war. He knew you were working on the story. You wouldn't make this up."

"But in practical terms, neither Bill Fulton nor I can prove anything."

She rested her face against his chest. "Oh, Mike."

They were silent for a few moments. She was at a complete loss. Mike's world was tumbling sideways—first the briefcase, then Mar's brush with the Monsignor. And she hadn't even told him about her visit with Dr. Maggio. She knew he was seconds away from asking, but she just couldn't bear adding one more piece of bad news to his load.

"Would it help if we took a walk after supper?"

Mike shook his head. "Sorry, Et, I'm all in. Carnavan was the frosting on the cake. As God is my witness, I'm struggling with everything in me not to hate that man. Or Loughlin either.

I have one power-hungry guy at work and one at church. Just dandy, isn't it? So many fine, dedicated priests out there. I was thinking about Father Paul today. What a true servant he was."

"He married us," Etta said wistfully.

"How a good man like that dies in a foxhole consoling the wounded while this one becomes Monsignor is beyond me."

She kissed his cheek. "What happens now?"

"It's going to get worse…you can be sure of that. Once Loughlin puts that series together, he'll be the golden boy. He'll have to get me out of there. He won't want me hanging around, knowing that he's a liar and a thief. It'd be too risky."

"How could he do that? The story's one thing, but he isn't your boss."

"Et, do you doubt that this man might be capable of anything? When this exposé hits, he'll quickly have friends upstairs."

"Can't Bill help?"

"Loughlin's a slacker and Bill knows it, but with no proof it's just…c'est la vie.

The doorbell rang. "Oh, what now?" Etta quietly snapped, then called out, "Mar, look down and see who that is, please." Etta looked up into the eyes of the man she loved. "You're the best writer they've got."

"Everybody's expendable, Et. You know that. This story will give Loughlin a lot of clout."

Margaret called from the kitchen. "It's Mrs. Steich."

"God save us. What does that woman want?" She gave Mike's arm an affectionate squeeze. "Might as well let her in, Mar." Margaret hit the buzzer that unlocked the double glass doors at the entry to the brownstone.

"Whatever happens, Mike, it's going to be all right. It will. I adore you. That child out there adores you. Remember that. We're going to get through this. All of us, all of it. You and I have been through worse."

Their eyes locked. Mike nodded and pressed her hand to his lips.

She turned toward the kitchen, but he gripped her.

"Et, forgive me, I didn't even ask about...I'm so sorry, I..."

She smiled. "It's okay. We can talk about it later." She headed for the kitchen. "Hello, Viola."

Viola Steich, who Mike referred to as a woman of dubious thoughtfulness, lived with her husband above the hardware store that had been in Russell Steich's family for three generations.

Theirs was a corner apartment with windows on both the avenue and the side street, where Viola positioned herself daily as if in a command post. From that vantage point, she monitored the neighborhood, any and all things, any and all people, while her husband found relief from her incessant gossip in the less volatile banter of the neighborhood men who came in for drill bits, socket wrenches and benign small talk.

"Hello, dear Etta. Just thought I'd stop by with a nice, fresh onion cake. It's still warm."

"That's very thoughtful, Viola. You didn't have to do that."

"What better time to do these little things for nice people than when times are...well, you know...a little tough."

"Tough?" Etta's heart skipped a beat. Was it possible she knew about the petition to the Bishop? Margaret's run-in with Monsignor? Could she know that already? Etta smiled. "How so?"

Viola Steich looked at Margaret and shrugged awkwardly. "You know. The Bishop and everything."

"Yes, confirmation is a big day, isn't it?" Etta hoped to deflect. "It really has come up fast, but I wouldn't say it's been tough." She was inches away from being furious not just with Viola Steich but with Margaret, as well. "I think Margaret's ready for the Bishop's questions." She patted Margaret on the

arm. "And by the way, Viola, the onion cake smells delicious."
Etta stood between Viola and the kitchen table, knowing that
if this rattle-tongued woman got to a chair, they'd be trying to
get her out of the house for the next hour.

"Well…I meant…you know…that trouble with the Bishop,"
Viola said, trying to regroup.

"Oh, it's no trouble at all. I think the Bishop is a good man;
he'll be kind with the children." Etta fought to keep her smile
from fading.

"Well, I meant…"

"And you have certainly meant well, Viola. Mike will love
the onion cake." Etta inched the woman closer to the door.

"That's comforting news," Viola said, clearly feigning relief,
"that Margaret will be making her confirmation, after all." She
moved slightly to the side and Etta moved with her, blocking
her path farther into the room.

"I'm so sorry there's no time for a chat right now, Viola. But
I do thank you again for thinking of us."

"Well, then," Viola said, the frustration showing in her sigh,
"if there is anything at all that you need, just come get me. I'm
always happy to help a neighbor."

"Thank you, Viola." Etta gently pressed the woman
backwards toward the door.

"Russell's not doing so well, you know."

"Oh, I didn't know." Instantly, Etta had pangs of guilt for
hurrying the woman off. "What's wrong?"

"Well, you know my Russell, always lifting things beyond
himself. He never listens to me. Now he has a hernia and they
have to operate."

"Well, I am sorry to hear that, Viola. Please give him our
regards and be sure to let us know if there's anything we can
do. Truly."

When she had gone, Etta turned to Margaret. "It's too bad
about Mr. Steich. He's a nice man, but I hope you see why

she came by in the first place, Margaret. And I hope you can understand why your uncle is so upset. It's things like this— busybodies like Viola, who take one little piece of gossip and spread it everywhere. They hurt people. We don't want to see you get hurt."

Mike came into the kitchen. "Or thrown out of school."

Margaret looked down and traced a line with her finger on the tabletop. "Sorry," she said quietly.

CHAPTER SIX

Late into the night, Margaret pondered the unanswered question she had asked Uncle Mike. *"What problems?"* Maybe it had to do with this person, Mr. Loughlin, but maybe there were other things. It bothered her to think of Aunt Etta or Uncle Mike having any kind of trouble, and now she felt doubly bad because of the trouble she had caused with Monsignor.

Aunt Etta was good to everyone; Uncle Mike was strong and smart. He wrote about important things for the newspaper and everybody read what he had to say. He was sure of things. He knew homework answers and helped her figure them out on her own.

Mike could fix anything. She had seen him take little parts out of the back of the radio and when he put them back, the radio worked again. Same with the kitchen faucet. Sometimes all he needed was his little oil can that he kept under the kitchen sink. He knew just where to point the squirt for the clothesline wheel or the front door hinges. *What problems?*

If Mr. Loughlin was causing trouble for Uncle Mike, Margaret didn't know how she could ever like him or forgive him. "All things through prayer," Lolly would say. Lots of people said that. But it was Aunt Lolly saying it that made her want to believe it. Lolly always had a thought to brighten things. "Find the good," she always said. "Find the good."

Margaret prayed for Uncle Mike and Aunt Etta all the time. And for Lolly. She prayed for the Bishop and for Junie's dog,

Tippy, with his one bad paw. And for Mr. Steich, who had to put up with Mrs. Steich, and once ran out all by himself to lift a car off a run-over boy on a bike.

You weren't always going to get what you wanted when you prayed, she knew that. She had prayed for Mrs. Piro but she died anyway of something in her head. Lately, she prayed a lot for the Russian immigrants, and Mikhail and Stanny and Peter were sent over to St. Vincent's just the same. Maybe Uncle Mike was right—she was just a troublemaker. Maybe that's why she was waking up so much in the middle of the night, worried about the immigrants, worried about being ready for confirmation. Maybe God was punishing her with worry.

At times like this, with lots of feelings and thoughts tumbling around, she wondered what her real mother and father had been like. Aunt Etta was all the mother she would ever want or need. And no one could be a better father than Uncle Mike. Still, she couldn't help wondering what Daniel Ferry was like. And Mary Ferry. Aunt Etta wasn't at all comfortable talking about it. Why speak of such painful loss, she would say. "Wait till you're older, Mar."

She could see why Aunt Etta never wanted to talk about the death of her parents. It must have been too much of a shock for everyone in the family. Margaret couldn't imagine what it would be like to lose a brother or a sister, a parent, a child. She couldn't imagine anything happening to Junie. And then for Aunt Etta and Uncle Mike to take her into their lives and raise her. Everything tumbled in her mind.

What problems?

———◄•►———

Loretta Ferry lay beside her husband in the bed they had slept in from the day they were married seventeen years earlier. They had met when she was twenty-two and in her first year teaching elementary school. Mike was twenty-five and just promoted to obituary writer for the Syracuse *Post-Standard*.

They had each gone to the New Year's Eve dance at the Hotel Beauclaire in downtown Syracuse, and would later say they knew from the moment they saw each other that they were meant to be husband and wife. She was Loretta O'Donnell, there with her two best girlfriends, he with a few of the guys. They had noticed each other from across the room and gradually made their way to the center of the floor, where he asked her to dance.

For the remainder of the evening they danced only with each other, and when the horns sounded at midnight, they shared a long first kiss, which they would have shared even without the ringing in of a new year. They married a month later at St. Cyril and Methodius, the same church where Etta had been baptized.

Etta wore white *po de sois* with a chapel train, and a veiled crystal tiara laced with tiny white rosebuds. She carried a cascading bouquet of pink and white lisianthus and Queen Anne's lace. Her parents paid for their reception at the very place they had met, the Beauclaire, with eighty-five people in attendance, mostly family and closest friends. Mike and his younger brother, Dan, had lost their parents years earlier, but there were plenty of aunts, uncles and cousins. A gold-framed photograph of the happy couple standing outside their honeymoon cabin in the Poconos in full winter gear still graced the living room mantel.

All those years ago, they had shared their dream of having a large family. Their hope was to have a little Michael Ferry, a Kevin, Brigitte and Kathleen Ferry and perhaps even a Thomas and Brian Ferry. On their long evening walks in spring and summer, with Mar up ahead snipping sprigs of forsythia, they had kept hope that maybe one day soon they would have good news.

Etta turned and put her arm across Mike's chest. In the

shadowy bedroom, lit only by the blue-gray wash of moonlight, she could see his eyes fixed on the ceiling. He had been silent since hearing of her visit with Dr. Maggio.

He stroked her arm, then turned to her. "You're all I need, Et," he whispered. "You and Mar. That's all. You're everything. You know that."

There was just enough light for her to be sure he could see her smile. He held her close and she truly understood that it didn't matter to him that there would not ever be a baby. It was final now—the test results had verified it. Dr. Maggio had made it clear—whatever physical impediments had made it impossible, there was now her age. She would soon be forty. She'd had many years to become used to the word "barren," a horrible tag for a woman with such precious hopes of motherhood.

She'd had to be careful not to commit the unforgivable sin of diminishing God's gift of Margaret, their child by the most odd and unfortunate circumstance, but no different than if she had been their very own. That in itself was a situation with worrisome potential that she always prayed she and Mike had handled well, without ever being sure. Her best hope was to deal with it in the years to come, when the time was right.

They dropped off to sleep in each other's arms, but not before a single tear trickled down Etta's cheek and fell onto Mike's chest.

CHAPTER SEVEN

Wallace Loughlin looked up when he heard the door to the copy room fly open and saw Bill Fulton plowing across the crowded floor in his direction.

"My office," Fulton said, his deep voice low and stern, as he passed Loughlin's desk.

Fulton may have been in a rush this morning; Wallace Loughlin was not. He took his time getting up, pushed in his chair, and pulled on his brown suit jacket before strolling across the smoke-filled room to the Managing Editor's office. Amid the frenzy of typewriters clacking and voices raised to deadline pitch, Loughlin smoothly sidestepped desk chairs that had rolled out askew into the aisle and wastebaskets overflowing with discarded drafts. Fulton rarely gave him the time of day anymore except to ream him out and he was probably about to do it again, but it was beginning to matter less and less to Loughlin—things were about to change. He straightened his tie and paused in the doorway of Fulton's office.

Bill Fulton, a scowl on his face and a pile of Tootsie Rolls in the oversized glass ashtray on his desk, grabbed his ringing phone. "Not now," he said and hung up. "Come in and close the door."

Loughlin closed the door and took a seat.

Fulton planted his elbows on the desk, his muscular forearms straining in the rolled-up sleeves of his crisp white shirt. "What are you working on?"

"Central Commerce Trust."

"Since when?"

Loughlin shrugged. "Weeks." Loughlin knew he had to be careful—Fulton was a cat-and-mouse kind of a guy, savvy enough to catch any missteps. He reached in his suit jacket, removed a pack of Camels, and held the pack out to Fulton, who ignored the offer. He should have remembered that Fulton had quit a long time ago.

"That's Mike Ferry's story."

"Is it? I've made some good contacts, strong leads. I thought it was up for grabs. It's the pearl a few of us are after. First come, first served. No?"

"No. I assigned you the school board piece and you're late. Don't bother lighting that in here. There's no ashtray for it."

Loughlin put the cigarettes back in his pocket. "I think Mr. Stockton would want me to handle stories more fitting to my talents."

Fulton narrowed his eyes and gave Loughlin a long, steady look. "Since when are you running in John Stockton's circle?"

"Oh, I've run into him in the elevator a few times. We've talked. He encourages me. I like that."

"Well John Stockton may own the paper, but as long as I'm Managing Editor I run things in this office."

Loughlin nodded pensively. "I believe that is true. As you say...as long as you are the Managing Editor."

"If I were you, Loughlin, I wouldn't overplay my hand. You've had your chances, plenty of them, but you've never shown me much of anything. Now you're telling me you're putting together one of the biggest stories of the year."

"That's what I'm saying."

Fulton leaned back in his chair with a smirk. "You'd be pretty damned good, then, huh? A guy who hasn't been able to hit his way to first base suddenly ends up MVP?"

Loughlin was determined to remain cool and steady. "I

guess all things are possible."

"Yeah, well, my job is not to wait around for what's possible. My job is to get the guy who gets the story. From what I've seen, you haven't done much getting."

"I believe I'm about to surprise you. Trust me."

"Trust has been a hard thing to have where you're concerned, Loughlin. I don't know exactly why that is, but I've always had a good gut about things like that. And I guess it's the same reason why I don't especially like you either."

Loughlin faked a smile, seething.

Fulton got up, walked behind his chair and looked out his third-floor window at the snarled traffic of midtown Manhattan threading its way up to Central Park like a poorly stitched seam. "Ferry's briefcase went missing yesterday." He turned and looked at Loughlin. "Know anything about that?"

Loughlin didn't flinch. "Only that Mike claimed it contained months of research. If it's true, that's a real tough break."

"What do you mean 'if it's true'? I've never doubted Mike Ferry's word. Why would you?"

Loughlin leaned forward and laced his fingers, feigning reticence. "Forget it."

"If you've got something to say, say it."

"I..." Loughlin intended to milk the hesitation as long as he could. He shook his head and got up to leave.

"Hold on, we're not through. You have something to say and I'm waiting for you to say it. Now, let's have it."

Loughlin ran his fingers through his hair. "Mike..." He stopped.

"What about Mike?"

Loughlin sat back down heavily. "Well, it's like this. I had this article I found in an out-of-town paper, all about some poorly run mental hospital. I figured it could make a good exposé series. So, yesterday after lunch, I brought it over to show Mike." Loughlin wished he'd been able to light that cigarette. He was treading in deeper and deeper water, but here was his chance.

"Go on."

"I…I'm sorry I brought it up. I'm just not comfortable with this."

"Well, you're going to sit there until you do get comfortable with it."

Loughlin took a deep breath. He rubbed his hands together, summoning his best nervous gesture. "I suggested to Mike that he hold onto the article. I was too busy with the bank exposé, but didn't want to lose track of this other possible story. I figured Mike and I could work on it together at some point. I handed him the article. He reached down behind his desk, which only had a legal pad on it and a couple of loose papers, and picked up his briefcase." He stopped.

"And…"

"And when he opened the briefcase to put the article in, I couldn't help notice that it was empty. The briefcase was empty." He sat taller and gave Fulton his most innocent look. "It wasn't an hour later that he claimed it had been stolen with all his papers. But I can tell you, there were no papers in Mike Ferry's briefcase. No journal. Nothing."

Fulton wagged his finger at Loughlin. "Listen here, I've known Mike Ferry a helluva long time—he doesn't have a dishonest bone in his body."

Loughlin put his hands up. "I knew I shouldn't have said anything. You'd believe Ferry, no matter what. I'm being square with you. And there's more." He looked at Fulton as if waiting for approval to continue.

"Go on."

Loughlin could see how unsettled Fulton was hearing this about Ferry—the perfect time for Loughlin to shore up his tale. "It's like this. A few days ago, I was working on the bank story at my desk. I'd spent weeks on it and I had notes everywhere, papers scattered all over my desk. I went out to the men's room and when I came back...well...there was Mike standing at my desk, looking over what I'd written."

"That's not like Mike either."

"That's what I thought. Mike always struck me as being a prince of a guy. He really helped me out when I first started here. But...well...this is a big story and..."

"Did you see him touch anything?"

"No, he just stood there looking down at what was on my desk." Loughlin shook his head. "I have no idea what might have happened if I hadn't returned when I did."

"Did you say anything to him?"

"I didn't have a chance. It was clear he was uncomfortable when I walked in. He said he came over to get a pencil."

Fulton's mouth tightened into a hard line. He sat down and moved a stack of papers in front of him. "You can get back to work now."

Loughlin stood and offered his hand. "Thanks for listening. I appreciate it. And I'll try even harder from now on not to disappoint you." The words burned in Loughlin's throat. He had learned the hard way that trying harder and being better were dead end streets he'd been down before. But that was another time and place. This was here and now and things had gone exactly as he'd hoped. He'd nailed it.

Fulton hesitated, then accepted Loughlin's handshake. "Just make sure you don't let the paper down with this story. The stakes are high, and trust me, you'll be the first one to feel the heat."

Loughlin nodded and opened the door to leave.

"One more thing," Fulton said. "If I find out that you've had any part in the disappearance of Mike's briefcase, John Stockton or no, you'll be gone before the next tick of the clock. Count on it."

Loughlin made his way back through the maze of crowded

desks, confident that his tale had planted an idea about Ferry that could serve him later should Ferry make any accusations after the story ran. He'd be spending the next few weeks burning the candle until morning using Ferry's notes to put the story together. He had looked everything over the night before; he'd have to do more research and summon every bit of what Ferry had taught him over these months. There had been only a few fleeting moments of guilt realizing how much hard work and expertise Ferry had put into this story. He himself would not have had a clue where to start on a story this big. He had never even worked for a newspaper before this gig. A phony resume and a few good lies had gotten him in the door. What would a research chemist know about a good headline? What did pharmaceutical formularies have to do with reporting on three-alarm fires or jewelry store break-ins?

The little he knew about reporting Mike Ferry had taught him. Oh, he had put many a decent White Paper together. That had been a requirement in his eight years of research work at Harden-Leland. But had they stood by him when his work was stolen? Had they even believed him? It was devastating. It would suit him fine if he never laid eyes on any of them again. Not Isabella, of course. He ended up breaking her heart along with his own when he took off halfway across the country. Beautiful Isabella. She had done him no harm, but he'd had to let go. Their wedding day had come and gone. It was all too crushing. Honesty, years of learning and hard effort had not paid off; he would have to be comfortable as the thief this unscrupulous world had turned him into.

He knew Ferry had no way of proving that he had taken the briefcase. Ferry had somehow gotten to one of the highest-level people at Central Commerce Trust, but he would never be able to go back to her, and without those details, he'd never be able to put the story together now. Still, when the time came, Loughlin would have to see to it that Ferry moved on. On one level, it didn't feel right, but that kind of thinking hadn't gotten him anywhere. The colleague who'd cheated him out of his discovery didn't hesitate a minute to take over everything he'd put his heart and soul into. But that was the past. Wallace Loughlin was on the way up. And neither Mike Ferry nor Bill Fulton could stop him.

Loughlin removed his suit jacket and draped it over the back of his chair, then loosened his tie.

"How long do you think it'll take to work over my notes and leads?" It was Mike Ferry.

Loughlin jumped, and tried hard not to show his discomfort in Ferry's presence. "Yours? Please, Mike, give it up." Coming face-to-face with Ferry made him realize that this thing might be a little hard to go through with, but he was determined all the same.

"Whose work will you have your eye on next time?"

"I have no idea what you're talking about." Loughlin took the pack of Camels from his pocket, removed a cigarette and tossed the pack onto the desk. "And I'm busy right now."

"If you think I'm going to give up on all my hard work with a nasty brush-off, think again." Ferry's voice was flat and quiet.

Loughlin leaned back and laced his fingers behind his head. "Sounds like sour grapes to me," his words squeezing around the cigarette dangling from his mouth. "You're just not used to being second dog."

"You may think you're riding high right now, Loughlin, but when you come crashing to the ground, I can promise you I won't be laughing—it will be all too pathetic to laugh about."

Loughlin watched Mike Ferry walk away, feeling only slightly sorry that his first big hit had to come at the expense of the guy who had taken him under his wing. To Ferry's detriment, he was principled, not at all a backstabber. Loughlin had been like that once, but what was that old saying? *Nice guys finish last.*

What a trusting fool Ferry had been to leave his briefcase

under the desk, unguarded, even for so short a time as it took to take a telephone call. Luckily, with the office in a deadline frenzy, most had been on their phones or zeroed in at their desks rapping out copy, unaware. Loughlin's movements had had to be swift and smooth to get his hands on the briefcase, cover it with his trench coat, and make it to the elevator and out of the building. Jackpot. No one saw and no one would ever be able to prove a thing? Poor Mike Ferry. Those are the breaks.

More than once, Isabelle had crossed his mind, but he'd had to put that behind him too. This was a new life, a new line of work, and a whole new way of living. If life was going to throw mud in his face, he'd throw it right back.

Mike Ferry was halfway across the office, when Fulton waved him over. Loughlin sat up straight to watch, wishing he could be a fly on the wall.

———◆———

"Have a seat, Mike."

Mike greeted Fulton soberly and sat down, but said nothing.

Against an impressive windowed cityscape, the office was a bland but efficient looking square with a couple of chairs and file cabinets. A well-used wooden coat rack stood in one corner. A side table held a couple of stacks of file folders and on the credenza behind Fulton's desk a photo of a young man in a football uniform and another of the same man dressed in army greens.

Fulton, his laced fingers resting on his desk, looked across at Mike. "How are you doing?"

Mike took a deep breath. The tension that he'd felt in his neck and shoulders all day had just worsened after his exchange with Loughlin. What was there to say?

"You all right?" Fulton pressed lightly.

"I'm all right."

"I'm not buying it," Fulton said. "Loughlin was just in here. I want to hear your side."

"You already know my side. My briefcase was stolen. Three months work. What more is there to tell?" Mike had never felt so outside of himself, as if someone had locked the door to his own private control room. Fulton was like family to him, a caring, sensitive man and trusted friend of many years, yet Mike didn't want to be there; didn't want to be anywhere right now. Loughlin was like Kryptonite, the strange poison that Mike couldn't counter. He felt betrayed and bereft, beaten to the ground with a cudgel of his own making.

"Loughlin's admitted he's working on Commerce."

Mike moved in his chair, then got to his feet and paced the room. "So I heard. That's laughable—the guy wouldn't have a clue."

Fulton tapped a pencil idly on the edge of his desk pad. "He says he gave you something to hold onto after lunch yesterday and when you opened your briefcase, it was empty. He says he caught you looking over all the work on his desk."

Mike stopped short. "And you believe him?"

"Not on your life." Fulton tossed the pencil onto the desk blotter. "I should have fired him weeks ago."

"Yeah, well, how would you know? When was the last time any of us had to worry about having a thief in our midst? And now he's trumping up stories to inoculate himself against any accusations I might make."

"Have you got any proof, Mike? Anything at all, extra copies, anything official that's dated?"

"Nothing. I've always kept my work tight, contained, so I'd never lose a stray note that could betray a confidence." Mike walked to the window. "Oh, I can give you names, but he's already covered himself. He'll say I saw the names on his desk."

"The problem," Bill Fulton drew in a deep breath, "is that without proof, my hands are tied. It's…"

"I know what it is. I didn't even want to go down this road. I told Etta I'd just sound like sour grapes."

"That's not what I was going to say. I know you better than that, Mike." Fulton leaned forward. "I don't mean to pile on, but you know the top floor. They're all about circulation. And when Loughlin turns that story in, they'll be in love."

"You realize he'll need to have me gone."

Fulton tightened his lip and nodded. "I believe you're right about that. If he clipped your papers, he's not going to want you around."

Mike threw up his arms in surrender.

Fulton came around the front of his desk and put his hand on Mike's shoulder. "I never thought I'd be saying these words to you—we go back a long way, and I've never had the first thought that you were anything but first rate both as a reporter and as a man, but if you're smart, Mike, you'll start looking. You know you can count on me for a glowing recommendation. As if you'd need it—everyone in town knows your work." He ran his hand across the top of his head. "Wallace Loughlin will find any way he can to be rid of you. What's more, you're not the only one he'll have in his crosshairs. Frankly, that scares the heck out of me because I suspect he'll go to any extent to get what he wants."

CHAPTER EIGHT

Margaret walked the three blocks to the subway station to meet Mike. She had gotten so little sleep the night before that she had overslept and hadn't seen him before he left for work. She needed to tell him how sorry she was for causing so much trouble with the Bishop and Monsignor.

It had not occurred to her that her actions would upset him and Aunt Etta, the two people who loved her more than anything. She had disappointed them at the worst possible time, a time when something was wrong that they didn't want her to know about, and she felt guilty and scared.

Mike usually got off the train around six. The large round clock at the top of the Dime Savings Bank building across the street said twelve minutes after six. She looked down over the top of the solid iron structure that surrounded the subway entrance on three sides, and there he was, his dark gray fedora bobbing with the others as the rush-hour crowd made its way up the stairs to the street.

When he reached the top, she fell in step beside him and took his hand. "Hi," was all she said, looking up at him.

"Hey. This is a surprise. It's been a while since you came to meet me."

"That's only because of all my confirmation studying." She felt relieved that he didn't sound angry, although he did look tired. "I'm sorry for being a troublemaker."

He squeezed her hand. "Well, that's something I'm glad to

hear, and have you learned anything?"

"Yes. I learned that no matter how important my Russian friends are, I should have thought about how upset you and Aunt Etta would be because of what I did."

"Good start." His smile had already made her feel a lot better.

"Aunt Etta had to go with Aunt Jo at the last minute to pick out some curtains. She has meatloaf on the stove, but said if we wanted to stop for pizza that would be fine with her."

"Pizza sounds good to me."

There was a lift in his voice. "We'll go to Barsotti's. How was school?"

"Good. I did my work and minded my own business, just like you told me."

He laughed.

As they turned the corner, they heard loud voices and scuffling coming from McGrath's Bar & Grill. A tall, unshaven man with dark hair stumbled out onto the sidewalk. Mike held Margaret back and crossed to the other side of the street.

"Stay outta here, Herring," a man with rolled-up shirtsleeves and a white apron tied around his waist yelled from the doorway. "I don't want to see your lousy drunken mug in here again. Next time, it's the cops you'll be dealing with."

Mike had hold of Margaret's hand as they crossed, but she was looking back over her shoulder.

"You know who that is, Uncle Mike? That's Johnny Herring's father, I just know it is. People say he drinks all the time and that he's mean to Johnny, and that his wife left him and everything."

"The boy who threw your books into the street?"

"Yes. Mine and Junie's. We never like it much when he's around because he makes trouble but if that's his father, I feel really bad for him."

Mike nodded. "Sad." He turned to see the man stagger out

of sight around the corner. A few minutes later, they reached Barsotti's, making their way down the three worn stone steps and over to their favorite place, the corner booth by the window that looked out onto a brick patio rimmed with potted evergreens and pink rhododendron coming into bloom. Little white lights flickered amid the greenery.

Margaret sat with her hands in her lap and looked around with a satisfied smile. She loved the red and white-checkered tablecloths and the round wine bottles wrapped in net and caked thick at the neck with candle wax, but the aromas were the best—rich garlicky smells, yeast dough and cheese baking in the old heat-scarred ovens behind the counter. Scenes of Italy hung in frames on the dark red walls along with autographed photos of famous people standing next to Mr. Barsotti—Frankie Laine, Patti Page, Perry Como, Victor Mature, and others she had only seen in the movies or heard on the radio.

Mr. Barsotti was a round, happy man who stopped at tables and talked to the customers. Margaret was glad he wasn't there this evening—she needed all the time she had to talk with Uncle Mike.

"Tell me more about your day," he said, after they had placed their order.

"I got a B plus on my history test."

"That's better. It was a B last time."

She nodded proudly and he smiled, but she could see that his eyes were heavy and that it wasn't a very happy smile.

"Uncle Mike, can I ask you something?"

"Sure," he said. He took a sip of the steaming black coffee the waiter had brought.

Margaret nervously rotated the glass of orange soda set before her on the table. "What kind of problems are you and Aunt Etta worried about?"

Mike chuckled. "What makes you think we're worried about anything...except maybe when you go at it with

Monsignor Carnavan?"

"Because when you were mad at me last night, you said something about problems. I wish you would tell me. I'm almost twelve. You don't have to keep things from me anymore."

"That was nothing, Mar. Sometimes things said in anger sound worse than they really are."

"But sometimes aren't there things that really are worse?"

He reached over and patted her hand. "Nothing for you to be troubled about. Truly."

Margaret fidgeted with the corner of her white cloth napkin and tried to smile because she thought it would make him feel good. "I had the feeling that something awful might happen."

"Grown-ups almost always have serious sounding things to think about and deal with. It doesn't mean something awful is about to happen. It's just the ordinary ways of life. And one reason we don't want children to know is that they would worry for no reason, just like you're doing now." He stroked her cheek. "So cheer up, or you'll get those funny little lines up here." He pointed to his brow and smiled.

"Well, I just wish you'd tell me things."

"Hey, kiddo, do you tell Aunt Etta and me everything?" He gave her a coy look. "Huh?"

She looked down with a sheepish grin.

"Do you tell us when Mr. and Mrs. Wortman make you leave because you and Junie get too noisy?"

She shot Mike a surprised look. She should have realized that he and Aunt Etta knew most everything—Brooklyn was such a small place and things often got home before she did. Like the time she and Junie and two other friends had a cupcake battle up on the avenue. Or the time they had taunted that man who opened the new key store because he looked like Josef Stalin. She didn't get in trouble for the cupcake battle, but she did for Josef Stalin. No Saturday afternoon movie that week. Plus, she had to go and apologize to the man, which was one of the most embarrassing things she'd ever had to do.

The pizza came and she could tell Uncle Mike was happy that they might change the subject. She was too, except that there were still a couple of things she needed to know.

"*Mmm*, looks and smells great, doesn't it?" He put the first slice on her plate. "Best pizza in all of Brooklyn, and I'm hungry as a bear."

"Me too," she said, happy to enjoy their meal and their playful chatter for a while.

Then she asked, "Did that Mr. Loughlin do something to hurt you?"

She could tell the question took Mike by surprise.

"What made you think of him of all people?"

She looked down, embarrassed. "Because you and Aunt Etta mentioned him last night in the living room, when I walked in. Remember? You sounded upset."

Mike looked at her and for a long moment sat perfectly still. "Mr. Loughlin is a man I work with. He's not a very nice man. There are probably a few people you might not be crazy about. Johnny Herring, for example. Mr. Loughlin's kind of like that—he does things that sometimes bother people. But that's nothing for you to worry about."

She picked at a piece of crust on her plate. "It's just that I thought maybe…"

"Maybe what?" His tone was soft and sympathetic.

"Maybe I might lose you." She could feel the tears building.

Mike looked at her for a moment in silence, then went and sat beside her. He put his arm around her and brought her close. "Never, Mar. Never. What could ever make you think such a thing?"

She leaned her head against his chest. "I was thinking about how I lost my real mother and father."

"But that was a long time ago, and what happened was very…unusual. There's absolutely nothing going on that would be anything like that, Mar. You've got to believe that. What happened with Mr. Loughlin is just…just grown-up annoying kind of stuff."

They were quiet for a moment. Then she looked up at him. "You knew my father better than anybody."

Mike looked down and nodded. "Yes. Yes, I did."

"You told me he was a good ballplayer."

"The best there was. Even though he was my younger brother, he could outhit me, outpitch me and outrun me, and anyone else for that matter. Brooklyn scouted him; he might have gotten to play with Pee Wee Reese and Gil Hodges. Imagine Joe DiMaggio chasing one of your dad's fly balls." They chuckled. "Anyway, there was a lot going on in the world—this was right before the war—and he ended up going into the Navy. Your father was a good man, Mar, and he would have loved you more than anything in the world. Your father and your mother."

"Tell me again how he met my mother."

"What brought all this up?"

She shrugged. "I don't know. But sometimes when I worry, they come to mind more than other times."

He nodded his understanding, as the waiter refilled his cup. He pressed her hand. "Your dad was with a couple of his friends. He had a lot of friends. He was always fun to be around. One of his friends had a sister, and one of her friends was your mother. And, boy, did she catch his eye. She was a pretty woman with a great smile and a great personality. Smart and lots of fun to be around. He fell head over heels in love, much the way it happened for Aunt Etta and me. I guess us Ferry boys were just big pushovers."

They laughed.

"Then what?"

"Well, you know…they got married. Things happened fast. You were on the way."

"And then?"

"And then…" was all he said, his voice dropping off.

They sat in silence looking out at the patio, where the black wrought iron tables had begun filling with customers.

"There were two questions about the war on my history test today," she said. "John O'Malley's uncle was killed too. He never met his uncle either, same as I never met my father."

"A lot of good men…and women…died in the war, Mar. All through Europe and in the Pacific. When you die for your country, you're a hero. Your father was a hero like the rest."

She sat up straight and smiled at him.

"Hey," he said, "your pizza's getting cold."

"You all liked my mother."

"Very much."

"Especially Lolly."

He drew a deep breath. "Especially Lolly. They were a lot alike, your mother and Lolly—the same age, same happy disposition. Guess that's why it hit her so hard when…"

"When my mother died?"

He nodded.

"Aunt Etta said Lolly almost died too."

"Yes," he said and fell silent again. Margaret had heard the story only once from Aunt Etta, but remembered every word of it. Lolly had been sick with the flu for weeks before it all happened. When Margaret's father was killed, it was a terrible shock to everyone. But when Margaret's mother died giving birth to her shortly afterwards, it was more than Lolly could handle in her weakened state. She suffered a stroke and was rushed to King's County Hospital, where she stayed for weeks before they moved her to a place that helped her to walk and talk again. A few months later, she was moved to St. Clement Home for the Disabled in Pennsylvania.

"Was Aunt Lolly ever in love? Did she ever have a boyfriend?"

"Yes, she did." He curled the corner of his napkin. "There

was one young man. I remember him well. He was very special to her."

"What happened?"

"Well, after her stroke, they weren't able to go on together. She never saw him again." Mike stared at his coffee cup, while strains of mandolin music played in the background. Now and then, one of the waiters sang a line or two and laughed along with the customers.

"I'm sorry that I made you sad, Uncle Mike. I really shouldn't have brought it all up."

He stroked her head. "Don't ever apologize for wanting to know about your family. But I do think it would be a good idea if we don't tell Aunt Etta that we talked about it. Those are memories that trouble her a lot. Let's just keep it between us." He winked.

Margaret smiled and nodded. It had always been easy to talk to Uncle Mike about things. He took time with explanations, where Aunt Etta was not so much of a talker. She just liked to get things done without a lot of words. "Will you let me visit you at work soon?"

Mike hesitated. "Why don't we wait a while, Mar. This may not be the best time."

"Because of Mr. Loughlin?"

"No. Not really. But...well..." He ran his hand across the top of his head. "What the heck. Let's plan on it next week, after confirmation is done with."

Margaret hugged him. "Thanks, Uncle Mike."

"And how about we take the rest of this pizza home with us." He waved to the waiter. "Maybe we'll just stick it in the oven and finish it up later."

"Great idea," she said, as they prepared to leave.

"Hey, and by the way," he said, nudging her, "remind me never to have a pizza date with you again. You're about as much fun as a stick in the eye."

She hit him lightly on the arm and out the door they went, laughing, both seemingly unaware of the growing chill of nightfall.

CHAPTER NINE

Nicholas Herring heard the boy stomping up the steps three at a time, and leaned down to set the half-empty bottle of Four Roses on the floor under the kitchen table. A moment later, breathless, Johnny Herring burst in through the door of the cold-water flat.

"You keep pounding those damn stairs, you'll get us thrown the hell outta here."

"Sorry, Pop." Johnny put his books on the kitchen table and went to the icebox.

"Did you chain up that damn bike?"

"I always do, Pop." The boy looked in at the dirty shelves, empty except for a catsup bottle lying on its side, the cap rimmed with dark red crust. The icebox was centered on a faded yellow wall between two wood-framed windows, one of them half covered with a water-stained piece of plywood where the glass was missing. The curtains, darkened with the soot of car exhaust and neglect, hung askew on bent rods.

"I don't know what you expect to find in there," Herring said. "I didn't see you bring in anything."

Johnny removed the bottle of catsup, and took it to the stove. "I thought maybe..."

"You thought, you thought. I guess you thought money grows on trees. You thought food just shows up."

"Pop, please don't start." The boy took a dented pot from the stove and filled it with water for the quick, familiar soup. "I didn't have anything to eat today." He ran his hand through his dark blond hair. "I had no money. I'm hungry."

"Whose fault is that? There's ways to get money."

"No there's not. Who's gonna hire a twelve-year-old kid?"

"I told you before—you don't have to earn money to get money. There's other ways."

"I don't like your ways, Pop. Piro is on to me. I copped an apple yesterday. He saw me."

"Then you better find another way." Herring rose from the table and picked up one of his son's books. "You think this is the way? Ever find any money in one of 'em?" He drew his arm back and flung the book against the kitchen wall, sending the clock above the icebox crashing to the floor.

Johnny ran at him. "Pop, don't!"

Herring pushed his son away with one hand, while picking up another book, and tore at the pages. "Here, how about this one?"

"Pop, please, they'll make us pay for them."

"Oh, yeah," he said, shoving his son against the sink, "how about they try makin' us pay for this?" With one great swipe across the kitchen table, Herring sent the rest of the books flying into the white metal cabinet.

"Please, Pop." Johnny bent down to pick up the torn pages and book covers, reaching under the table to retrieve the scattered pieces. A moment later, he rose slow and tight-lipped, the bourbon bottle in his hand. He narrowed his eyes and slammed the bottle on the table. "No, there's never any money for anything, is there—only your rotten booze." He moved in close, looking up into his father's face. "There's nothing for me to eat, but you always have yours." His face was hot, tears and rage building. "Who'd you steal from this time? What sucker turned his back so you could be the lousy thief that you are who can't even buy his own kid a piece of bread?"

Herring looked at the boy, cold-eyed. *Just like his mother—*

always crying about something. I'd like to smack the little rat's face the way I smacked hers.

"You're a bum!" the boy yelled. "That's what you are. That's all you'll ever be. Mom knew it. That's why she left. You drove her away, you bum!"

In a fury, Nicholas Herring tore at the belt of his worn gray trousers. "You don't talk to me like that, you no-good louse." He began chasing the boy through the rooms. "Don't you ever talk to me like that." He swung the belt as Johnny ran to get away from him. "You never learn, do you? This time I'll knock your rotten head off."

"I hate you! I hate you!" the boy yelled as the belt came down hard across his shoulders.

"Well, maybe you'll like this better." Herring's voice was loud and deliberate. He had Johnny trapped behind a lamp table in the living room. He picked up the lamp and smashed it onto the bare wood floor in front of Johnny. The boy threw his hands up to shield himself from the flying glass.

Herring grabbed the table and pulled it away, slamming it against the wall. Then he swung at the boy crouched on the floor in the corner, pieces of the shattered lamp mixing with the blows.

"Don't hit me! Pop! Don't hit me! The glass!" He pleaded, his face flushed and wet with tears. "Pop, please. Please."

Herring knew there was only one way to teach a boy. Fix him good. Break his will. Break everything if you had to, the same way he himself had been taught. "You never talk to me like that again, you hear me? Never." He kept swinging.

Someone yelled up from the street. A loud pounding came from the floor above, then from the kitchen door, followed by a neighbor's frantic call.

"Mr. Herring! Mr. Herring! Johnny! Open the door! Please. Open this door!"

"Leave us the hell alone," Herring yelled back. He reached

down and grabbed the boy by his hair, pulling him forward onto his knees amid the broken glass. "Don't you ever throw your mother up to me!" He dropped the belt and smacked Johnny across the face, clapping his ear and slamming him back against the wall.

Herring sneered at his son, who lay in a heap sobbing, sleeves torn, welts already visible on his arms and neck, his nose dripping blood. Slivers of glass had pierced the boy's shirt and trousers; a few stuck to his face and to his swollen, bloodied hands.

"How's that now?" Herring yelled. "And how's this, you lousy little creep—you steal or you starve. Your no-good mother left you behind. Now I'm saddled with you. And if you think I'm gonna be stuck feeding you and paying for your crap, you're crazy." Herring kicked the boy with the toe of his old thick work shoe, catching Johnny's anklebone.

The boy's whole body jerked. He threw his head back and, amid his breathless sobs, let out a tortured scream.

Herring kicked him again. "That's for good measure. I'd just as soon shoot you, you good-for-nothin' louse." He picked up his belt and began shoving it through his trouser loops. "And if I so much as hear one more word out of you, you'll find your teeth scattered across the floor like those rotten books of yours."

The pounding on the kitchen door continued. "Jesus, Mary and Joseph. Please, Mr. Herring, stop. Open the door. Please. The boy. Open the door."

Nicholas Herring did not open the door. He walked unsteadily through the dreary rooms to the kitchen, bumping the walls as he went, and made his way to the stove, where he slapped the pot of boiling water into the dirty porcelain sink. Then, kicking aside the scattered remains of his son's schoolbooks, he opened the bourbon bottle and took a long swig. He'd show that boy. He'd show them all.

CHAPTER TEN

Mrs. Paladino heard the apartment door slam and listened for the pounding of Nicholas Herring's footsteps down the stairs. When the outside door banged shut, she peeked into the dark hallway with its mixed smells of pork and roasted peppers, then opened her door cautiously to step out. She waited another moment, then went across to Herring's door and listened. Silence.

She took her superintendent's master key from her apron pocket, put it in the lock, gave it a turn and pressed open the door. She had not been in Herring's flat since Mrs. Herring left three months before, and was immediately caught by the total disarray and the odor of stale, foul air. Torn books and papers were scattered everywhere. An empty whiskey bottle lay on the kitchen table and just beyond the doorway to the adjoining room were piles of dirty clothes.

"Johnny," she whispered, "it's Mrs. Paladino." She walked a little farther into the apartment, checking behind her as she went. "Johnny, I came to help you."

She moved cautiously toward the center of the kitchen to look through the rooms. A white metal cabinet was standing sideways from the wall. She stepped over salt and pepper shakers and a catsup bottle. She knew the boy must be back there, but was afraid to go too far, knowing that if Herring returned she would have no way out.

"Johnny, please," she whispered louder. "I need to help you.

Please answer me. Can you hear me?"

After a few moments, she heard movement coming from the far room, then a groan. She waited.

"Johnny, I can't come back there. Please try to come out."

There were windows only at both ends of the flat, and in the fading afternoon light, it was hard at first for her to make out the figure of the boy pulling himself along the linoleum floor toward the kitchen. Once she realized what she was seeing, she blessed herself. "Jesus, Mary and Joseph." She hurried toward the boy.

A trail of smeared blood followed Johnny Herring, whose eyes were nearly swollen shut, his hair glistening with slivers of glass. She saw him reach for one of the drawer handles on the dresser to pull himself up, but he quickly fell back to the floor.

Mrs. Paladino rushed to his side, but there were so many tiny pieces of glass stuck to his clothing that she didn't know how to get him to his feet or if he was even able to stand. She could see that his injuries might be very serious.

She took a pillow from the bed and placed it beneath his head. The pillow was filthy and smelled sour, but she had little choice. She needed to get him out of there before his father came back. If only her husband were around. Her heart raced. She had to think fast.

She hurried across the hall to her own flat and picked up a scatter rug and a bedsheet. When she returned, she explained to Johnny that she would have to remove his shirt and trousers to get rid of most of the glass so she could roll him onto the small rug. Then, she would cover him with the sheet and drag him to her flat.

The boy moaned miserably as she worked, his face and lips too swollen and covered with cuts for him to speak. When she began to remove his trousers, she saw that his ankle was severely bruised. Her heart broke for him. "Mother of God," was all she could say or think.

She pulled him across the kitchen and out into the hallway to her flat, thankful that she was stout enough and he was scrawny enough for her to move him. She pulled him into the nearest bedroom and put a clean pillow under his head. Then she ran back to Herring's to return the filthy bed pillow. She picked the boy's clothing off the floor, along with any telltale signs that she had been there.

She knew it would take her more than an hour to remove the glass from his hair and skin. She would gently wipe away the dried blood and do her best to soothe his wounds. When her husband returned, she would talk to him about having Doctor Figueroa come, but Herring must not see him or suspect the boy was there. It would be too dangerous for all of them. She worried more for her husband and Johnny than for herself.

She knew they might have to call the authorities. The seriousness of that thought frightened her. In all her sixty-two years, no one in her family had ever had to call the police. But they had never encountered a monster like Nicholas Herring. She was also afraid of what he might do to them if he learned they were the ones who had made the call. She would wait and see how her husband wanted to handle this. In the meantime, she would put ice on the boy's ankle, give him warm broth and soothing words. She would cradle him and let him know he was safe. Yes, she would make sure he was safe, something she was certain his mother had not done.

CHAPTER ELEVEN

"Hold your finger here," Mrs. Addison said.

Lolly did as directed. "Isn't it a beautiful day?"

"Yes, it is, but we must focus right now. Mr. Grassley will be here shortly to drive you to Philadelphia."

Lolly pressed her forefinger hard against the brown paper wrapping, holding the double strands of white string in place, while Mrs. Addison tied a knot and a twice-tied bow.

"You know how to do everything, Mrs. Addison." Lolly believed if you thought something nice about someone you should tell them. "Thank you again for the blanket you made me."

Mrs. Addison looked up at Lolly and smiled. "Well, it was actually an afghan and that was three months ago. No need to keep thanking me."

"I keep thanking you because I keep liking it."

"You're a kind and loving person, Lolly.

Mrs. Addison had a way of making all the residents feel good about themselves, especially the ones with polio. None of them would ever be able to take the train from Philadelphia to New York City on their own the way she could, but Mrs. Addison helped make up for it by having Mr. Grassley take them on outings into town or to the park. Lolly usually went along, always trying to pay special attention not to lag behind talking to people she met along the way, like the man with the seventeen-year-old Irish Setter with one eye, and the woman with the picture of her dead husband stitched into the lining of her elegant black silk hat. Lolly tended to think that Life was an amazing blessed place.

She took the package and placed it in her brown cardboard suitcase.

"I think Margaret is going to be quite pleased with your gift, Lolly."

Lolly smiled and turned away, enjoying the thought. "She will, won't she." It was a statement not a question. Lolly was careful not to say too much or speak too fast and stumble over her words. "I tried and tried to think of that...just-so-special gift for Margaret, and all of a sudden there it was."

Mrs. Addison patted Lolly's arm. "Well, now it's all folded up so beautifully and you are going to have a wonderful time."

"I always do." Lolly paused. "I told you that Margaret is taking my name for confirmation, mine and Saint Anne's, the mother of the Virgin Mary—Margaret Anne Lorelei Ferry."

"That's beautiful, Lolly. I know she thinks the world of you."

Lolly's smile faded.

"What is it?"

"Etta worries when I'm around. She's afraid things will go wrong, especially now because Margaret is making her... confirmation, and everything has to go just so."

"Well, you can understand why that is. Right?"

Lolly looked down and nodded.

"You will have a good trip and a good time, Lolly. Stay focused and calm. Use your poetry."

"Yes. I will, Mrs. Addison. I have another that I've... memorized. Another Frost—"Once By the Pacific." Did you ever read it?"

"I don't know that I did."

"The crashing water made a misty din, great waves looked over others coming in..." She shook her head with an admiring smile. "Such short ordinary words to make such mighty images. The schoolchildren I taught loved the rhyme and rhythm of his poems. That was a long time ago, but," she gave a slight chuckle, "Frost is still Frost. When I get back, I'll write out a copy for you."

"Thank you, Lolly. I'm sure I'll like it as well as you do. A great one to recite on the train when you feel you need it."

"Frost is always a comfort. And you know that the train always goes right through, then Mike is there waiting for me." She remembered that Mrs. Addison had never made the trip. "New York City is not really so far, just a couple of hours. You would love Penn Station. It's a special place. I have so many memories there from...from...before."

"Well, we'll just have to go together one day and you'll show me everything."

As a girl growing up in Syracuse, Lolly had dreamed of one day going to Pennsylvania. She had heard about the Pennsylvania Dutch and imagined them with wooden shoes curling up at the toe and little caps pointing out at the sides.

She had come to live at St. Clement at the age of twenty-three, just months after suffering the stroke that left her with a few mild though likely permanent impairments—a slight limp, a need to speak her long words slowly and, less and less often over the years, an occasional lack of focus—a trait she believed she probably had long before the stroke, and laughed often about.

The stroke also tampered with the symmetry of her face, a flaw that was recognizable, though many thought not unappealing, especially when she smiled. Of course, the worst of it were the things she must not ever dwell upon.

She had been a resident worker now for ten of the twelve years she lived there with a corner window room of her own as living quarters, a stipend, and a shared office. She had lost the dexterity to type fast, but was good on the telephone and diligent about the paperwork she handled. They had appointed her the official greeter for the new arrivals, a duty she was called upon to perform only when someone "moved on." For some, like her, the rehabilitation helped them improve greatly. A few even improved enough to go back to a normal way of life. Most, though, did not.

Over the years, Lolly's sister Rae had invited her to come live with them. So had her sister Jo, generous offers but out of the question as far as Lolly was concerned—she wouldn't want to risk becoming a burden or to give up the freedom she enjoyed. The people at St. Clement understood her condition and all the ways she was *not* limited, something her family had yet to fully grasp. Mike and Margaret were the only ones who treated her the way people at the facility did. It was Mike who had found St. Clement through a contact at the newspaper where he worked.

Mr. Grassley announced himself with two taps of the car horn that sent them scrambling.

"Off you go now." The white-haired Mrs. Addison hugged Lolly and picked up her suitcase.

"Thank you again, Mrs. Addison." Lolly took the suitcase from her. "I'll see you in a few days." Then, in a more measured way, she said, "Please check on the linen delivery. I placed the order on Tuesday, and Mr. Haller...Harrelson said he'd be sure to have it here by the end of the week." She felt her face flush, stumbling over her words as she often did when rushed, and perhaps more so at the thought of Mr. Grassley.

"Good morning to you, Lolly." Mr. Grassley, with customary cheerfulness, took Lolly's suitcase. "And to you, Mrs. Addison." He put the suitcase in the back of the wood-paneled Ford station wagon, and off they went, Lolly waving goodbye from the front seat of the dark green car that blended in a way that she loved with the surrounding woods, as if it were part of the natural landscape.

"Looks like you're up for a high time there, Lolly."

"I believe so, Mr. Grassley. Margaret is making her confirmation." She spoke her long words carefully, not wishing her nerves to get the better of her.

"Very nice," he said. "Very nice. And I wish one of these days you would call me Andrew."

"Andrew," she repeated with a shy smile. Andrew Grassley never seemed to notice the way her mouth turned up a little more on one side than the other, an imperfection even she seemed to be unaware of in his presence.

He laughed. "See, that's not so hard."

"Not so hard," she said. She liked the way he looked, with his window rolled down and his shirtsleeves rolled up, his arm resting on the door, a single vein bulging in the smoothness of his forearm. The sunlight made his brown hair shine and the slight wind seemed to blow streaks of silver through it as they drove. When he glanced her way, she could see the tiny dark flecks in his hazel eyes, and this was not at all the first time she had noticed them.

"Now, tell me how you are this fine day, Miss Lorelei O'Donnell."

She pulled in a quick breath of air. "How did you know my name is Lorelei?"

"I know a lot of things about you."

"What kind of things?"

"Well, I know that you have the most beautiful gray-blue eyes that shine like starlight. I know that you laugh with the voice of the angels and that the merry heart in you dances for the joy of others."

Lolly felt her face burn with the excitement of hearing such words from him. She kept her head down, smiling, but could say nothing in reply.

"Now I'd like to ask you—is there anything you know about me?'

Lolly glanced at Andrew Grassley. "Well," she said, and took a deep breath. "I know that you are the best grounds...keeper St. Clement has ever had, and that you live in the dark red shingle cottage by the creek. You keep the box...woods trimmed and the flower beds looking quite...beautiful." She would have loved to mention the hydrangeas and chrysanthemums in particular, but didn't dare attempt them at this moment. The thought of even trying to pronounce them made her almost laugh out loud at herself. Why couldn't they have been roses or tulips? She could have said those names with no difficulty at all. "I know that you have a way of making everything prettier than it looked before you came, which was a year ago last week. You like to sing as you work and you have a lovely tenor voice that gets people to stop and listen."

She knew more than that, but would not say. People talked; she asked about the rest. She knew that the stiffness of his gait was due to the brace on his left leg, the result of being wounded at Normandy. She knew that he was away at war for three years and returned home to find that his wife had not waited.

"Do you stop and listen too, Lolly? When I sing, I mean."

"I do," she said, her eyes trained on him. His was what she called a warm caramel voice. She turned back and with her gaze fixed straight ahead through the windshield, added, "Maybe more than the others." Did she only imagine the sweetness of the brief silence that followed?

On an afternoon many months earlier, he had caught up with her on the path around the grounds. They walked along together until the sun began to set, and the chill caught them quickly. He gave her his sweater, which warmed her heart as well as her small frame, and she felt the strength of his arm as he set the sweater about her shoulders. She had watched him before that and liked his quiet, friendly ways. She knew that he watched her too. Since then, she felt the tease of longing that she had come to believe she might never experience again.

It was Andrew who broke the silence. "I was wondering, Miss Lorelei O'Donnell. I was wondering if you would allow me to take you to the spring dance at the Haverstown Hall next Saturday night."

"I...I don't know what to say Mr....Andrew." She looked directly at him. "You know that I'm not...that I don't walk very..."

"It wouldn't matter now, would it, if you were in my arms. That is, if I were to hold you."

"Oh," was all she said at the very thought of his arms around her, and again they were surrounded by a comfortable silence there in the dark green car, vanishing together into the rural Pennsylvania countryside.

Lolly closed her eyes and let the gentle rocking of the train soothe her with its hypnotic rhythm. Mr. Grassley's words—Andrew—Andrew's words—played over and over in her head, sweet and warm. Love. She was sure. It was a moment, a feeling, wonderful, thrilling and she had known it before. But that was another time, another life. *No.* She meant only to have her heart reference it, but gradually...*No...*

"Remember your poetry," Mrs. Addison had said. *Two roads diverged in a yellow wood, and sorry I couldn't take them both and be one traveler, long I stood...* She couldn't allow herself, even briefly, to be coaxed back. She mustn't think of it...of him. That was so long ago and Andrew was now...and maybe forever...who could say?

Some memories must live only in that small, cherished corner of your heart where there is no form, like a solid blue sky without a single cloud. Thoughts demand shape and color and the painful nuance of detail—a curl, a color, the blink of dark eyes; the scent of powdered manliness, warm skin. A touch, strong and tender. The talk, the plans, the dreams. A home, a child, a life. *No. The crashing water made a misty din, great waves looked over others coming in, and thought of doing something to the shore that water never did to land before...*

She looked at her shadowy reflection in the train window. The rapid flashing of sunlight through the trees clipped her image over and over into black and white still shots, like old photos she must never look at again. *The clouds hung low and hairy in the skies, like locks blown forward in the gleam of eyes...* But it was no use. No use at all.

He had dreamed of that faraway exotic place the way she had dreamed of Pennsylvania, silly little longings. She watched herself in the train window, remembering how they had playfully mocked each other's wishfulness and with a wry and crooked little smile—a smile now not so much gay as melancholy— she considered the irony of how both had gotten their wish.

CHAPTER TWELVE

The smoky incense rose like a sheer veil above the altar at St. Aloysius before drifting toward the crowded pews. Bishop Harriot, in miter and red-bordered chasuble, descended the marble steps and recessed up the center aisle toward the wooden doors standing open to the May afternoon.

The organ's celebratory thunder swelled above the strains of the bell choir. Thirty-eight children trailed in twos like ducklings, their expressions a mix of pride, self-consciousness and relief. The boys, all fresh haircuts, navy blue suits, and flushed faces; the girls in white organdy and lace, with veils that fell from flowered headpieces or tiaras, shimmering in the amber light below the church's vaulted ceiling.

Margaret straightened the fine white lace shawl that Aunt Lolly had surprised her with. Margaret could see Lolly seated alongside Aunt Etta and Uncle Mike, her shining face smiling broadly amid the dark suits, pastel dresses and flowery spring hats. The school had limited the number of guests each child could invite to the ceremony. Aunt Jo, Uncle Frank and the others were either on their way to Margaret's house or already there. It was a grand time that turned out just as Mike had predicted: the Bishop's questions were nowhere near as hard as Margaret and Junie had feared.

Margaret wondered if anyone had noticed that one long pause when the Bishop first read her name. He hadn't paused for anyone else. She'd felt the heat flash in her face, certain that he remembered the petition she had circulated. Maybe he would just stop right there and not let her make her confirmation. *That's what you get for being so impudent*, Sister Bernadine would have said and Uncle Mike would never have let her see another movie again.

Surely Aunt Rae had noticed, standing as Margaret's sponsor before the Bishop, her hand resting on Margaret's right shoulder. When the Bishop looked at Margaret, his eyes narrowed and he nodded ever so slightly. Margaret was sure one side of his mouth turned up in a smile. She wondered if she'd be in trouble with Sister if the Bishop smiled at her. Was a Bishop even supposed to smile in church?

"Margaret Anne Lorelei Ferry," Bishop Harriot had said, "what are the twelve fruits of the Holy Spirit?"

Margaret was relieved that it was a list. She could do a list much better than having to make some kind of a statement. She swallowed hard, her mouth dry as wood. "Love, joy, peace…patience." Out of the corner of her eye, she could see Monsignor Carnavan standing somberly. "Kindness… goodness." She took a deep breath. "Faithfulness…modesty… chastity…gentleness." She was aware of flashbulbs going off. "Generosity…and self-control."

The Bishop dipped his thumb into the alabaster pot of sacred Chrism oil and anointed Margaret by making the sign of the cross on her forehead. "Be sealed with the gift of the Holy Spirit," he said. Then, Margaret and Aunt Rae moved to the far side of the altar and took their place among the other children and sponsors.

"We're so proud of you." Aunt Etta was the first to hug her outside church, where the children were swallowed up in the noisy crush of relatives.

"What did I tell you?" Mike said. "You did great."

Margaret put her arms around him and saw Lolly off to one side, smiling. Her face had a glow about it that Margaret first noticed when she arrived from Philadelphia the previous afternoon. Lolly had stayed at Aunt Rae's that night, but not before spending time at Margaret's. That was when she had given her the shawl—the prettiest thing her niece had ever owned or even worn.

Margaret walked over and hugged her. "Oh, Aunt Lolly, you look so beautiful today. And I just love this shawl. I've never had anything like it."

"I'm so glad you do." Lolly's eyes glistened brighter than usual.

Margaret had wanted Lolly to be her confirmation sponsor, but Aunt Etta said no. "It's just too busy a day, Mar, and everything at church has to go precisely as planned. You know how that might turn out to be a problem for Lolly." Mike had agreed.

Junie made her way over. "I didn't know you were wearing a shawl." She touched the delicate lace edge. "When did you get it? It's so pretty."

"Aunt Lolly gave it to me."

Lolly patted Junie's shoulder. "You look lovely, Junie. Just lovely. Your parents…must be very proud of you today."

Junie smiled. "Thank you, Miss O'Donnell. You look lovely too." She turned to Margaret. "Come over later. We're going out to eat, but we won't be that long."

To Margaret this was a day of days. Confirmation was over, the spring air was warm and sweet, and she was surrounded by family. On the walk home, they would pass the airy ways in front of the brownstones with their garden boxes filled with early blooms of hyacinth and daffodils and forsythia hedges ready to burst with the color of sunlight. It was a day she truly believed could not be spoiled by anything.

Aunt Etta's new cotton curtains breathed with the warm air

coming through the kitchen windows. Margaret thought they looked like angel wings. She knew the angels were everywhere, especially today. She had thought of her mother and father and said a prayer for them during the confirmation mass.

Talk and laughter and the aroma of roast prime rib that lingered long after the dinner plates had been cleared and the strawberry sheet cake served up. Margaret could see that everyone was content—Aunt Rae and Uncle Howard talked about the new apartment they were getting in Forest Hills, Aunt Lolly included a prayer during grace for Carole Lombard, the famous actress who died in a plane crash in World War II, and Aunt Jo and Uncle Frank shared their plans for an Adirondack vacation that excited their son, Thomas, and daughter, Sarah.

"They have boats and horses and everything," Thomas said. He was nine and Margaret loved to be around him with all his boy talk.

"I hope I get one of those spotty brown and white horses," Sarah said, "like in the movies." At seven, Sarah was the picky one but Margaret loved the way she ended up being happy with everything that came her way.

Rae turned to Lolly. "I want to know where you found such a beautiful shawl."

Frank tamped his cigarette out in the glass ashtray. "There's got to be a story to it, Loll, and nobody can tell it better than you."

Lolly smiled self-consciously. Margaret sat near the end of the table and looked about at the happy faces of the people she loved, people who loved each other and cared so specially for Lolly.

Aunt Jo put down her cup and reached over to lift a corner of the shawl. "It isn't alencon lace. It's much finer."

"The stitching is so intricate and delicate," Rae said. "I'm not sure what kind of lace it is. It looks very old world, doesn't it? Did you find it in Haverstown?"

"I didn't exactly find it." Lolly laughed. "It found me." She took a deep breath. Margaret could see she was settling herself so she wouldn't stumble over words. "Mrs. Samuelson gave it to me. I can't imagine why."

There were some surprised looks around the table. "Do you mean Samuelson, as in the wealthy Philadelphia Samuelsons?" Jo asked.

"Yes. She's a lovely person. She's our main donor for St. Clement."

Frank leaned in, reaching for the cream. "She just decided to give you a beautiful shawl?"

"And a pretty expensive one, if I had to guess." Howard lit a cigarette. "Although I don't suppose that's an issue if you're a Samuelson. But still quite a generous gesture."

"Was it for some special occasion?" Jo asked.

"No, nothing special. I came out of the office to go for a walk...and as I passed that little...living room area that we have...you all know the one...I happened to look over and saw her." Lolly shrugged. "It was odd. We just stood there looking at each other as if...I don't know...as if there was something we were supposed to say. I walked over to her and she took my hand. She told me she had something that she...believed I would like to have. I had no idea what it could be or why. We had never really said much to each other, but we always smiled. And...and there were times I found her watching me, but it never made me...uncomfortable. She was always such a gracious person when she visited. And quiet. Never a bother the way we've all heard some people...can be when they have so much money and want everyone to know it."

As Margaret listened along with the others, she felt so proud of Lolly. Margaret didn't know anyone else who had such a condition, but she couldn't imagine that anyone else would be so pleasant about it, so full of joy and faith in all things, as if what was wrong with her didn't matter at all, as long as she spoke carefully enough.

"Then," Lolly went on, "she waived her hand toward the front desk and...Sally came right over. She asked Sally to please go out...and tell her driver to bring...the package from the back seat."

"Just like that?" Rae asked. "She didn't explain anything?"

Lolly smiled and shook her head. "No. The driver came in...he seemed like a very nice man... all dressed in black... with a cap on his head, just like in the movies. But he did take his cap off when he came through the door. A gentleman. He was carrying a package wrapped...in brown paper with a string tied around it. Mrs. Samuelson...handed me the package and said not to open it now. She said she had a feeling...it was going to make someone very happy."

Everyone looked around the table at each other.

"Did you say anything to her?" Jo asked.

Lolly squeezed her shoulders up into a slow shrug. "I felt I wasn't supposed...to say anything but thank you." She looked around at the puzzled faces. "That's what I felt."

Margaret watched the others. No one said a word, but she could tell they must have been thinking the same thing—what an odd story, and so like Lolly to have such an odd one to tell.

Lolly just smiled. "When I opened it later, I knew exactly what...Mrs. Samuelson meant. It was just the kind of special gift I wanted...for Mar."

"How strange," Aunt Jo said.

Sarah reached for a cookie. "Was she an old lady with a big wart on the end of her nose?"

Margaret laughed along with everyone else.

"Sarah, that's not nice," Aunt Jo said. "And no more cookies. You've had enough for one day. You won't be able to sleep tonight."

Lolly turned and touched Sarah's arm. "No, she looked to be about maybe your Mommy's age or Aunt Etta's or so, and she didn't have…a wart on the end of her nose. It was a lovely nose. And her eyes were a greenish gray and…brilliant. Such clear eyes that…I remember thinking they must have seen wondrous things."

"Well, it's a beautiful gift," Etta said, bringing the coffee pot to the table for a second round. "Margaret, if you're planning to stop around at Junie's, don't wait too long."

"But I want to hear the rest," Margaret said.

Mike looked up at Etta. "We all do. Go on, Lolly."

Margaret knew that look. It was the look Uncle Mike always gave Aunt Etta to remind her to be patient with Lolly. Uncle Mike knew, and so did Margaret, that Aunt Etta was nervous when Lolly went on about this or that, as if…well, Mar didn't know "as if" what. She never understood why Aunt Etta got so frustrated with Lolly, except that maybe she was afraid Lolly might do or say something to embarrass herself.

"Maybe I better not. You know how I can…"

"No, really, Lolly," Mike said. "We all want to hear the rest."

"Yes, please go on, Lolly," Etta said, her face softening to a smile. She rested her hand on Mike's shoulder.

"Well, there isn't any more to tell… except that she said… she had had it a very long time… and that now it was time to pass it on."

"Time to pass it on," Mike said. "That's a strange thing to say, isn't it?"

"The whole thing is strange," Howard said. Margaret could tell that no one really knew what to make of it.

"Did she have a big hump on her back?"

"Sarah, stop now." Jo looked up at the wall clock. "Go in and put on one of your radio shows. Maybe *Lone Ranger* is on. Or *Our Gal Sunday*. Thomas, go help your sister find the right station."

"What about the television set?" Thomas asked. "Can we watch that, Uncle Mike?"

"You sure can," Mike said, and headed for the living room with the two children.

Margaret rose from the table and hugged Lolly, then she turned and smiled at everyone. "I better go to Junie's. It's almost four o'clock. I won't be gone long." She went out the door and headed down the stairs, still hearing the happy chatter at the table. She pulled the shawl closer around her shoulders, smiling about Lolly's wonderful story. Sweet Aunt Lolly. Aunt Etta had no reason to worry. What could possibly go wrong on a day as perfect as this?

CHAPTER THIRTEEN

Margaret stepped from the brownstone into the afternoon sunlight, headed to Junie's. Two boys on a stoop ate Milk Duds and read their *Tales from the Crypt* comic books. On the other side of the street, Mrs. Schiano swept the sidewalk outside her house, while her old boxer, Stoogie, rested nearby. The woman waved and blew a kiss.

Margaret called over. "Hello, Mrs. Schiano."

"What a beautiful day you had for confirmation, Margaret. You're such a grown-up girl now. I remember you in the carriage."

Margaret smiled. "Did you get any letters from Danny?"

"Just yesterday, thank you. He's fine and says hello to everybody. He misses my cooking." She laughed. "There's no lasagna in Korea."

"I always say a prayer for him."

"You're a good girl, Margaret. God bless you."

Aunt Etta and Uncle Mike had often talked about buying a house on Long Island next year after Margaret graduated. It would be fun to have a basement and a front lawn and a back yard, maybe even an attic where she could steal away to spend afternoons reading Nancy Drew. But she would miss it here in Brooklyn, where everything was so nearly perfect.

A light breeze lifted her veil, and she reached up quickly to secure it, holding onto the edge of her shawl, which kept slipping off her shoulder. She looked down and noticed her right stocking bunched in a little ripple of creases around her ankle—the first pair of nylons she'd ever had.

An elderly man and woman, arm in arm, waited on the corner for the light to change. They turned to her and smiled. Margaret smiled back, feeling awkward—she hadn't thought it would be this hard to wear things that fluttered and moved all over the place. You had to keep pulling them up and holding them down, straightening and tugging the whole time. It wasn't anything like in the movies where June Alyson and Deanna Durbin could run up and down the stairs in a floor-length gown and never trip on the hem or have the flowers fall out of their hair.

"Congratulations," the woman said, "you're a beautiful young lady."

Margaret gave her a shy thank you, holding her headpiece in place with one hand and her shawl with the other. On her wrist, a little white satin purse containing some of the gift money Aunt Jo and Uncle Frank had given her swung from its braided silk strap. She was going to use the money to buy the red wallet she'd seen in Levin's window. Maybe Aunt Etta would also let her get that navy blue purse with the shoulder strap.

Sunday traffic was light—Sunday always had a different feel to it. Only the candy store would be open for business. Maybe she would stop in and let Mr. and Mrs. Wortman see her confirmation dress. She wasn't at all hungry for candy or anything else for that matter—the strawberry cake that Aunt Rae had brought was the most delicious she'd ever had. She was beginning to feel sorry that she'd had a second piece.

On the avenue, curtains billowing from apartment windows waved like flags along a parade route, while the aroma of Sunday dinners spilled out into the spring air. Three girls jumped double Dutch on the sidewalk as Tommy McGrath, with his bucket and rags, washed his black Ford coupe in a parking spot at the curb. Everything was just as it should be, even the occasional car horn, the pounding of tires over the potholes and the muffled roar of a ballgame coming from a window somewhere.

Outside the candy store, Johnny Herring, his bike sprawled beside him on the sidewalk, stood leaning against the wall, just far enough from the front door so that Mr. and Mrs. Wortman would not be able see him. He said something to one of the men coming out of the store, but the man just shook his head and walked away, a newspaper under his arm. Margaret had a jumble of feelings when Johnny Herring was around—he could be mean, and she was still mad at him for ruining her book covers and getting Junie's purse all muddy. But she had seen his father and now she felt bad for him, thinking that what people said about his family must be true—his father was mean and his mother ran off and left Johnny behind. Johnny went to P.S. 37, but Margaret had no idea if he even went to school at all. Maybe there was no one to care whether he did or not, not even a friend. She had never seen him with other kids—most were probably afraid of him, just as she sometimes was.

Another man came out of the store and Johnny said something to him. The man reached in his pocket and appeared to give the boy a coin. Margaret turned her head toward the street, so Johnny wouldn't notice that she had seen him ask for money.

When she reached the store, she decided not to go in, but she didn't feel right just walking past without saying anything. "Hi," she said, slowing her walk.

Johnny Herring stuck his chin up and narrowed his eyes. Margaret saw that he had cuts on his face, and stopped.

"Did you get hurt?"

"Keep walkin'."

A man entered the store. Johnny glanced at him, and Margaret knew that if she hadn't been there, Johnny would have asked for money again.

"Are you okay?" She didn't know why she was taking a chance talking to him, except that she had never seen him like this. His tan cotton shirt was a mess of wrinkles with grime around the collar and cuffs. It looked as if it hadn't been washed in days. Neither did his trousers, which were torn at the pockets. He was like a homeless cat out in the cold all night without any food or water, nowhere to sleep, no one to care for it.

"Beat it, will ya?" He turned and looked off down the street.

Margaret stepped closer and saw that his blond hair was matted, some of it missing in places. Maybe because she was looking at him, he grabbed a cap from his back pocket and pulled it onto his head. His hands were covered with cuts and bruises.

"Johnny, did something happen to you? Do you need help?"

"I don't need anything."

"But maybe I can do something for you."

"Yeah, you can get lost." He bent to pick up his bike.

He was moving slower than usual and his ankle was swollen.

"You *are* hurt."

"You're nuts." He got on his bike.

"How can you even pedal with a hurt foot?"

"You think I'm a crybaby? It's none of your business anyway." He began to push off.

"Wait," she said, opening her purse. She could hardly believe what she was about to do for a boy who was always so mean to her. "I've got something of yours."

"Why don't you get out of my hair?"

"You remember the day you rode by and knocked our books all over the ground?"

"Maybe that'll teach you and that other dimwit not to take up half the sidewalk."

She held out her hand. "Well, you dropped this. You probably didn't even realize it till later, but I kept it for you."

Johnny Herring stared in silence at the crisp five-dollar bill in Margaret's outstretched hand. He crinkled his brow and pulled his head back.

"Take it," she said, "it's yours."

"Aw, what are you talkin' about? Why don't you leave me alone?"

"Why should I? We all need friends, don't we?"

He looked away. "I don't need anybody." He started again to push off.

"Johnny, wait. Please."

He stopped and crossed his arms, still looking away.

"I have an idea." She stood in front of him and put a light grip on his handlebars.

"Hey," he snarled.

"I'm awfully hungry," she said, still holding on, "and Mrs. Wortman makes really good grill cheese sandwiches. Why don't you come with me and we'll both have one? I don't like eating all by myself."

There was a long silence. Johnny Herring turned and looked at her, his eyes less angry, maybe curious. They were the color of a blue dress she'd had a long time ago, the prettiest dress she'd ever had—prettier even than her confirmation dress. His lashes were dark blond like his hair and his face had a straight-line look about his nose and chin. She had never thought until now how nice looking he was, even with all the bruises, cuts and scrapes, dirty clothes and all. And there was something else—when his eyes got softer the way they did, she could tell that deep down he really wasn't bad at all. "Find the good," Aunt Lolly always said.

"Please come with me, Johnny." She could hardly believe her own words. What if he just reached out and hit her? He could knock her to the ground. "Please?"

Neither of them noticed that her shawl had slipped from her right shoulder and fallen to the ground between them.

After a long moment, his lips tightened and the look in his eyes grew hard again. "I don't want your lousy money or your grill cheese." He raised his voice and she took a step back, startled. "And I don't want to be friends, not with you or anybody else. You hear me?"

Johnny Herring pushed off on his bike, and headed across the street just as the light changed. It was in that flash of a moment that Margaret gasped, seeing her shawl, its delicate lace caught on the rear wheel of his bike, dragging along the sidewalk behind him. She grabbed at it but missed.

"Johnny, Johnny," she yelled. "My shawl." She began to cry as she took off after him. He didn't turn around. She felt a wave of panic and dread—her beautiful shawl, Lolly's precious gift. Everything blurred as though she were lifted out of herself. "Johnny!" she cried again, calling his name over and over, as she ran out into the street.

———◆———

Johnny Herring knew that sound—the blast of a car horn, the squeal of brakes. The thud. He stopped short and turned quickly, shocked also by the sight of Margaret's shawl hanging from his rear wheel. His mind raced. Holy...She's been hit. He thought of riding back, but stopped. He couldn't fully grasp what had taken only seconds to happen. His heart beat so fast he thought it would explode.

There was a commotion, people running, but all he could see of her was the white of her dress on the ground, the other side of a dark blue DeSoto, whose driver, pacing frantically back and forth, cried his apology to the gathering crowd.

Mr. Wortman hurried out, removed his sweater, and did something with it. Covered her body maybe. How was this possible? They were just talking. She had tried to be nice to him, but he wouldn't let her. *Oh, God, please.*

Would they blame him? Would they think he'd stolen her

shawl? He hadn't taken it on purpose. He didn't know what
to do. The shawl was filthy now from being dragged along the
street. He reached down and tore it from his wheel. If someone
saw him with it, he'd get the blame for sure. He pitched it to
the side of the building, where it landed out of sight between
two banged up metal garbage cans.

She had tried to be nice to him. She had tried. He began
to tremble. What if she was…if she was…? He couldn't bear
to even think the word. And why wouldn't he be to blame?
He took off his cap and slapped it against his hand again and
again.

He had heard her yelling his name, but he never even
bothered to turn around. All she wanted was her shawl—he
knew that now. That stupid shawl stuck to his stupid wheel.
He got off his bike and kicked it over onto the sidewalk. Then
he leaned against the wall and threw his hands over his eyes.
She had tried to be nice to him. No one was ever nice to him.
She had offered him money. She knew it wasn't his; she had
to know. She made it up just to help him. She wasn't like a lot
of other people. She was okay. Why did he have to be such
a rat? "Please, God, please." He said it out loud. He couldn't
remember the last time he had asked God for anything.

As the scream of sirens grew louder, Johnny Herring
lowered himself to the ground and sobbed. Sobbed until his
body shook. And prayed. He did not notice a certain waft of
air that arrived gently in a cool and quiet swirl, lifting the shawl
from the place where it rested, and carrying it along, carrying it
as if on wings. Carrying it back to the place where it belonged.

CHAPTER FOURTEEN

St. Peter's Hospital was a massive six-story red brick building with a front tower, tall double-hung windows, and a handsome austerity that typified institutional architecture of the previous century. A majestic though brooding structure, it occupied an entire square block along Henry Street, looming above the neighborhood sidewalks in the Cobble Hill section of Brooklyn.

A long stone staircase led to the entrance, where heavy wooden doors opened onto a wide center corridor with high ceilings, a gray linoleum floor that shone like a mirror, and the lingering scents of ether and Pine Sol. The three-story crucifix mounted on the far wall nearly dwarfed the broad circular marble staircase.

Mike Ferry stood at the window of the first floor waiting room, staring into the dusk, his outstretched arm braced against the wooden frame, his eyes thickened by the tearfulness he fought so hard to hold back for Etta's sake. It had been nearly two hours now. He and Etta were exhausted from the tension and the terror of the moment, she fidgeting with her rosary or picking mindlessly at the crocheted edges of her handkerchief, he offering her comfort while struggling to find the strength to handle what was going on. Now and then, he'd had to step away before he broke down in front of her.

Across the softly lighted room, Jo and Rae took turns pacing and sitting with their sister, as Frank attempted to be a voice of reason and hope. He was a bear of a man with caring eyes and a heart to match, a man accustomed by trade and dedication to carrying people out of burning buildings and, when needed, breathing life back into the near dead.

"Listen," he had whispered to Mike and Etta, "this is a good hospital, and Vianney's one of the best. He's the one who took out Sarah's appendix two years ago. Remember? And that was pretty serious."

Howard had remained back at the apartment with the children, while Lolly, silent in her desolation, had gone to the chapel at the rear of the hospital. She had not uttered a word following the horrific news, and Mike feared it might all be too much for her. Frank had offered to go to the chapel with her, but she had put up a gentle hand and gone off by herself.

Tommy McGrath had seen the whole thing and tore around to the Ferrys' house with his breathless account of what had happened—Johnny Herring had taken off with Margaret's shawl.

That shawl, Etta now thought, her eyes red-rimmed and blank. "That shawl," she murmured.

"What is it, Et?" Jo leaned closer.

"Somehow, it's always Lolly," Etta said in a low voice, speaking into space. "No matter what…that's just the way it is. Mike always said I worried too much."

Jo caught Rae's eye, both aware of Etta's meaning, aware also that it seemed to be true—when Lolly was involved, things happened. Even something as simple as a beautiful shawl, Lolly's special gift, with its lovely, almost mystical story, had somehow led to disaster. What must Lolly be feeling right now? Lolly, of all people. Jo put her arm around Etta. "It's no one's fault. It was an accident."

A statue of St. Peter stood on a shelf within an alcove centered on one of the pale blue walls, on another wall, a framed painting of the Immaculate Heart of Mary. In the half-full room, a middle-aged woman sat alone and dabbed her eyes with a handkerchief, while a young, solemn looking husband and wife held hands. A large man with his hat in his lap and his jaw resting on his fist slept. Others read the paper or skimmed through the outdated issues of *Look*, *Good Housekeeping* or *Field and Stream*. They all waited.

Now and then, the loud speaker sounded the name of a doctor or a code, which Mike Ferry, his stomach twisted into knots, interpreted as meaning that something somewhere was going wrong. He ran his fingers through his hair, wondering if she was in pain. What if she were suddenly gone from their lives? How would they ever deal with losing her, the child they loved above all else, the only child they would ever have? And what about Lolly, poor Lolly? Margaret meant everything to her. What must she be going through? Lolly, so well-meaning yet always somehow on the wrong side of things, now once again to blame in Etta's mind. She had gone off by herself to…what? To cry, to pray, to beg, to make a bargain with the Lord as likely they all were doing?

Had he been too hard on Mar about the petition to the Bishop? Beautiful, stubborn Mar. Had he shown her how much he loved her? Wallace Loughlin flashed through his mind and Mike didn't need a single second to ponder how very insignificant he was, he and his lie, the paper itself, the whole damn job. What did any of it matter? He felt terrified and sick. Frank went to stand beside him and put his hand on his shoulder.

Now and then, the double doors swung open and every head jutted up expectantly, usually seeing a nurse or doctor enter. This time it was one of the nuns, in black habit and starched white bib, Sister Teresa, the same one who had come to them at the very beginning. She was carrying Margaret's shawl, folded into a square, a puzzled look on her face.

Etta rose quickly, and Mike hurried over.

"I'm sorry, still no news yet," Sister said softly. She handed the shawl to Etta. "I was sure I had given this to you earlier when I gave you the purse."

Etta looked about, certain that was true. Margaret's smudged white purse lay on the seat where Etta had been sitting. The shawl, torn and dark with street soot, had been there too, she was sure of it. But how had it come to be with Margaret in the first place, if that boy had run off with it? "I...I don't know." Her voice was low and dull.

"Please trust that the doctors are working very hard," Sister said with a sympathetic smile. She turned to leave. "Everything is in God's hands, you can be sure."

"Thank you, Sister," Mike said, his arm around Etta, his eyes filled with tears. *Working very hard, she said.* Dear God, please, he thought, please. *I'll be better. I'll be whatever you want. I'll do whatever you lead me to do. Only, please.*

For another half hour, they sat. "How could such a thing happen?" Etta muttered, trance-like. "We were all just together, talking and laughing. She was so happy." Her thoughts were chaotic, full of fear and melancholy. She thought of how much she loved brushing Margaret's silky hair, how much they enjoyed picking out clothes together, making popovers, Margaret's favorite. What if they lost her? How could she bear any of it? She thought about how Margaret had come into their lives, how her life with them had begun with a tragedy. Would it end with one, as well? How could they ever deal with such a loss? How could Lolly?

God forgive me for being unkind to Lolly. Etta sobbed against Mike's shoulder, wondering how he could possibly bear up if the worst were to happen. Poor Mike, always so in charge. She would have to be strong for him—he had no idea how fragile he was.

To everyone's shock, the doors again swung open and Viola Steich's shrill voice pierced the quiet like a buzz saw in a forest.

She scanned the room quickly, then with small hurried steps and a black purse swinging from her thick wrist, went directly to Etta and Mike. "I cannot believe it. I'm so very, very sorry. I can't imagine what you're going through."

Etta buried her face in her hands as Mike moved quickly to act as a buffer between her and Viola. "I'm surprised to see you, Viola. This is not a good time for us. You understand." His voice was deep and on the edge of cracking. For an instant it flashed through his mind that if the worst came to pass, there would be encounters just like this, over and over—people wanting to know and their having to talk about it, talk about what would be impossible to talk about. It would kill Etta. They would have to go away, move somewhere else. How was it even possible now to have to deal with this woman?

"I understand," Viola said, looking around Mike to see Etta, who didn't look up. "My Russell is here. He had his hernia surgery on Friday."

"Oh, I'm sorry to hear that. I hope he's okay." Steich was a good man. Mike liked him. And no surprise at all about the hernia—he had actually lifted a car off a boy. The boy had lived, and now all Mike could think about was if that would also be true for Mar. "We just can't talk right now, Viola."

Another one of the nuns came in and went directly to the young married couple. Mike saw the smiles, the instant relief. The two hugged each other and thanked Sister, following her out. "God please," Mike thought.

Then, one of the doors opened slowly and Lolly came in, appearing so dazed and disconsolate that it frightened him even more. She looked at no one but went straight to the far window and stood there as if frozen. Right behind her, a distinguished looking man of about fifty with meticulously trimmed silver hair entered the room. Doctor Andrew Vianney, his face solemn, went immediately to Etta and Mike, his stethoscope dangling from the pocket of his white lab coat.

"Mr. and Mrs. Ferry."

They stood before him, hearts pounding.

He reached for Etta's hand and took a breath. "Margaret… is in very serious condition. We've moved her to Intensive Care just down the hall."

"Is she…will she be all right?"

"I'm sorry to say we don't know at this point. We have done all that we can." He looked from one to the other. "It will be important for you to prepare yourselves for…whatever may come. The priest will be here shortly."

Etta's legs began going out from under her. Mike held her and in so doing kept himself from giving way. A wave of nausea swept through him. Everything around them was disappearing, walls, people, sounds. He could barely comprehend Vianney.

"I can assure you, Mrs. Ferry, Mr. Ferry, we have done everything possible for your beautiful child."

The words and emotions cut through the silence of the room. The middle-aged woman with the handkerchief made the sign of the cross. Jo and Rae held each other and sobbed. Frank went to the window and put his arms around Lolly, who remained transfixed.

Viola Steich backed away, speechless. The man who had dozed stirred from his rest at the sound of Etta's mournful cry.

Doctor Vianney took Etta and Mike aside. "I can't tell you how sorry I am." He opened his hands in a gesture of helplessness. "Your daughter's injuries are…extensive. She hasn't regained consciousness…except." He looked away, reticent.

"Except…?" Mike pressed.

"Something very unusual happened that startled us actually, but at first gave us hope."

Across the room, Lolly lifted her head and turned slowly toward the doctor, as if she could hear what he was saying.

"Margaret did speak," Vianney said, thoughtfully. "Just once."

Mike shot a look at Etta, then drew his hand across his eyes, as if to better see what the doctor was telling them. "What was it? What did she say?"

"She said, 'I promise.' That's what she said. 'I promise,' as clearly as you or I would say it. We were all shocked. But that was all." He touched Etta's arm. "Why don't you both come with me. I'll take you to her."

With his arm still around her, Mike guided Etta's halting steps. He turned and extended his arm, beckoning Lolly to come. But just as they reached the waiting room doors, a nurse pushed through, frantic. "Doctor, come quick." There was no need for her to explain.

Beyond the open doors of the waiting room was the sight that sent gasps up and down the corridor and caused Etta to faint. Two of the nuns hurried over, as Mike stared down the hall in disbelief. The people in the waiting room, aware that something was going on, rose and began gathering at the open doors.

The woman with the handkerchief got down on her knees. "Jesus, Mary and Joseph," she said and blessed herself again.

Lolly had come to Mike and Etta's side. Medics, patients and nuns, stone still, looked on as Dr. Vianney, himself clearly stunned by the sight, walked slowly down the corridor to the place where Margaret Ferry stood.

CHAPTER FIFTEEN

Margaret Ferry stood barefoot in the center of the corridor, her face as luminous as the moon, her hair floating out, as if by static charge, like a diadem of silken riplets. Her hospital gown, white and radiant, hung at an angle, nearly touching the floor. The lace shawl, perfect again in its vintage delicacy, encircled her shoulders with a soft pulse of light that moved like a wave of energy about her entire body.

Some went down on their knees, breathless, mystified.

"Mother of God." Sister Teresa's words were barely audible.

Dr. Vianney walked slowly toward Margaret, Mike close behind. Etta, resuscitated with the smelling salts the nuns had administered, sat half-dazed, Lolly at her side.

"Am I ready to go home now, Dr. Vianney?" Margaret's voice was mellow with all the innocent inquisitiveness of youth.

Mike gasped, overwhelmed with euphoria, a mixture of tears and laughter welling up in his throat. "Margaret," he cried. "Mar.

Her hair had settled itself and her look returned to normal—normal for a girl of eleven who had made her confirmation on a beautiful spring day.

Dr. Vianney extended his arm behind him, gesturing for Mike to wait. "Well, Margaret," he said, "you certainly seem to be feeling much better."

"What happened?" She looked past Dr. Vianney to Mike. "Uncle Mike," she said with excitement, and took a step forward.

Dr. Vianney put his hand up. "Try not to move, Margaret. Let us come to you."

"Aunt Etta's here too, Mar," Mike said, his voice cracking in a burst of tearfulness. "She's right here. Lolly too. We're all here, Mar."

Etta, elated and confused, walked unsteadily toward them, clutching Lolly's hand against her side. Lolly had a wondrous look on her face, a serene smile as of one satisfied by the surprise of understanding.

"Let's go back into the room, Margaret." Dr. Vianney said, guiding her down the short side hallway to the operating room, where for more than two hours six people had worked frantically to save her life. "I...I want to ask you a few questions."

"They can come with us, right?"

"Your parents can, of course, but..."

Etta spoke up. "Lolly will have to come too, Doctor. She and Margaret are very close." She squeezed Lolly's hand as if to affirm her own words.

"That's fine," said Vianney. "Although, you'll all have to step out when we examine Margaret."

Etta nodded, looking to Mike and Lolly for agreement.

"Why do I have to stay? I'm not sick."

The murmur of voices in the crowded corridor was gaining volume as stunned onlookers buzzed about what they had witnessed.

One of the nuns led Margaret into the room, while Vianney turned to the three of them. "I'd like for the others who were in the emergency room with us earlier to join us. You can imagine that it's important for them to...well...to bear witness to this, if you will." He stroked his chin and looked at them thoughtfully. "It's clear that something has taken place here that none of us has any medical or even rational explanation for. It's something I've certainly never experienced before in my thirty years of practice…or in my lifetime for that matter. And it's clear that the ramifications will extend beyond St. Peter's."

Etta touched Vianney's arm. "Doctor, I'm wondering. Is it at all possible that you…well, that you were…"

"Wrong, Mrs. Ferry?" Vianney took her hand. "Your niece was hit by a car. You may read the police report. Her left arm was shattered from the impact. Her left leg broken in four places. Her ribs were broken. Her spleen was ruptured. She had a concussion, along with considerable internal injuries and loss of blood."

Etta threw her hand to her mouth, horrified.

"She is lucky to be alive," Vianney said, "…let alone…"

"Her appearance," said Mike, shaking his head as one searching the unknown. "It was as if she were glowing; her hair was…"

"And the shawl." Etta looked at Lolly. "I'd had it in my hands—it was filthy. It was torn. Doctor, I…I can't imagine. I don't understand."

"You're not alone, Mrs. Ferry, believe me." Vianney patted her arm. "We're going to keep your niece under observation. Perhaps we'll learn something. Frankly, I'm not sure we're… any of us…capable of coming up with an explanation for what has occurred."

Etta's eyes filled with tears. "I don't know what to think, what to feel. I'm so very grateful. All we can do is thank God… and yet, I…I just can't imagine."

Once again, a feeling of helplessness swept over Mike, unaccustomed as he was to being so completely at a loss. Etta was strong and smart, but Mike knew he was the one she always looked to for final decisions, the one to make sure things worked. On the job, Fulton counted on him to delve into a story and find the core in order to glean the deepest meaning. But this? What sense could he make of this? What help could he provide to Etta, to Lolly and the rest of the family? To Margaret herself? This was so far beyond reason or comprehension. Like an earthquake when there's no place to turn for solid ground, everything was shifting underfoot. Shock and aftershock—nearly losing Mar, then miraculously having her back as if nothing at all had happened.

Vianney took a deep breath. "I've seen people rally from the brink of death. I've seen babies, others, young and old, with life-threatening conditions, snap back. I've seen healing where we didn't believe healing was possible. This is different. This is spontaneous and profound.

He started into the room, then stopped and turned, shaking his head. "As for the lace shawl...you're right, Mrs. Ferry. It was in such poor condition it looked like a rag. It was removed from the room several times; I believe you know that. Sister Teresa said she gave it to you more than once. Yet...somehow...it was back in the room with Margaret." He ran his hand across the top of his head. "You saw it. It's perfect now."

They looked at each other, but could say nothing.

"There is one other thing," Vianney said. "If word of this gets out, it will likely cause a tidal wave of curiosity and interest that may become quite burdensome for all of you. The hospital will do everything it can to keep it quiet, I promise, but right now, our priority is your daughter.

Viola Steich hurried toward the bank of pay phones located around the corner from the main hospital corridor. She had not yet been up to the third floor ward where her husband was recovering. There was time for that later. Russell would be fine. There had been no problems following his surgery on Friday. This, on the other hand, was urgent. A terrible boy, a delinquent, had nearly killed a lovely innocent girl by stealing her shawl, but then...

She stepped into one of the phone booths, and shoved the heavy glass-paneled folding door closed. Then, she turned quickly through the pages of the directory. Russell always complained that she talked too much about people. He called her a gossip. What did he know? Tools and motors, wires, cords and screws, not much else. Was it gossip to share news about people? Gossip had a mean sound to it. She wasn't mean and she never gossiped. In any case, Russell would be proud of her this time. Everyone would be. She had witnessed something unbelievable firsthand and it could not be denied. A miracle had occurred right before her eyes—the type of thing that could make history and she was part of it. Some of the other phone booths were occupied. For all she knew, people were already calling about this very thing. There was no time to waste.

Once she found the number, she spilled her change purse onto the phone shelf. She always carried plenty of change for bus and train fare—plenty of coins to tell her story without interruption. She was still amazed not only by what had happened but by the fact that she had been right there with the Ferrys. Right there. She was definitely part of it. That made it her story as well as theirs. Poor Russell, up there on the third floor with no idea what had occurred. Neither did a lot of other people, but she was about to change that. This was the biggest news ever.

Viola Steich dialed and waited. After a few rings, a man's voice answered, "City desk."

BOOK TWO

CHAPTER SIXTEEN

Bill Fulton's cabin in the Catskills had an unexpected charm, which immediately made it clear to the Ferrys that the harmonious and cozy surroundings Elaine Fulton had created were still intact. The Fultons had lost their only child, Tim, at Omaha Beach. Now, nearing fifty, Bill and Elaine rarely spent much time there anymore. Once an avid fisherman in love with the outdoors, the veteran newspaperman had allowed his work to take over much of his life. It was his idea that Mike and Etta steal away with Margaret to escape what was bound to be an onslaught of prying reporters and zealous miracle seekers. They agreed it might be best. Any notion that this was to be a springtime vacation in the mountains never entered their minds—the cabin's woodland setting was just remote enough for the privacy the Ferrys required, and that was all they could hope for. They needed time to absorb and process the incredible, realizing that time itself could not possibly equip them with an understanding of all that had happened. For Margaret it was different. Margaret appeared to be very nearly her normal self. Very nearly.

They rose each chilly morning for an early breakfast before walking one of the wooded trails or casting a line into the nearby stream. In the few days they'd been there, they had become more comfortable in town, where they cautiously learned that no one knew who they were. Mike had checked the local papers and only once found a short article buried between a carpet ad and a political story carried over from page two. Most fortunately, the first woman to break the sound barrier captured the headlines and lead stories.

Doctor Vianney, himself still pondering the unexplainable, gave Margaret a clean bill of health with the promise to personally attend to the child if anything were to suddenly change. He wanted to see Margaret for a check-up in a few weeks. They had told no one, except Vianney, where they were going. Bill Fulton would know how to reach them if that became necessary.

A priest from the Bishop's office had telephoned before they left to set up a home visit. That visit would now have to wait, regardless of how eager Etta and Mike were to know what the Church made of this.

Margaret had no recollection of the accident, only that she had awakened in a hospital bed. They asked her, perhaps too often, how she was feeling. She always replied with a delighted "fine." It was Doctor Vianney's recommendation that they go easy in explaining the extent of her injuries to her. "Let's allow her to settle in," he'd said. But Vianney remained as curious as the Ferrys about the "promise" she had made in the operating room, and suggested that they might try somehow to bring that up in a conversation with her.

Unlike her aunt and uncle who were still dazed from the entire experience, Margaret was on a pleasure trip. She did, however, recall her conversation with Johnny Herring and the fact that he had been begging on the street, covered in cuts and bruises, something Mike promised to look into when they returned home. But for now their main goal, apart from protecting Margaret from any sensationalism, was to observe her closely. While grateful beyond all measure for her miraculous recovery, they harbored no small level of anxiety that something could go wrong again as quickly and inexplicably as everything had all gone right. Was Margaret really well and back to normal?

Was that truly possible? Had all this actually happened? And why? Why?

Their intention was to stay only a week, hopeful that any interest would die down by then. Mike's deep-rooted experience with the largely fickle reading public made him optimistic that people would soon move on. The Ferrys couldn't stay away forever, and if the story were to receive the kind of attention that Mike believed it truly warranted, he and Etta knew they would have no choice but to move away. One bit of mercy was that the downstairs apartment in their brownstone was unoccupied, saving them from prying eyes much too close to home—the owner was saving it for his soon-to-be-married daughter, who would not be moving in until fall.

Soon after the accident, while Margaret was still under observation in the hospital and word had begun to spread, Junie's mother came by the apartment, unable to fathom what she and her family had heard. Viola Steich had dutifully spread the word, boasting of her firsthand account.

Mrs. Giordano's visit had been the first indication that Bill Fulton was right—they had to get away. Not that they didn't find her curiosity reasonable at first. Junie was Margaret's best friend, after all. Some neighbors had actually been there when the car plowed into Margaret. Mr. Wortman had personally attended to the girl as she lay unconscious in the street. So indeed, there was more than a solid foundation of truth to the story. The difficulty for the Ferrys was in trying to explain how one minute Margaret lay there awaiting last rites, and the next she was standing fine and radiant, bearing not the slightest sign of any injuries whatever. They decided to skip over the "radiant" part.

Etta and Mike found it harder and harder to hear themselves talk about it—the absurdity was astounding—and from all indications, Junie's mother found it harder and harder to believe what she was hearing. What they realized was that ultimately Junie's mother was concerned for Junie, and what it would mean for their daughter to be mixed up in such a swirl of sensation that might turn out to be an outrageous piece of fiction. Etta and Mike could certainly understand how a parent might wonder if Margaret could ever again be a really normal friend. Losing Junie's friendship would break Margaret's heart and raise all kinds of questions in her own mind about what exactly was going on, questions that Etta and Mike likely might never be equipped to answer.

"So, if that's true," Mrs. Giordano had said, her brow furrowed, "then what you're telling me is that Viola was right? There was a...a miracle?"

"We can only tell you what occurred." They found themselves as uncomfortable with the word "miracle" as they did with the word "if." Their instincts told them that, in general, people tended to regard anything supernatural with skepticism and even suspicion. As for Mrs. Giordano, the stakes were clearly higher—like them, she had a daughter to protect.

"Forgive me," she'd said, "but this is very hard to grasp. Margaret and Junie are just...I don't know...just ordinary young girls. What can account for such an unbelievable thing happening...if indeed it did? Where is Margaret now?"

Etta and Mike could see what they were up against. "She's still in the hospital being checked out."

"So, she hasn't actually recovered. She's still being treated."

"She's completely well, Vivian. The doctors are as amazed as the rest of us. They wanted to keep her for an extra couple of days for observation, to try to determine how such a spontaneous healing could have occurred."

"Spontaneous healing," Mrs. Giordano repeated flatly.

There was a momentary silence. Neither Etta nor Mike offered any further information or comment.

"Well, it's all so incredible. All I can say is that I am deeply sorry about the accident." She gave a thin smile. "Margaret was such a special friend to Junie."

Was?

"I'd better be going. It sounds like Margaret is getting the best of care. I certainly hope she's better soon." She moved to leave, then turned back. "I...I think it might be best if Junie doesn't come around...for a while at least...you know...just till everything gets sorted out." She touched Etta's shoulder. "My best to you both, and to Margaret. I'll be praying for her recovery."

The cabin door swung open and Margaret came in, full of excited laughter. "Guess what happened to us."

Mike was right behind her, a big smile on his face.

Etta turned from the kitchen. "I can't imagine."

"A very special bird," Mike said.

"An Indigo Bunting." Margaret peeled off her sweater and tossed it onto the back of a kitchen chair. "It's the most amazing blue. And I don't think they even have them in this part of the world. Can you imagine? We saw it along the trail where that old well pump is, and it came and landed right on my hand. Right here." She pointed to her right thumb. "I never had a bird do that before, not even that little gray and yellow one with the funny wing who comes to our birdbath every year. You should have seen it."

Etta put her arm around Margaret's shoulder. "That is pretty amazing. I never met a girl so full of the most enjoyable surprises."

"I wish Aunt Lolly had come with us."

"We asked her, but she said it would be nice for us to have this time to ourselves."

Over a lunch of chicken sandwiches and potato salad, Etta gave Mike the high sign, his cue to broach the question Dr. Vianney had suggested. "I'm curious, Mar. Dr. Vianney told us that when you were asleep in the hospital, you said, 'I promise.' Do you recall saying that?"

"Oh, yes," she said, without hesitation, her mouth half full. "The lady wanted me to do something and I promised her I would."

"The lady?" Etta put down her fork and gave Mike a look.

"Yes, she had the sweetest voice."

"Who was she?" Mike asked. "Had you ever seen her before?"

"I couldn't see her at all, but I kind of felt...well, it's hard to explain... I...I was far away, but very close. That's the best way I can explain it. Like being wide awake inside a deep, deep dream. And when I heard the lady's voice, I felt like I had always known her."

Etta smiled. "What exactly did she say?"

Margaret stopped. She looked straight ahead, squinting, thoughtful. "Well, that's the funny part. She never said anything." She paused. "She was giving me a gift, some kind of a special gift." She stopped again, and after a moment simply shook her head and shrugged.

"What do you mean a gift? And how could you know all that if she never spoke to you?"

"I don't exactly know. It was all like one big..." She rolled her hands searching for the right word, "...feeling."

"Has she let you know anything since then?"

"No. But sometimes I can tell she's around, though she isn't really. This potato salad is so good, Aunt Etta."

That night, they put on light jackets and sat out on the plank deck, the first night that it was not too cool to do so. The spring air was redolent of pine and musk, and the nearby stream, barely visible through the trees, glistened from the light of a half moon. Etta brought out hot tea and cookies, and they spoke quietly about the day. It had been a good one. They had gone into town in the afternoon, stopping for ice cream, and wandering in and out of the local stores. At one point, while Mike and Margaret were picking up a few things at Goff's

Hardware, Etta browsed a small shop where an antique baby carriage gave her a brief moment of melancholy.

"Well, what do you think of this place, Mar?" Mike asked.

"I love it here. I hope Mr. Fulton lets us come back again and again." She turned to Etta, reached over and touched her arm. "As long as there's nothing here to ever make us sad."

Etta gave her a curious look.

"I think Mr. Fulton is so nice for letting us come."

Mike leaned back in the Adirondack chair and looked up at the night sky. "Bill Fulton is a good man, Mar. He's always had a way of putting others first. Some people don't know that about him because in his job he tends to be a bit gruff. But I've known him a long time. He was a great baseball player in college and later on coached at the school his son went to. An all-around good guy."

"Not like Mr. Loughlin, I guess." Margaret took them by surprise. In the light of the porch, they could see that when she mentioned his name, her hair flared out slightly the way it did that day in the hospital.

Mike and Etta caught each other's eye. "What on earth made you think of Mr. Loughlin?" Mike asked.

Margaret picked up a sugar cookie and dunked it into her warm tea. "I was just thinking. Sooner or later he'll have to give you back your briefcase, right?"

⸻

Mike stood in his pajamas at the bathroom sink, drying his face with a towel. "For the life of me, Et, I don't know what's going on. She looks so normal—nothing more than a scratch on her arm from a pine tree. How does she know about Loughlin taking the briefcase? I never told her that. And what about the lady's voice...or whatever it was?"

Etta folded down the bed covers, then stopped. "But we

didn't come here to figure this out, did we? It's beyond us, Mike. We knew that from the start. We came here to get Mar away from…who knows what?"

"And to observe her behavior," Mike said, "which is pretty mystifying."

Etta went to his side. "There's one important thing we mustn't lose sight of."

He turned to her, a questioning look on his face.

"This child, for reasons known only to God, experienced a miracle. No one is likely to ever know how or why…not you, not me, not a doctor or a priest or a bishop. We're looking for answers that will never be there. Beyond all the reasoning in the world, Mar is well."

"But that thing with Loughlin. What else might she know that there's no way she could? Not logically, anyway."

Etta put her head down. "Did you see the way she touched my arm and said something about not being sad?"

Mike nodded. "What was that about?"

"I stopped into that little antique store while you and Mar were at Goff's. I saw a baby carriage, and… it caught me for a moment. I felt, you know…I think Mar somehow picked up on that."

Mike shook his head. "How on earth…"

"Logic is out the window here. Whether anyone else in the world believes a single bit of this is not our problem. All we need to do is just accept it and be thankful till the end of our days that she's alive and well. That's it."

"This could be a long, winding road, Et, and we don't know what's around the curve."

"But it's a road that we'll travel together."

He put his arms around her and held her close. After a few moments, he looked at her square on and smiled. "Well, then, I think I'd like waffles for breakfast."

Margaret stood at the open window of her cabin bedroom, looking out into the dark mountain night, and pulled up the collar of her bathrobe. The chill gave her a momentary shiver, but she didn't mind. She liked everything about being so close to nature, hearing the trees move with the moon blinking through them, the soft lap of water in the stream, or possibly a small fish leaping. They had been in the Catskills more than a week, a place she had barely imagined before, and now the only place that could ever make her want to leave Brooklyn. It had been one of the happiest times of her life, filled with what she loved most, birds and wooded paths, the smell of cedar and pine, the crackle and crunch under foot. A running brook. Fish caught for supper and, at night, cookies and hot tea on the porch with Aunt Etta and Uncle Mike. Too bad Junie and Aunt Lolly couldn't see all this.

She had thought about St. Aloysius and Sister Bernadine, about Stanny and Mikhail and Peter, about Johnny Herring, and Uncle Mike's briefcase, and about Mr. Wortman, whom she now understood came to her aid. She had thought about them all and her heart felt so full of love.

The curtains billowed and she tilted her head back to feel the rush of air. She closed her eyes and took a deep breath. A small leaf blew in and startled her. She smiled, pressing it to her lips. Something extraordinary had happened to her that brought them here, and though Uncle Mike had only told her a little about all that had taken place, it didn't matter. She was excited to be away in this wonderful woodsy heaven with the two of them...to feel so happy and...and...what? She opened her eyes and cocked her head, as if to listen for a moment to her own thoughts, waiting. Happy and... She stood perfectly still and listened as the air itself sang around her like some melody her heart could sing forever. She nodded slowly, contentedly, then shut the window and climbed into bed at peace with the world.

CHAPTER SEVENTEEN

"We forgot the ZuZu crackers," Margaret said, as she and Etta made their way out through the red double doors of the A&P. "I'll go back."

"Stay here, Mar, please. I don't want you walking away from me."

"But they're Uncle Mike's favorite."

"I'm not comfortable right now when you go off on your own." Etta wished they were still in the Catskills, safe, private, not having to deal with one more...thing. No questions or curious glances. No looking over their shoulder. They'd been back in Brooklyn a week and their lives were still upside down. Mike remained on leave from work, and she rarely left the house except to go to the grocery store, thankful that most of the overly sympathetic though inquisitive attention was decreasing. Margaret was not yet back in school and was only permitted to go out if Etta or Mike were with her.

Though Etta's name was little known before, shopkeepers and even occasional strangers now smiled and greeted her politely as Mrs. Ferry. She much preferred anonymity. Still, she and Margaret returned the politeness and the smiles, albeit with restraint. It was only natural, after all, that people would be awed and curious.

There had been the more or less expected number of people astonished at the sight of this child so perfectly and incredibly normal, not the least of whom was Mr. Wortman.

He had actually backed away slightly the day Etta and Mike went to the candy store with Margaret to thank him. They had gone at night, as close as they could to closing time so as not to attract attention, and the two customers who left with their cigarettes and newspapers seemed to have no idea who the girl was. Mr. Wortman, on the other hand, had remained anxious seeing Margaret, even as he expressed agreement that it surely was, indeed, a miracle. They had not seen anything of Junie.

Lolly called nearly every day, comforted that Margaret's spontaneous recovery was sustained and that maybe things would soon level out and become more or less normal again. Sister Bernadine had called several times and a priest from the Bishop's office, a Father Desmond, had finally come to the house, having already heard firsthand accounts, including Doctor Vianney's detailed medical report. Father Desmond, polite and cordial, impressed them with his sensitivity in questioning Margaret, and was himself impressed by the condition of both the child and the shawl. He then spoke privately with Etta and Mike.

They mentioned the briefcase incident—how Margaret knew about it without being told.

"Most unusual," was Father Desmond's thoughtful reply. "Have you noticed any other changes? Is she otherwise happy or sad or different in any other way that you can tell?"

Mike shook his head. "She's always been a lively kid, full of enthusiasm for the things she considers important. Extremely compassionate. She loves helping people, especially if she believes there's some bit of injustice going on." Mike explained all that had happened about the Russian immigrants, including Margaret's letter to the Bishop, which took Father Desmond by surprise.

The priest shook his head in amusement. "She really is passionate, isn't she?"

"She can get on a soap box quicker than anyone I know,"

Mike said, with an admiring tone in his voice, "but now and then the right amount of mischief too. We've never had much to complain about. She's always been a respectful, happy kid. It appears she still is."

"Except…" Etta started. She picked at her fingernail. "Except…since the accident, she's just very…I don't know… serene. Nothing seems to bother her or upset her. Everything else appears normal. Eating, sleeping, playing. She isn't back in school yet, and we have no idea how that's going to work out. She's taking everything in stride; we're the ones trying to adjust."

Mike put his hand on his wife's shoulder. "And we're not even sure exactly what it is we're adjusting to. Everything kind of looks the same, yet it's all changed, hasn't it?"

Etta admitted she was scared. "Something as extraordinary as this…so unbelievable…makes me wonder, Father, if a person can really ever be normal again. I had vowed to simply be grateful for the blessing, but…"

"Hold onto your blessing, Mrs. Ferry."

Mike nodded. "Believe me, Father, we're trying."

Walking down the avenue with Margaret on what appeared to be just a normal spring afternoon, having done something as ordinary as buying milk and eggs, it was hard to rise above the reality of occasional prying eyes and probing questions. Yet, Margaret was clearly oblivious to all of it, commenting as she always did on the color of the spring flowers in the window boxes and airy ways, smiling as people walked past with a dog she could pet.

They crossed Ninth Street and made their way past Meyer's fabric store, where a man stepped out of the doorway. "Excuse me, Mrs. Ferry." He wore a suit and hat and a badge that said Press. "May I please have a word?"

"Keep walking, Margaret." Etta shifted her paper grocery bag, to put an arm around her niece, and quickened her pace.

"I promise it'll only take a minute." He followed along, holding a small pad and a pencil.

Etta marched straight ahead, nearly pulling Margaret, who kept watching the man.

"What has it been like, Miss Ferry, coming back as you did from…from death's door? Do you feel any different? You look so normal, quite pretty."

Etta walked faster. "Leave us alone. Margaret, hurry along." A small number of passersby had taken notice and began to loosely trail the threesome. A few cars slowed, likely realizing something was happening on the sidewalk.

The man was unrelenting. "Do you believe you've changed? I just need to ask a few questions."

Finally, Margaret stopped.

"Margaret!" Etta snapped.

"It's okay, Mrs. Ferry," said the reporter, who appeared to be in his late thirties. "I mean no harm." He took a step closer. "What was it like to be so near death, then suddenly wake up completely healed?"

The crowd had moved in closer as well, a tighter group now, their curiosity heightened as they realized who the girl was.

Etta looked about, panic-stricken. "Margaret! Come with me now," she commanded, but Margaret, still holding one of the grocery bags, had stepped away from her.

"He's right, Aunt Etta," Margaret said, almost playfully. "He means no harm." She turned to look directly into the man's face.

More people gathered. A car stopped, double-parking at the curb, and rolled down the window.

Etta was frantic. "I want you to leave us alone right now or I'll call a policeman."

"No need to worry, Aunt Etta. There's something he needs to know. Isn't that right, Mr. Young?"

The man jerked his head back. "How do you know my

name?" He chuckled nervously and checked his Press badge. There was no name on it. Margaret stood perfectly still, smiling. The crowd suddenly grew silent, seeming to sense that something odd was going on here.

"Margaret," was all Etta could say, almost pleading.

"Like I was saying, Miss Ferry," said the reporter, a touch of nervousness in his voice. "What I'd like to know..."

Margaret's hair lifted softly, but there was no breeze. People looked at each other, but said nothing. A few took a step back. Etta put her hand to her mouth, alarmed, and placed her grocery bag on the ground. "Please..."

The man hesitated, much less sure of things. "I...I just wanted to know about...about..."

"About Nathan." Margaret's voice was low and calm.

The man's brow furrowed. "Who?" He gave her a long, steady look, his eyes never leaving hers. "No, I just wanted to know about..."

"Nathan," Margaret repeated. "Nathan Greenstock."

"Margaret," Etta took her arm. "What are you doing? What are you saying?"

The reporter froze. "Nathan Greenstock," he said, as if dumbfounded, and allowed the pencil and pad to slip from his hands.

"Isn't that right, Mr. Young?" Margaret said softly. "You've wondered about him for such a long time."

"How could you possibly..."

"You've never forgotten him," she said.

"What is this? What's going on here?" He looked about as if someone lurking in the crowd would say this was a practical joke. That someone could explain the craziness of what was taking place.

"Nathan Greenstock," Margaret said again. "He saved your life at Omaha Beach. Isn't that right, Mr. Young? I'm sorry you've been so unhappy since then because you've never been able to find him."

"I tried to find him; I tried everything," he said frantically. "Everything." His voice was deeper now, a mournful pleading. "He took the bullet that should have killed me. They carried him away. But how could you know any of this? How...?"

"Nathan is very well. You won't have any trouble finding him in Rhode Island. That's what you really needed to know, wasn't it, Mr. Young? All these years you've wanted to know how to find Nathan Greenstock."

For a long moment, the man stared at Margaret, then nodded slowly, half dazed. "Yes. Yes...I...I..." He took off his hat, removed his handkerchief from his lapel pocket and wiped his face. "This is all too...I...it's...I don't know what to say. I don't know how you know all this."

Etta could say nothing. There were murmurs from the crowd, confused looks mingled with half smiles.

"Would you mind picking up my aunt's grocery bag please, Mr. Young?"

Without hesitating, the reporter picked up the brown paper bag and handed it to Etta with an awkward half-smile.

"Thank you so much, Mr. Young." Then Margaret gently took Etta's arm, and they continued on down the avenue with their groceries.

"Thank you," they heard the man call out. "Thank you," he said again, his hat still in his hand.

When Etta looked back, she saw him standing there perfectly still with the crowd behind him, all watching them walk away.

———◆———

Etta lay on the sofa, a cool towel on her forehead, Margaret at her side. Mike walked across the living room, then back again. "You're confounding us, Mar," he said. "We're not saying you've done anything wrong. Just...well...very unusual." He was still pacing. "You know that, don't you? We're not used to all this."

Margaret nodded. "Then you're not mad?"

Etta reached over and took her hand. "How could we be mad? You helped that man, even though he rattled me. I worry when strangers come up to us on the street. We don't want anything to happen to you. But you just know these things and...and we don't understand how. It's a lot for us. I was terrified."

"How did you know this man...or anything, I mean?" Mike asked.

Margaret rubbed her ear and shrugged. "I'm not sure, Uncle Mike. But I...I think it might have something to do with what I promised. I have a kind of feeling about it. But it's a good feeling, honest. I'm just sorry it upset you, Aunt Etta. I didn't mean to."

"It's all right. Here, take the towel. I'll just rest here a little before supper."

Margaret took the towel and kissed Etta on the forehead. "I love you, Aunt Etta."

"Please don't worry, Mar. I'll get used to things. We all will. We just need some time. We want to make sure you're safe. We love you." She closed her eyes.

Mike pressed Etta's hand. "You rest here a while, Et. I'll heat up the chicken soup that's in the refrigerator." He headed to the kitchen with Margaret right behind him. But along the way she stopped and glanced back over her shoulder at Etta. Etta seemed so fragile right now. Beautiful Etta, the best mother she could ever ask for.

Margaret went to the dresser, removed the shawl, and held it against her cheek. There was a certain aroma to it, what she thought of as a kind of ancient sweetness. She went back into the living room and carefully covered Etta, so as not to wake her. "This will make you feel much better," she whispered and blew her aunt a kiss.

CHAPTER EIGHTEEN

Sunlight streamed across the Ferrys' kitchen table, where Mike sat skimming the morning *Tribune*, and Margaret, dressed but sleepy-eyed, turned through the daily comic strips with an occasional chuckle.

"Anything?" Etta scooped scrambled eggs from an iron skillet at the stove, a warm spring breeze at her back from the open window.

Mike turned the final couple of pages. "Good news—nothing."

"You mean about us?" Margaret took a bite of her raisin toast.

"That's right, kiddo. No mention for the last three or four days. You must have scared off that reporter of yours pretty good."

"I didn't mean to. I just had something important to tell him."

Etta brought the plates to the table. "Oh, you told him all right."

"Extra bacon for me, please," Margaret said.

They still wondered, marveled at how this child could be so normal. How was all this possible—comic strips and extra bacon, like nothing at all had rocked their world? As if they weren't praying thanks every single day from the deepest part of themselves for the miracle that had delivered this child back to them. Still…every morning before Margaret woke up,

Etta and Mike slipped into her room to check on her, briefly observing her for any sign that there might be some kind of a change, a relapse. Could something end up going wrong after all? The fact that the miracle was holding was only beginning to quell their anxieties and put the memory of those horrific hours at the hospital a little farther behind them. There was a growing sense, fragile as it was, that somehow all might be well again in the Ferry household. Mostly. They still couldn't explain what had happened with that reporter, or how she knew about Mike's briefcase being stolen and connected it to Wallace Loughlin, or even about Etta's "sadness," as Margaret had put it. Margaret herself couldn't explain it. Mike's work situation at the paper was in disarray, but during the agonizing wait at the hospital, he realized how ultimately unimportant all of it was by comparison.

They had talked about having Margaret see someone, a professional of some kind…a doctor, but exactly what kind? A priest? They'd already met with one. Just who was there to make sense of any of it? Who could possibly offer a rational explanation for Margaret's encounter with the reporter? No, they would simply have to settle for whatever one could make of a miracle. Settle, as well, for what lay ahead.

He reached over and patted Margaret's shoulder. "Just a couple more days until we have you back in school and I head to the office. Let's shoot for Monday. We'll let Sister Bernadine know." Sister had been by to visit and, like everyone else seeing Margaret for the first time, could hardly contain her amazement. Margaret's return to her classroom would be the first time on her own since the accident, but they knew they could count on Sister to monitor things.

"I can't wait." Margaret nibbled on a strip of crisp bacon. "But remember, Uncle Mike, you promised me a trip to your office."

Etta jumped in. "But that was before…"

Mike put his hand on Etta's arm. "I think...well...I think it might be all right, Et."

"Are you sure it's a good idea taking her into the City? What if someone recognizes her? What if some other...crazy thing happens?"

He poured a glass of orange juice. "It looks like things are under control. It's been nearly a month since the accident, and Manhattan has so many fast-moving parts and people, I don't think anyone is going to take notice. We can go in next Saturday. How does that sound?" He looked to Etta for approval. She knew in her heart he was the less rigid one with good judgment that usually eased her anxiety and won her over. After all these years, she had not gotten over his charm. She gave a somewhat reluctant nod and squeezed out a smile.

"Thank you, Aunt Etta. Two happy things in a row—I get to go to Uncle Mike's office and then I go back to school. I really miss Junie and Sister Bernadine. But first, I get to see Mr. Fulton again. I can thank him for our really nice trip to the cabin. I wonder if the eggs in the nest have hatched yet. I wish I could tell Peter and Stanny and Mikhail about it. I really miss them too. But it will be so nice to be back at St. Aloysius."

"Now, don't get all excited about school," Etta said, always the one to add a dose of reality and caution. "Remember, things might be a bit different. Sometimes even the people we know very well change when odd things happen. We don't want you to be disappointed."

"I know, but I'm going to be twelve soon. You don't have to worry. Everything will be okay."

Etta and Mike gave each other a look, clearly not at all sure about that.

"And please, please, Mar," Etta said, putting her hand over her heart to underscore her plea, "just try to put the whole Russian immigrant thing aside for the time being. Don't do anything that might...you know...shock anybody, least of all

Monsignor. Just please stay out of his way."

"Well, okay, but if he…"

"Did you hear what your aunt just said about Monsignor?"
Margaret nodded.

"And for heaven's sake, don't be telling him anything."

"Anything like what?"

"Like those things you told the reporter," Etta said. "Things
you're not supposed to know. It makes people nervous." She
got up to get the coffee pot and stopped behind Margaret to
give her a hug. "We don't want to be hard on you, Mar. Just try
to lay back a bit."

"But Mr. Young was happy about what I told him." She
looked from one to the other. "Wasn't he?" She looked off
toward the window, a puzzled scowl on her face. "I can't even
remember exactly what I said to him."

Mike scratched the side of his chin. "Well…if there's any
way you can feel it coming on…like when that thing happens
with your hair." He wiggled his fingers about his head.

"I don't know why that happens." Margaret put her hand up
to her head. "It's not doing it now, is it?"

"No. But just try to…"

The doorbell rang, and they all jumped. Mike nearly spilled
his coffee. He laughed. "Who ever thought one harmless little
doorbell could get such a rise out of us?" He went to the front
window and looked out, but saw no one. He went to the door
to look down the stairs. Through the curtained glass of the
vestibule entry, he saw two figures. "Not sure who they are,
but they don't look like reporters." He hit the buzzer and a
stout little woman, who appeared to be in her sixties, entered
the hallway.

"Can we help you?" Mike called down.

"Mr. Ferry?"

"Yes."

"I live a few blocks from here. May I please have a moment

of your time on a very important matter?" She sounded a little breathless, no doubt from climbing the brownstone's outer staircase.

"I'm sorry, but we're not seeing anyone right now."

"Oh, please. I'm not one of those nosey people. I...I must speak with you."

Mike hesitated. The woman stood perfectly still, waiting. After concluding that she appeared harmless enough in her matronly flowered dress, stocky black shoes, and gray hair pulled back neatly in a bun, he nodded, and she made her way up the stairs with a spry step and a warm, but tenuous smile.

"What do you need to see me about?" Mike asked. Etta stood behind him in the doorway. Margaret was still at the kitchen table engrossed in *Gasoline Alley*.

"I wouldn't bother you for anything in the world," she whispered, "but my husband and I have been helping Johnny Herring and..."

"Johnny Herring? I've been looking everywhere for that boy."

"My husband and I live across the hall from where Johnny lives." She put her hand to her cheek and shook her head. "A terrible situation, Mr. Ferry, just terrible."

"We wanted to talk with him, to let him know everything is okay. I'm sorry, I didn't get your name."

"I'm Mrs. Paladino. Josephine. My husband and I have been helping the boy what little we can. Everybody heard all kinds of stories about what happened, and they blame Johnny. That gossipy woman...her husband owns the hardware store..."

"Viola Steich," Etta said flatly.

"Yes and shame on her," Mrs. Paladino said, "for spreading such terrible things. My husband and I believe the boy. He's been so upset and worried, not being able to make things right. He wanted to come here, but he was afraid." She looked at Etta. "He's a good boy, Mrs. Ferry. So much has happened."

Etta came forward and touched the woman's arm. "Come in, Mrs. Paladino. And please forgive us—have your husband come up, as well."

"My husband? Oh, that's not my husband," she said, looking behind her down the stairs. "That's the boy. That's Johnny."

CHAPTER NINETEEN

Mike turned to Etta, then bounded down the stairs to open the vestibule door. Johnny Herring, gaunt and frail, backed away.

"Johnny." Mike's voice was sympathetic and cordial, "It's okay. I'm Mr. Ferry, Margaret's uncle. Please come in. I've been looking for you for days."

Johnny's brow furrowed. He didn't move.

"But only for good reasons." Mike caught himself quickly. "Nothing bad. We wanted to say how sorry we are for all the trouble you've been through. Margaret told us what happened, that none of it was your fault. You have nothing to fear from us. Please. Come."

Mike led the way up, with Johnny following cautiously. Margaret, still engrossed in the comic strips, out of earshot, was unaware of what was going on, and when Mrs. Paladino entered the kitchen with Johnny Herring at her side, she jumped to her feet, nearly knocking over her chair.

"Johnny," she gasped.

Johnny Herring, equally stunned, stopped cold, seeing for himself what he had heard but couldn't believe—she looked exactly the same as before the accident, not a mark, her skin spotless white, eyes bright and warm.

Margaret's gaze never left his. He looked very different from the last time she had seen him, his clothes now clean and tidy, his dark blond hair combed back off his face. There were scars.

Mrs. Paladino, speechless, blessed herself.

Mike spoke up quickly, putting his arm around Margaret's shoulder, protective in a way. It made him uncomfortable, as it did Etta, when people openly expressed their amazement in front of Margaret, although it hadn't ever seemed to bother her. "People are quite surprised," he said, "when they first see Margaret since...since everything happened. But she's okay, as you can see, and we're all very grateful." For a moment, there was an awkward pause, the two visitors gazing at the girl.

"Come. Sit," Etta said. "Have some breakfast with us."

Mrs. Paladino explained that they had already eaten, but Etta managed to coax the boy into having bacon and eggs— "Young men always need a lot of food." She poured a cup of coffee for Mrs. Paladino, while Margaret remained silent, taking in the boy with whom she had come to feel such a close bond, a great sense of having shared an amazing thing. She wondered if in some way he felt the same.

"Johnny," Mrs. Paladino said, "would you like to tell everyone what you've been wanting to say? You can see these are nice people."

Mike gently reached out to touch Johnny's arm, but the boy snatched it away on impulse. It startled them. "I...I'm sorry," the boy said timidly. "I didn't mean to..."

"It's okay," Mike said. "I mean no harm. I just want to encourage you to say whatever is on your mind. You're among friends."

Johnny Herring put his head down, then began slowly. "I...I didn't mean for anything to happen to you. I swear."

Margaret smiled. "I know."

"Honest—I didn't know till I got across the street and heard...I heard, you know. And soon as I turned around, I saw the shawl stuck to my bike wheel." He pressed his fingers against his eyes.

"It's okay, Johnny," Mike said.

The boy lifted his head, tearful, and took a deep breath, looking around the table. "I don't think it's okay." He swallowed hard, glanced momentarily at Margaret, then put his head down. "You tried to be nice to me. Nobody was ever that nice to me. You tried to buy me a sandwich with money you said was mine. You knew that wasn't my money." He picked nervously at his fingernails. "I had no money. You were willing to give me yours. But I yelled at you and took off." His voice cracked. "I yelled at you. And then everything happened and I wished I was dead." He put his head in his hands.

"But that's all behind us now, Johnny," Etta said. "Margaret is fine. You can see that. You're not to blame for anything. Besides, accidents happen all the time. I spilled a whole pot of hot soup one time on Mr. Ferry's foot. I panicked and felt terrible. It was awful. He had to go to the hospital. He still has a small scar. I didn't mean to do that anymore than you meant for Margaret to get hurt. Please don't punish yourself any longer over this."

"But people say I stole the shawl." He looked at Margaret again. "I would never do that to you. They say it all happened because of me. People…"

"Johnny, Johnny." Etta put her arm around the boy's shoulder. "Please. People will come around. We'll see to that. It's going to be all right."

"I promise you we will make sure people know the truth," Mike said. "The important thing right now is that you're okay. And, by the way," he said with a wry smile, "you can see that Margaret is too."

Johnny looked up into Mike's face, and after a moment, allowed a hint of a smile.

"I have an idea," Etta said. "Since all is forgiven, let's cheer things up a bit. Mar, why don't you take Johnny into the living room? Maybe see if there's anything on the television."

"Okay." Margaret got up and put her hand on Johnny's

shoulder. "Come on. Maybe there's a movie on. Do you like the *Three Stooges* or the *Lone Ranger*?"

Johnny rose slowly, nodding respectfully to the others before leaving the kitchen. Mike could understand what Margaret saw in the boy. Once away from the wrath and violence of his father, he appeared to be courteous and appreciative of everything that was done for him, and was certainly remorseful.

"I can see he's been through an awful lot," Mike said. "I imagine you and your husband have too. I agree with what you said, Mrs. Paladino—I think he is a good kid. Margaret said the same thing long before today. Our niece has always had a way of seeing the good in people."

"She looks like a wonderful girl, Mr. Ferry. I'm so happy for all of you. A great miracle. I wish we could dare to pray for another one." She took a crochet-edged handkerchief from her purse and dabbed her eyes. "The situation with Johnny has been terrible. It still is."

She had a quiet and gracious way of speaking with measured words that revealed a hint of an Italian accent in her broken English. She went on to tell them about Nicholas Herring and the way he treated his son. "The man is a terrible drinker. He beat the boy without mercy." She told about the day that Johnny was so badly injured, when she moved him to her apartment, hid him, and spent several hours removing the slivers of glass from his head and legs, before she could even tend to his wounds.

Etta sat stone still with one hand over her mouth, the other holding onto Mike's arm.

"We had the doctor come secretly, but no police. We were afraid of what that monster of a man might do for revenge. I was afraid for my husband." Mrs. Paladino shook her head. "He thinks he's still as strong as he used to be. We decided to hide the boy—we couldn't let him go back home. But as soon as Johnny was able to get up and around, he ran off. He was so ashamed of being a burden. My husband found him in the alley behind Longo's grocery store, eating scraps of food, but he ran off again. That was around the time, I believe, when your lovely niece was talking to him…her confirmation day. He ran back to us that day and told us everything. He was beside himself with guilt and worry, Mrs. Ferry, and terrified that your poor niece would…would…you know…" She dabbed at her eyes again. "But then, thank God, we read about what happened in the hospital, and that she was alive.

"Where is Nicholas Herring now?" Mike asked, lowering his voice. "Have you seen him?"

"No, we have not seen him. I hope we never have to see him again." Mrs. Paladino leaned back to look toward the living room, then went on in a whisper. "I don't want the boy to hear us talking. That monster is in jail and he's going to be there for a long time, thank God."

Mike looked at Etta, then back at Mrs. Paladino. "Well…I can't say we're surprised."

"What did he do?" Etta asked, leaning forward, her brow furrowed.

"He tried to rob a liquor store…that one by the park. Mrs. Wortman said he hit the man over the head with a bottle." She made the sign of the cross. "Herring almost killed him. They say robbery and attempted murder. That poor man. He's still in the hospital."

"Does Johnny know all this?" Etta asked.

"Oh, yes. We had to tell him. He doesn't say anything about his father, but we know he's relieved that he won't be around. We all are. There's a lot of feelings tumbling around inside that boy, you can understand that. It's still his father." She twisted the edge of the handkerchief. "At least the man won't be hiding in some dark corner. It was such a frightening thing."

A surprising burst of laughter came from the living room and made them smile. "Maybe things are looking up." Mike took Etta's hand, then grew serious. "Except, of course, what's going to happen to Johnny now? Where will he go?"

The woman shrugged wearily. "That's a big problem, Mr. Ferry. Their apartment is still there, but he stays with us. He has no one. We feed him and look after him. Gladly. How can a boy keep an apartment on his own? The rent will come due soon, and when there is no one to pay it, then what? My husband's father lives with us. He's ninety-three. We don't have the room. We won't be able to continue this. We don't know what to do. It's only a matter of time before they realize the boy is on his own, even if he's with us. Right away, they'll put him in a home, and we don't know what will happen to him. I cry in my prayers every night for this boy." She pressed her handkerchief to her eyes and muffled a sob.

Etta put her arm around the woman and looked at Mike. They both took a deep breath.

Margaret came into the kitchen laughing, Johnny Herring close behind, wearing a shy smile. "They are so funny," she said. "I like Moe; he's so mean."

"I never saw a television set before, except in the store windows," Johnny said quietly, appearing self-conscious.

Margaret put her arm through Mike's. "Uncle Mike, I've been thinking. Why don't we let Johnny come with us to the City? He's never seen a real newspaper office before."

"Oh, Margaret," Etta said, despair in her voice. "I don't think that's such a good idea with everything that's going on."

"Well...." Mike hesitated, looking at Etta. "Maybe it's not really such a bad idea, Et." He waited until Etta shook her head slowly and smiled, signaling her acquiescence. Mike looked at Johnny. "What do you say, Johnny? Have you ever been into the City?"

"No, sir."

"Would you like to come with us...if it's okay with Mrs. Paladino?"

The boy put his head down and shrugged.

Mrs. Paladino touched the boy's shoulder. "It's a nice idea, Johnny. Don't you think?"

He looked up at her, then at Mike, and shrugged again.

"I'll take that as a yes," Mike said, laughing. "So, it's all set then."

The woman, obviously cheered by the unexpected lightness of the moment, nodded her approval, then rose to leave. She took Mike's and Etta's hands in hers. "We have to be going now. I can't thank you enough. You'll never know."

They left with Mike's discreet offer of money, which Mrs. Paladino graciously declined, and his promise to help, although at the moment he could not quite imagine how.

As they headed toward the door, Johnny turned, looked at Mike and Etta, then at Margaret, and nodded his thanks. They had barely closed the vestibule door behind them when the phone rang. Bill Fulton had some bad news.

CHAPTER TWENTY

Margaret sat at the small square corner table in Sister Bernadine's office, alphabetizing folders. Across the room at her desk, Sister organized records and scrawled her meticulous fountain pen cursives, now and then glancing in the girl's direction, wondering. *How can all this ordinary business go on as if nothing has happened, as if this child is not a marvel?*

It was an endless puzzle to Sister, as she was sure it must be to others, how very little Margaret had changed since her... well, she was thinking recovery, but, of course, the mystery of it all was that there was no recovery. No sign whatever of the horrific accident and the injuries the girl had sustained.

Michael Ferry's paper had been considerate of the family in deciding not to run the story, while the prospect of ongoing front-page sensationalism had vanished overnight in the face of other headlines, including the brutal murder of a prominent bank executive and his family in Westport, Connecticut. Sister wondered if the world might not have benefitted from a first-class miracle.

In any case, Margaret was here. She was well, a bit quieter perhaps, yet she seemed at ease and happy. There was something that might occasionally happen with her hair; Michael Ferry had alerted her, but she hadn't seen it yet and couldn't imagine. All in all, the whole thing was unfathomable, even for one who lived daily with the understanding of God's hand in all things.

"How are you today, Margaret?"

Margaret looked up with a serene smile. "I'm fine, thank you, Sister."

"I believe I miss your chatter."

"I wanted to surprise you, Sister. Look." Margaret held up two manila folders. "Sullivan and Vitale—the last of the new families. I'm all done."

"That's wonderful. You are so helpful, as always."

"And they're a lot easier to pronounce." Margaret laughed. "Even though I did get used to the Russian names."

One change Sister noticed about Margaret was the surprising absence of impatience and frustration with regard to the Russian families leaving St. Aloysius. It was a relief to Sister not to constantly have to defend Monsignor's actions. Still, Sister was intrigued.

"What's your next project?" Margaret asked.

Sister had known this was going to be the hard part. She had tried to change Monsignor's mind, but he was adamant about not wanting Margaret to be privy any longer to school or church business. Monsignor had also changed since Margaret's accident. It was clear that he did not know what to make of all that had happened. Odd that he should be so uncomfortable with the prospect of a miracle, even as the Bishop's office had been conducting its own inquiry and appeared unusually optimistic that, indeed, a miracle had occurred, although the Church rarely declared such things, leaving people to believe what they would.

It had been over a month since the accident and the girl had been back to school now only a few days with a clean bill of health, unwittingly and quite naturally inviting the curiosity of teachers and classmates, who had the strictest orders from the Bishop's office not to bother her in any way or ask a lot of questions.

There were so many things that people were eager to call miracles—Christ's face in a slice of wedding cake, The Blessed

Mother appearing on the outside wall of a laundromat. Nearly all were, at best, up for debate. From the evidence so far, this was not, but for some reason, it did not sit well with Monsignor Carnavan, who appeared irritated at any mention of the incident, dismissing it as so much exaggeration and folly. In the face of such incredible circumstances, was he still stewing about Margaret's petition to the Bishop? With more important things to focus on, surely the Bishop himself must have forgotten about it.

"But what of the firsthand witnesses? Sister had asked Monsignor.

"People see what they want to see," had been his reply.

"The Bishop is taking it quite seriously."

"I leave the Bishop to believe what he will; I myself will not be taken in so easily." Somehow, that line of thinking had caused Monsignor to distrust Margaret, though it made no sense at all to Sister. He appeared to place no credence in what the doctors reported, and on more than one occasion challenged the accounts of eyewitnesses to both the accident and the incident at the hospital.

He questioned Sister about the girl's behavior at school, but there was nothing to report. Still, he kept at it as if trying to trip her up, as though she might be covering for some unacceptable activity on Margaret's part. How would she now break the news to Margaret that she would no longer be allowed to help in the office?

"I've been thinking, Margaret—with school ending in just about a month, I...I'm not sure there is really so much to be done, after all." It wasn't a lie. Sister was quite capable of handling most of her office needs on her own—she had simply enjoyed Margaret's company over these many months. She relished the girl's indomitable passion, which reminded her of the exuberant spirit of her own youth. She had come to like Margaret Ferry very much.

"The work should go fast then, Sister, shouldn't it?"

Before Sister could answer, she was startled to see Margaret's hair gently fan out, as if by static charge. Margaret didn't appear to be aware of it. "Monsignor," the girl said matter of factly, her attention still on gathering up the files.

"What about Monsignor?" Sister asked.

The answer came in the form of a sharp rap on the door as Monsignor Carnavan pushed into the room. Sister flashed a look at Margaret, who appeared to be unaware of her own prescience.

"Good afternoon, Monsignor." Sister gave a slight nod. "I didn't know you were coming over."

"Clearly," he said, turning a stern eye to Margaret.

Margaret got to her feet. "Good afternoon, Monsignor."

The priest looked at Sister Bernadine with a scowl. "We had an understanding, Sister, did we not?"

Sister flushed. "Yes, Monsignor. I..."

"Please don't be mad at Sister," Margaret said. "She was just about to tell me when you came in."

The two of them gave Margaret a puzzled look.

The Monsignor stepped closer. "Tell you what, exactly?"

"That she isn't allowed to have me come and work with her anymore."

"But how did you know that?" Sister asked.

Margaret shrugged. "Sometimes I just know things."

Monsignor narrowed his eyes. "Listening at doors, no doubt. Be very careful with what you think you know, Miss Ferry. Now, leave us please."

Sister half expected Margaret to defend herself—of course, the girl had not listened at doors. But Margaret said nothing. Sister didn't know what to make of any of it, standing there with her fingers pressed against her lips. Monsignor was too stern with Margaret. Here was a girl, who from all appearances had come by some rare and special ability, gift perhaps, but how and to what purpose, Sister Bernadine could not begin to understand, any more than she could understand Monsignor's harsh reaction.

Margaret picked up her schoolbooks as Sister Bernadine stepped forward. She was about to put her hand on the girl's shoulder, but stopped. Should she touch this child?

"I'm sorry, Margaret. I have no way to account for all that has happened, but I think you are a very special girl and you have been a great help to me. You have performed every task given to you with excellence." She moved as if to push a curl of hair behind Margaret's ear, but again drew her hand back. "Your uncle will be here shortly to pick you up. Please just wait outside and let me know when he arrives."

This was another change—Margaret was no longer free to walk home without an escort. Since the incident, at the Bishop's request, a police officer was posted at the school to fend off any reporters who tried for a photo or a comment. Either Margaret's aunt or uncle had come for the girl each day. They would leave by the back door and steal across to the churchyard to take the longer, more circuitous route home. The last thing they wanted was for a reporter to find out where they lived. So far it had worked, and they all hoped that what little interest remained would soon fade completely.

Margaret smiled on her way to the door, and as she passed Monsignor, she stopped and gave him a long steady look. Sister saw a certain knowing in the way Margaret took him in, as if searching something behind his eyes. Her hair fluttered as if by a slight breeze and Sister's mouth opened in a gasp. There was, of course, no breeze.

Monsignor took a step back, but Margaret's eyes never left him. "God bless you in all good thoughts and intentions, Monsignor Carnavan. In all your deeds and decisions, may you discern His purpose." Then she turned and walked out the door, closing it quietly behind her. Sister Bernadine had a worried smile, as Monsignor drilled the door with his glare.

"How dare she." His tone was quiet and hard.

"She's only a child. She…"

"She is impudent and disrespectful."

Sister Bernadine felt extremely unsettled by Monsignor's reaction. She tunneled her hands into her sleeves. "Could you not sense the purity of her words? Did you notice the light in her eyes?"

"You have greatly disappointed me, Sister. You continue to harbor this girl in spite of…"

"Harbor?" Sister Bernadine struggled not to raise her voice. "You mean as one would harbor a felon? Is that what Margaret Ferry has become for you, Monsignor? With all due respect, your reaction to this child escapes my comprehension."

"Anyone can see she is…she is…"

"Blessed?" She walked toward him. *Holy Spirit, hold my tongue, hold my tongue.*

"That you could believe such nonsense makes me think you are…"

Sister stiffened. "The Bishop does not see it as nonsense. How is it that you do, Monsignor?"

Monsignor's lips tightened into a thin line. "It is clear to me, Sister Bernadine, that you have lost not only your perspective but every shred of reason, reverence and sense of duty."

His words came at her like spears. "My sense of duty is ultimately for the Almighty." The toxic swell of anger had overtaken her. "And let us not forget that there…is…only… One."

They were silent for a long moment, the air stifled by the heat of their words.

"You may as well know right now, Sister—Margaret Ferry will not be returning to St. Aloysius in the fall."

Sister Bernadine struggled to keep the bitterest of words from spilling out. "How will you possibly rationalize this to the

Bishop with all that's going on? The inquiry? With what cruel authority can you justify sending her away?"

"She is disruptive to the other students," Monsignor said. "Let the Bishop find a suitable place for her...elsewhere. I won't have a child here who is...is...possessed."

"Ah, yes, then that must be true, Monsignor Carnavan, possessed. And by what? The Holy Spirit? And who is the mysterious woman they say spoke to her? Is that what's bothering you? That perhaps God has graced this...this... impudent, unworthy child with a blessing of which you, in all your great kindness and compassion, are so much more deserving?"

Even as she felt the shame of her wrath, she was incapable of stopping herself. She felt the heat in her face. "Be careful, Monsignor, that your jealousy does not consume your soul."

Monsignor Carnavan glared at her through narrowed eyes. "When Mr. Ferry arrives, you will let him know that his niece will not be returning to this school next year. And I, Sister, I will call Baltimore and inform the Mother House that you will not be returning either. You will be reassigned at the end of this school year." He stomped out, slamming the door behind him.

Sister stared at the closed door in astonishment. Then, after a long moment, she slowly went to her desk and sat heavily, her shoulders slumped. Once, when she was a child growing up in rural Connecticut, she visited an aunt and uncle whose neighbors had the biggest dog she had ever seen, a wooly brown Akita named Wolf, around whom she had never felt at ease. One day, without warning, Wolf charged at her, knocked her to the ground and pulled her around by the clothing with his teeth. She screamed until both her voice and her breath were gone. It took three people to get the dog off her, and although she suffered only scratches and bruises, it took years to quell the anxiety of those desperate moments. Now, with her face buried in her hands, and her elbows planted on the desk she had occupied for more than fifteen years, she remembered Wolf.

The telephone rang and Sister Bernadine let it, uncertain that she had the voice to speak. What could she make of any of this? She had been defiant. She had been dismissed. She had failed her Order and her students. Yet, how could she have remained silent in the face of such...such utter ...oh, what was the point? Her time here was over. Just like that. The Lord's way was a mysterious one, indeed.

There was a knock on the door and she had to respond; it was likely Margaret wanting to let her know her uncle had arrived. Sister Bernadine patted a tear from the corner of her eye. How was she to explain Margaret's expulsion in any reasonable way to the Ferrys? Such a good family. And to have raised such a delightful and special child. Now, after all they had just been through, to turn them away from St. Aloysius. What was she to tell them that wouldn't reveal her disdain for their pastor? She stood erect, and went to the door.

"Hello, Mr. Ferry," she said, feigning cheerfulness. "Please come in."

"Oh, I don't want to take up your time, Sister. I just thought I'd say hello and let you know we were leaving."

"Yes...well..."

"Are you all right, Sister?"

Margaret had remained seated in one of the chairs outside Sister's office, thumbing through her social studies textbook.

"We'll just be a few minutes, Margaret," Sister said, and closed the door.

"What is it, Sister? Is anything wrong?"

"Please forgive me, Mr. Ferry. I'm sorry to say I have some... some disappointing news."

CHAPTER TWENTY-ONE

"Your chocolate soda is ready, Margaret." Mrs. Wortman placed the glass on the counter, along with a cup of coffee for Etta. "Cream and one sugar, I remember."

"Thank you, Mrs. Wortman." There was a sweet sadness about this woman that Etta suspected a lot of her hurried customers didn't notice.

Margaret looked over from the comic book rack where she had been thumbing through the latest issue of *Brenda Starr*, and smiled. "Thank you, Mrs. Wortman."

"I gave you a cookie." The woman looked at Etta and shrugged. "What could it hurt?"

"Not a thing. That's fine."

"And bring the book. I'll give it to you," the woman said plainly.

"Oh...no...we're happy to buy it," Etta said.

"Please." Mrs. Wortman tapped her hand against her heart.

"That's very kind of you." All the years they lived here, Etta had never really spoken with Mrs. Wortman outside of a courteous greeting. She felt ashamed now, realizing how she had misjudged her. She was a plain, strong-looking woman, with a Jewish accent as thick as her bones, and hair like fine gray wire. Yet Etta could see she had a kind of grace about her that was hinted at in her eyes—deep, soulful eyes that looked at people more attentively, maybe even caringly, than they gave her credit for, no doubt because of her hard edges. There were no children that anyone seemed to know of, only rumors through the years about a family tragedy.

"This is my favorite cookie," Margaret said. "Chocolate drizzle. That makes it an almost perfect day."

Etta could believe it. School was done—Margaret's first week back—and tomorrow was a big day, going to the City with her Uncle Mike and Johnny Herring. She could no longer help Sister after school, and she still wasn't allowed to play with her best friend, but it didn't bother her. Nothing seemed to bother her these days. What would she think when she learned she would not be returning to St. Aloysius in the fall? There was a time when Etta knew this child inside and out, but that had changed. She and Mike no longer had any idea what their niece might do next. They weren't even sure if Margaret knew—apparently some things just came to her, whether it was a mood or as Sister Bernadine had called it, a *knowing*. Odd as it was, Margaret didn't seem to know what she knew until the moment she knew it.

They had seated themselves at the far end of the counter, away from the easy glance of customers who came and went. So far, no one had noticed who the girl was. Perhaps it no longer mattered to anyone, and for that Etta was extremely grateful, especially now with everything else that was going on. She was afraid to ask herself what more could possibly go wrong, fearing that she would quickly find out. Little by little, things had been getting back to normal. Now, everything was upside down all over again. What logic could Monsignor Carnavan have possibly used to come to such a decision at this of all times? Sister had explained everything—everything that was possible to explain.

"More coffee?" Mrs. Wortman offered.

"I'm fine, thanks."

"There's much on your mind," the woman said quietly, only half asking.

Etta nodded. Somehow, she suspected this woman was well acquainted with pain. "Much." She took a deep breath and thought about Mike. Mike, of all people, to have worked so hard and have his story stolen right out from under his nose. She could only imagine how hard it was for Bill Fulton to tell him that Loughlin had turned in The Central Commerce Trust story and that it would start running the week after next. Loughlin had been bragging about his secret meetings with the bank's CFO and main whistleblower, someone that Mike and Bill Fulton knew Loughlin had never laid eyes on. Once that series ran, Loughlin would get the promotion and Mike's future with the paper would be history.

"I'm sure it'll have your fingerprints all over it," Bill had told Mike, "—the detail, the depth of research—all you. Loughlin wouldn't have gotten a sideways glance from their CFO."

But what did it matter? There was no proof. The news had come at a time when Mike and Etta had hoped, with Margaret back in school, to have a few days alone together, something that hadn't been possible since the accident. Mike had tried to put on a happy face, but she knew his anger and frustration. She could see it in his eyes. He had written a number of pieces during these weeks away from the office, and Etta tried not to overplay her praise for how good they were, which was true, but that bank exposé would have been the plum.

"I'm going to the City tomorrow," Margaret said, her whispered enthusiasm overruling the momentary seriousness.

"How nice." Mrs. Wortman's questioning look brought Etta back.

"She's been asking for a long time. My husband didn't see a problem with it since things were…well…mostly settling down."

Mrs. Wortman leaned toward Margaret. "You shouldn't make such noise in the City that you always make here."

"No," Etta said, giving Margaret a half smile, "I think she'll promise to behave herself, right Mar?"

Margaret nodded and took another sip of her soda, while Etta watched admiringly the way Mrs. Wortman busied herself with the heavy ice cream bins, moving them easily with her strong hands into their stainless steel wells behind the counter.

"I think I'll call Uncle Mike," Etta said, getting up from the stool. "Let him know we have one more stop to make—we need a new curtain rod for the bathroom.

"Oh, let me call him, Aunt Etta."

Etta reached in her purse and gave Margaret a few coins for the telephone, then sat back down. "Mr. Wortman isn't here today."

"This is the day for errands."

"I just want to say again, Mrs. Wortman, that we'll never forget how he helped Margaret."

"He's good, my Isador—people don't know." Mrs. Wortman shrugged. "I guess he doesn't let them." The two women smiled wryly.

"It's a good thing he's not here right now," the woman said, looking around the store. "He would worry there's no business."

Etta looked about, only now aware of the unusual quietness of the place. "Oh. Where did everybody go?" Except for the three of them, the store was empty. She glanced at the faded Coca-Cola wall clock. "Ten to four, an odd time for no one to be here."

A moment later the front door swung open and they turned to see Viola Steich enter in a huff, head down, chattering away in her own thoughts. She sat quickly, peeling off her white gloves without noticing who it was at the far end of the counter.

Mrs. Wortman rolled her eyes and proceeded to wipe the counter.

"I'll have an egg cream, please. Just an egg cream. What an exasperating day."

Etta slouched a little, hoping to shrink from sight at least for a few minutes, but the moment the woman glanced along the counter, she shrieked. "Oh, my gracious, my gracious, there you are. I have been by so many times, but no one ever answers the bell." She picked up her gloves and purse and moved to a stool closer to Etta. "I've been wondering when I would get to see my very special friends. You know, Mrs. Wortman, I was right there at the hospital when it all happened."

Etta wasn't sure what to say or do. Margaret would come out of the phone booth any minute, and there was no telling how outrageously Viola would behave seeing her for the first time. "How is Mr. Steich doing?"

"Oh, he's all right," she said, swiping at the air with her hand. "But he's not the problem. It's that awful, awful Herring boy. Some nice family took him in. I just heard. The husband's father lives with them. He's ninety. God only knows what can happen with a boy like that living there. What are they thinking? You know he's just a younger version of his father, that monster. Begging. Stealing. He needs to be put away, like his father. You see how he almost killed your beautiful niece. Well, I can tell you, Mrs. Ferry, if I have my way, the police will know exactly where he is and see that he goes to reform school where he belongs."

Before Etta could get a word in, the door to the phone booth slid open with a low screech and Margaret stepped out, her hair fluttering for an instant. Etta moved swiftly off the stool before Mrs. Steich noticed. "We have to be running along now."

"Hello, Mrs. Steich." Margaret had a look on her face that immediately gave Etta an uneasy feeling. She had seen it before a few days earlier when the reporter came up to them. A wide-eyed inquisitive look, radiating a gentle exuberance that Etta now understood to be disarming. Etta grew more anxious.

Viola Steich stared at the girl, mouth open, as Etta took

Margaret by the arm.

"My gracious, it's you, Margaret. I have been hoping and hoping to see you. I was there at the hospital, you know. I…"

Mrs. Wortman banged the glass of egg cream onto the counter in front of Viola to distract her. "Can I get you something else?"

The woman, momentarily startled, went on anyway. "You look like nothing at all happened. Nothing at all. Who would believe it, except that I was there myself…at the hospital."

Margaret looked at Etta. "I think we need to stay for a minute, Aunt Etta."

Etta opened her mouth to protest, but Margaret lifted her chin and smiled, her eyes glistening. "Just for a few minutes."

Etta followed her back to where they had been sitting. This time, Margaret chose the stool between her aunt and Mrs. Steich. "Doesn't Mrs. Wortman make the best egg creams?" Margaret said. "They're so sweet."

"We really have to run along now, Margaret. Uncle Mike will be waiting for us. Really."

"I was just telling your aunt about that Herring boy. How absolutely awful that he…"

"Would you pass the salt, please, Mrs. Steich?"

A look of bewilderment crossed the woman's face, since the girl had nothing to put salt on, but she passed the shaker anyway, accidentally tipping it over in the process. Salt spilled across the counter in front of them.

"Oh, I'm so sorry," Mrs. Steich said, flustered.

Mrs. Wortman picked up a towel to clean it, but Margaret put up her hand. "It's okay to leave it, Mrs. Wortman."

As if without knowing why, Mrs. Wortman did as Margaret said, and the girl began slowly moving her finger through the salt in small circles.

Etta rubbed the side of her neck nervously, but knew better than to interfere. *Lord have mercy, what now?*

"Tell me about Johnny, Mrs. Steich," Margaret said quietly without looking up. Her hair lifted.

"Well," the woman began, her eyes fixed on the swirls of salt Margaret was fingering. She was clearly elated by the prospect of having others hear her well-repeated condemnation of the boy. "I can certainly give you an earful." She took a deep breath. "He...he...h...h...." She leaned forward and threw her hand to her throat. She tried again. "I can only tell you that he...h...h...." A look of panic crossed her face as Etta and Mrs. Wortman reached toward her in astonishment.

"Are you okay?"

"I don't know what it is. I don't seem able to...to...." Red-faced, the woman tried a third time. "What I am trying to tell you is that the boy is...uh...uh...." She leaned her head forward, struggling to push the words out, but it was futile.

Mrs. Wortman set a glass of water on the counter, which Margaret gently slid to the side.

"Maybe something sweet would help," Margaret said.

"Yes. Yes. I don't know what it is. My throat must be dry." She patted her chest, then tried once more. "Johnny Herring is a...a...a..."

Margaret turned and looked directly into the woman's eyes, pushing the glass of egg cream closer to her.

The woman looked steadily at the girl, then picked up the glass of egg cream and took a sip. "Yes," she said, calmly. "Yes, that's better." She took another sip. "That's much better."

Etta and Mrs. Wortman glanced at each other, mystified and motionless.

"I definitely want to hear more, Mrs. Steich," Margaret said.

"Yes, well." She set the glass of egg cream down. "That boy...that boy...he...he has been through so much. He really has. His father, such a sick and miserable man, treated him so badly."

Etta and Mrs. Wortman stared at the woman, disbelievingly.

Margaret listened intently to Mrs. Steich.

The woman lifted the glass to her lips again. "Yes, that feels better. I suppose what I'm trying to say is it was such a terrible situation for the boy." She shook her head. "How else could he possibly be expected to behave with no one at home to care for him or feed him? He's really not a bad boy, is he?" She looked to the others for agreement. "Thank God a good family has taken him in."

"Yes," Margaret said.. "That's so compassionate of you, Mrs. Steich. So sweet of you to understand."

"Yes," Etta and Mrs. Wortman repeated, low and in unison.

There was a brief silence before Margaret said, "See, Mrs. Steich? The salt is gone."

The counter was perfectly clear. The women looked at each other.

Viola Steich slowly ran her hand across the smooth Formica countertop. "Yes, the salt is all gone now." She looked into Margaret's eyes, then at the clock. "Oh, dear, I must be going. I want to stop by Mendel's before it closes and pick up a nice new shirt for that boy." A moment later she was gone.

Margaret Ferry took another bite of her cookie, and breathed a satisfied sigh. "If you ever tried Mrs. Wortman's chocolate drizzle cookie, Aunt Etta, it would be your favorite too."

Etta and Mrs. Wortman stared at the girl in silence. A moment later, the door swung open. A man in a business suit entered and picked up one of the evening papers. Two others entered shortly after, and the customary stream of afternoon customers resumed.

CHAPTER TWENTY-TWO

"Do you realize how crazy that sounds, Et?"

"Crazier than her telling that reporter about some long-lost friend from the war? I'm telling you, Mike, I saw it with my own eyes." They'd been taking an evening stroll along the tree-lined sidewalk outside Greenwood Cemetery. "Mrs. Wortman was as shocked as I was. There was no doubt. I'm telling you...she changed Viola's words, changed her mind. Salt and sugar; salty and sweet. I can't explain it. And meanwhile...meanwhile, did you ever know the candy store to be empty, I mean completely empty, no one around...and on a Friday afternoon? Not a soul that whole time?"

"Do you think maybe we should...I don't know...see somebody...get some help? We've talked about it before. Maybe a psychiatrist?"

"God, Mike, Mar's not crazy. She's not doing anything wrong. She's somehow helping. Isn't that the pattern? Think about it—whatever she's doing, it ends up with good results. The reporter found his friend. Viola changed her mind about Johnny."

Mike tapped his thumb against his lip. "I just wish we could find something normal here. I feel as though we're treading water out in the middle of the ocean with no lifeboats in sight. And look at her." He motioned down the street. "Happy as a lark, looking at crocuses and pansies. Petting that couple's boxer. What do we do with this?"

They were quiet for a long moment.

"Okay," Etta said, "let's think about it. Why do we have to do anything? Just because this is strange to us, it doesn't seem at all strange to her. She isn't causing trouble. She's not hurting anyone. There's no danger that we can see. What makes us think we have to do anything? The diocese knows about her. They know how rare it is. The Church has dealt with this sort of thing, and they don't seem alarmed or shocked or confused."

"But I'm worried about something else, Et. What if...what if she were to know everything?"

"Everything, like what?" She stopped abruptly and looked up at him with fearful understanding. "Oh, Lord."

"She knows other things that don't seem possible for her to know. What if she knows about...Syracuse and...?"

They searched each other's eyes, then continued along in silence, she with her arm through his, tucked in close.

CHAPTER TWENTY-THREE

In all the world it was her favorite place—New York in the springtime. Well, maybe New York in the fall too…and Christmas with the tree and the ice rink at Rockefeller Center and the windows all decorated at Lord and Taylor. What's wrong with people having lots of favorite places? Just like food—sometimes spaghetti was her favorite, sometimes pot roast. The cabin in the Poconos—definitely a favorite. But today she was here in the City with Uncle Mike and Johnny and happy as could be. They had taken two different subway trains to land at Grand Central Station. From there, they walked over to Lexington Avenue, to Kopley's art supply store that she liked so well, and couldn't wait to show Johnny. This was the best day.

Johnny Herring, his head tilted back as far as it could to see to the very top of the tallest buildings, said little, but she could tell he was happy to be there too. A couple of times he nudged her to look at something odd about a person passing by on the crowded avenue—a hobo-looking man carrying a little gray and black dog in the pocket of his oversized coat; a woman so tall he joked about her joining the Harlem Globetrotters. It was nice to see Johnny smile. She would eventually want to show him every place she knew and loved—the Statue of Liberty, the Coney Island Parachute ride, the Brooklyn Botanical Gardens, the Central Park Zoo where you could sail a toy boat—maybe Uncle Mike could get him one. The wonderful New York

Public Library—Uncle Mike had once taken a picture of her sitting on one of the lions. The Metropolitan Museum of Art with paintings the size of an entire wall. She had a feeling he would really like Rembrandt—right up against the dark, dark part was always a brilliant sunny gold color that lit the faces.

He had come along with a haircut and a brand new shirt and trousers, limping less than when she had last seen him the morning that Mrs. Paladino had brought him around. Mr. and Mrs. Paladino were taking good care of him. Mike had put five dollars in a wallet he bought for him, a gift that made Johnny blush and nod his thanks.

There was a change of plans because of what was happening at Uncle Mike's job, which probably involved the bad things Mr. Loughlin was up to. They wouldn't be going to the newspaper office but would meet Mr. Fulton nearby at Mar's favorite restaurant, the Horn and Hardart Automat on 42nd Street and Third Avenue. But first to Kopley's.

"Did you ever see so many different kinds of pencils and paints and brushes?" Mar asked Johnny.

Johnny Herring shook his head and looked the place over. A visiting artist worked at an easel in one corner of the shop, and Johnny couldn't take his eyes off him. "I never really saw anybody draw or paint anything," he said as Margaret thumbed through a large drawing book with a picture of a pumpkin and a sombrero on the cover. "Can you draw?" he asked her.

"Not really. I just like to copy pictures, especially from the bird and butterfly books I get at the library."

"Would you like to pick out something, Johnny?" Mike asked. "Maybe give it a try when you get home? My treat."

"I wouldn't know what to draw."

"What about those old cars you like so well," Mar said.

Johnny glanced about quickly for whatever it was—some kind of a breeze—that made her hair flutter, and gave her a curious look. "That's weird. How did you know I like old cars?"

"I don't know," she said with a shrug. "It just came to me that you would like that kind of a car. You do, right?"

"I guess," he said. "Yeah...I do...but how...?"

"Ok," Mike cut in, "let's start picking out a couple of things you'd both like to have." He looked at his watch. "We don't want to keep Mr. Fulton waiting."

A little while later they left the store, Margaret and Johnny each carrying a Kopley's Art Shop paper bag, and headed to Horn and Hardart for lunch.

———

Bill Fulton met them outside the busy Automat entrance with his arms outstretched for Margaret, and fussed about how much taller and prettier she was than the last time he had seen her a few years earlier. Mike had cautioned him not to make too much of all the miracle stuff, to just keep things on an even keel. He had also filled him in on Johnny's background to prevent any awkward questions or comments, and Bill greeted the boy with a pat on the back and a warm welcome.

"What are they feeding kids nowadays that they look so grown up," Bill said. "You're a pretty fit young man there, Johnny."

The boy smiled self-consciously, wondering how it was that he kept meeting so many nice people. All he had ever heard from his father was how mean and greedy people were, but now, time after time, he could see that wasn't true. Most people were kind and generous to him, and it had all started with Mrs. Paladino and Mr. and Mrs. Ferry—well, actually, it all started with Margaret that day she offered to have a grill cheese sandwich with him, that day that everything happened.

"We'd better get inside," Mike said, laughing. "We're blocking half the sidewalk."

Once they had made their way through the revolving doors, Margaret lit up and tugged Johnny's sleeve. "Look, Johnny.

Look at that wall of little window doors." All along the entire wall to the left of the entrance were rows of little square glass doors trimmed in brass. The place bustled with customers moving here and there from one door to another, putting in coins and taking out food.

"I never saw anything like that. How does it work?" Johnny asked.

"You look through the little glass windows to see the food you want, you put in the amount of nickels it says. Then the door opens and you take out the food. Isn't it the best? Come on, we'll get our nickels over here."

Mike had given them each an extra dollar bill for the coin changer, then he and Bill followed along.

"You can get chicken pot pie or a cheese sandwich or anything," Margaret said. "Look, here's the pea soup, my favorite. It's only four nickels. Then, I'm getting apple pie a la mode, which is only another four nickels."

Johnny picked up a tray and looked over all the choices before selecting a cheese sandwich, a glass of milk, and a brownie. "This is pretty neat," he said to her, quietly. "And I still have nickels left over."

After they made their selections, they saw Mike waving them over to a table on the other side of the crowded restaurant, near the windows. He and Bill had gotten roast beef sandwiches and hot coffee.

"So, tell me," Bill said to Johnny, "do you like to play sports?"

"I...I think I'd like to. I really haven't had much of a chance."

"Well, maybe we can do something about that. What do you like best—football, baseball?"

"I like baseball...but I can't play till my ankle gets better. I...I fell and sprained it."

Over sandwiches and soup, they talked about DiMaggio, Campanella and Rizzuto. Johnny said that his favorite was Gil Hodges, and Margaret poked him in the arm saying he was her favorite too—he and Johnny Mize. "I'll have to show you my picture cards. I have two of theirs. I'll give you one."

"I used to have some picture cards," Johnny said, "but...but I don't know what happened to them."

"No matter," Mike said. "We'll just start a new collection."

Bill put his arm around the boy's shoulder. "I think we might be able to do better than that. The Yankees are out of town next week; so's Brooklyn. But the week after, how about we all go see the Yankees play?

Johnny and Margaret looked at each other in amazement, laughing and both saying "yes" at the same time.

It was mid-afternoon when they exited the restaurant onto Lexington Avenue. Johnny looked up and down the crowded street. "Why are so many people wearing business clothes? It's Saturday. Don't they get a day off?"

"New York is an odd place, Johnny," Mike said. "Many people do have the whole weekend off, but many others work on Saturday. Not all businesses close for the weekend around here, like our newspaper, for example. It's open seven days a week. Doesn't mean we all work seven days a week though."

At Margaret's request, Mike had agreed that they would walk with Bill the few blocks to the newspaper building without going inside, so they could show Johnny where the two men worked. He pointed out that the paper's offices occupied eight floors of the twenty-story art deco structure, and while he and Bill were preoccupied telling Johnny a little about the building and the newspaper, Margaret caught sight of a man turning into a nearby Rexall drugstore.

"Uncle Mike, could I go into that Rexall to get some Juicy Fruit?"

Mike looked about, then agreed. "Don't go anywhere else. And come right back."

She nodded and hurried off.

CHAPTER TWENTY-FOUR

The man Margaret saw entering the Rexall drugstore stood in line at the checkout counter paying no attention to the girl looking at the chewing gum selections on the rack to his right. The store was busy, too busy for anyone to notice how the girl's hair fluttered as if in a breeze, though there was no breeze. The only person in line behind the man suddenly hurried off to the far end of the store, apparently having forgotten something, and Margaret Ferry took the woman's place in line.

When it was his turn, the man asked for a pack of Camels and slid a quarter across the counter. He was a nice looking man, Margaret thought—about as tall as Uncle Mike, but with sandy-colored hair. He slipped the pack of cigarettes into the pocket of his suit jacket and walked over to the magazine displays, which took up nearly half of aisle five.

After handing the cashier a nickel for the Juicy Fruit gum, Margaret followed. "I don't think I've ever seen so many magazines in one place," she said, putting the pack of gum into her small denim purse.

The man looked at her with a thin smile, then turned away and picked up a copy of *Argosy*.

"Oh, I've read that one," she said. "My uncle had a copy."

He put the magazine back on the rack and picked up *Rod and Reel*.

"Fishing is fun, isn't it," she said.

He turned to her. "Do I know you?"

She shook her head.

"Well, then, if you don't mind, why don't you run along?"

"Oh, I can't run along just yet, Mr. Loughlin."

Wallace Loughlin shot her a surprised look. "How do you know my name? Who are you?"

Margaret picked up a copy of *McCall's* magazine. "This is one I like."

"I asked you how you know my name."

She flipped through some of the magazine pages. "I know a lot more about you than just your name."

He took the magazine out of her hand. "Is this some kind of a joke? Have I met you before?" He looked about. "You mentioned your uncle—is he here with you?"

She gestured to the magazine he'd been holding. "Do you still go fishing, Mr. Loughlin?"

He put the magazines down. "I don't know what you're up to, kid," he said, walking away, "but I don't have time for this."

"Isabelle would love to know if you still like to go fishing. You always had such fun together."

Loughlin stopped and turned sharply, as Margaret strolled farther up the aisle. "Hey." He pushed past a few shoppers, calling to her again. "Hey."

She kept walking, drawing him toward the back of the store where it was less busy.

"I'm talking to you." He touched her shoulder and she turned around, her hair lifting in a swirl of soft waves. He pulled his hand away and stepped back.

"What...what...who are you? What's going on here? What do you know about Isabelle?"

"I know that she believes you are the kindest, most wonderful man," Margaret said, her voice low and gentle. "I know that she has always been proud of you, Mr. Loughlin, but that she remembers you with a broken heart because you left and you didn't even say goodbye."

He searched her face. "How do you know her…or me? Who put you up to this?"

"Isabelle loves you very much."

He glanced behind them, a look of hopefulness briefly crossing his face. "Is she here?"

"It's only me."

"I must be crazy having this conversation with a kid." He pointed at her. "If you think you're going to get away with any kind of a scam, I'll have a cop in here so fast it'll make your head spin."

"Isabelle knows that Edward stole your idea. She never doubted you, no matter what Edward told you."

He walked toward her. "What are you talking about?"

"Isabelle has never given up on you, Mr. Loughlin. She loves you too much."

Again he tried to leave. "This is a bunch of crazy nonsense. I don't know where you're from or what makes you think I should believe…"

"Edward cheated you out of your discovery—he claimed it was his idea; you know all that. What you don't know is that the company found out you were telling the truth. They've been trying to find you. They know all about Edward." She stepped in and eyed him more closely. "So many people get hurt when someone lies and cheats and steals someone else's work. Don't you agree, Mr. Loughlin?"

He stared intently at her. "How could any of this possibly concern you? It's none of your business."

"Oh, but right now you are my business. You and Isabelle. You could call her. You'd see I'm telling the truth. There's a pay phone right back here. She still lives on Jasper Lane in Cleveland."

"Does Isabelle know where I am? Did she send you?"

She shook her head.

Wallace Loughlin's eyes narrowed. "How…when did you

meet her?"

"I have never met her."

"Well, I don't know what kind of a game you're playing, but…"

She put her hand up and he stopped. "You can believe me or not, Mr. Loughlin. You may do as you like. But remember— if you should call this beautiful woman, who loves you with all her heart, and whom you love with all of yours, please make sure you are still the kindest, most wonderful and honorable man she has always been so proud of. You wouldn't want to break her heart twice, would you?"

Wallace Loughlin ran his fingers through his hair and said nothing. He looked toward the front of the store, pensive. It was still busy, people coming and going. Amid the noise and bustle, the two looked at each other, she with innocent knowing, he with a look of anxious incredulity, and…perhaps…a flicker of hopefulness. After a moment, his shoulders drooped and he leaned against the wall, rubbing his brow. "This is crazy. I don't know what to think."

"I know how shocking this must be for you, Mr. Loughlin, but it is the truth."

A store clerk with the name Rexall stitched in red above the pocket of his shirt came down the aisle. "Is everything all right, Mister?" He looked at Loughlin then at Margaret. "Any problems here? You need help?"

Loughlin straightened himself. "No. No, I'm fine…it's okay…thanks. We're okay. I just got a little overheated. Must be this warm weather. Everything is okay."

Margaret smiled and the man returned to the front of the store, twice looking back over his shoulder.

"You show up out of nowhere," Loughlin said in a loud whisper, gesturing to the surroundings, "on an aisle in a drugstore for God's sake. It's crazy. Or maybe I'm the crazy one. I don't even know who you are, and…"

"Does it really matter where we are or who I am, Mr. Loughlin? Would you rather not have known? I thought this was happy news."

Wallace Loughlin looked at the child, a long steady look, as if something might be revealed in her face that could be taken as truth. Finally, he nodded slowly. He walked a few feet away, came back, and nodded again. "Yes," he said, "it might be...it might be very good news." He looked at her. "But how do you know? Who are you?"

"I'm only the messenger, Mr. Loughlin, and if I were you, I wouldn't want to waste a single minute."

Loughlin hesitated, then he made his way to the pay phone, just as Mike Ferry entered the store. Margaret hurried to join him.

"What in heaven's name is taking you so long?"

"Things took longer than I thought," she said, and off they went to say goodbye to Bill Fulton.

Johnny Herring was all smiles and wonderment as they boarded the uptown bus to finish their day with an afternoon carriage ride around Central Park.

CHAPTER TWENTY-FIVE

On Monday morning, Andrew Grassley's green station wagon carrying Mike, Etta and Father Desmond, slowly made its way up the long winding drive as Lolly eagerly watched from the doorway of the main building at St. Clement. This was the day Mike had planned to officially return to the office, but Bill Fulton understood that Father Desmond's late-announced trip to meet with Lolly and Mrs. Samuelson about the shawl took precedence.

St. Clement occupied a cluster of quaint stone and timber buildings on the property still affectionately referred to by locals as the Samuelson estate. The charming two-story gabled structures with their deep sloping eaves and wide rows of white-trimmed windows stood invitingly in a sprawling pastoral, tree-lined setting. Three of the buildings originally had been guest and servant quarters, the two more extravagant sized structures family dwellings, one of which now housed eighteen residents and administration that included Lolly's office and modest living quarters.

After being greeted by Mrs. Addison with pleasantries and introductions all around, they made their way to a table in the dining room, where lunch would be served. It was a large cheerful space of polished dark pine, white crisscross sheers, flowered carpet, and plentiful sunlight. Fresh daisies were set on each table in small colorful rustic vases made by some of the residents in one of the twice-weekly pottery classes.

"This is so pretty, Mrs. Addison," Etta said. "Nicer each time we come. Thank you."

"It's good to see you again, Mrs. Ferry. I hope you all enjoy your visit." She explained that the residents were in the far meadow for their long-awaited first picnic outing of the season. "So you'll have all the privacy you need." Then she departed.

"What do you think of Mr. Grassley?" Lolly whispered to Etta, the moment she had a chance.

Lolly and Etta had become much closer since those horrific hours at the hospital, perhaps when Etta realized how fragile and fleeting life truly was. Etta had visited her sister many times over the years, but often with an undercurrent of anxiety on her own part that had been hard to shake. It felt a bit different now and she was glad. "I have to say he's every bit as nice and as handsome as you said he was. And..." she gave her sister a sly grin, "he had wonderful things to say about you, Miss Lorelei O'Donnell." Etta caught herself. "Oh, Lolly, forgive me," she said softly. "I didn't mean..."

"Please don't feel bad. It's okay." Lolly smiled, clutching Etta's hand. "Never feel bad about...any of that."

"We're very grateful that he was able to meet us in Philadelphia," Etta said, recovering.

Father Desmond settled into a seat at the table. "Seems that there are lots of nice people here, Lolly, with you at the top of the list, I'd say."

Lolly smiled shyly.

"She's the best," Mike said, patting his sister-in-law's arm.

Father Desmond looked over at the ornate wooden grandmother clock on the wall. "Did Mrs. Samuelson say what time she would be here?"

"Any minute, I think." Lolly turned to Mike. "I wish Mar had come."

"I know, but she needed to be in school. She just started back."

"She was disappointed," Etta said, "but felt better when we reminded her that you'll be coming next weekend."

Lolly gave Etta a worried look. "Where will Mar go after school today if you're not there?"

"There's a nice couple in the neighborhood," Mike said. "Mr. and Mrs. Paladino. They're going to meet Mar at school and take her to their house. We'll pick her up when we get back later today. That boy is there too—Johnny Herring. And it's all good. We'll tell you about it later."

"You're a good and loving aunt to worry so, Lolly," Father Desmond said.

"I've always tried to be."

The sound of cheerful voices drew their attention to the entry where Mrs. Addison greeted a woman dressed smartly in a light tan blazer and skirt. The woman, who looked to be in her forties, had auburn hair that curled softly just below her ears. She came toward them with a bright smile and a lively step, and it was clear to Mike and Etta that Lolly had been very accurate in describing the brilliance of the woman's hazel eyes. Everyone stood to greet Mrs. Ryder Samuelson.

"This is quite an honor, Mrs. Samuelson," Mike said, shaking hands.

"Everyone calls me Berry," she said, greeting the others. She gave Lolly a hug before they all settled themselves. "I must first ask about your niece, Margaret," she said, looking to Etta then to Mike. "How is she doing?"

"To say she's very well would be an understatement," Mike said.

Etta smiled and shook her head. "You know, of course, that it's all been nothing short of a miracle. That's why we're here actually. We're hoping you can give us some information that might help us...understand."

"But first," Mike said, "we want to thank you. You've done a wonderful thing here with St. Clement. No one appreciates your generous efforts more than our family. I'm so glad to finally get to meet you."

The luncheon of roast chicken proceeded with small talk, along with Berry Samuelson's casual summary of the planned upgrades to the facility due to take place over the next two years. Finally, over coffee and lemon pound cake, they discussed the shawl.

"I guess by now you pretty much know everything that happened, Mrs. Samuelson." Mike quickly corrected himself. "Berry."

"There were a couple of brief stories in the Philadelphia paper," the woman offered. "Then one or two shorter pieces just for a day or so after. A few eyewitness quotes. Nothing front page. Then, the story was gone. I suppose that's a good thing. Of course, I learned most of the details from Lolly." She reached across and touched Lolly's hand. "It was quite a roller coaster for all of you. I can only imagine," she said. "I'm curious. What have you noticed so far with regard to Margaret?"

Mike looked to Etta. "Well, for one thing," Etta said, "there's not a single…let's say…physical sign that anything ever happened to her. She's happy as ever, a bit more serene, we notice, but still girlish in the way that girls her age are, and yet sometimes mature beyond her years…or understanding. She'll be twelve on her next birthday."

"And," Mike added, soberly, "there have been these odd occasions where she knows things…before they happen… or that have already happened that she couldn't possibly have any knowledge of." Mike and Etta went on to explain the encounter with the reporter on the street and the incident with Viola Steich at the candy store, among others. "The latest one just happened yesterday. Her aunt and I were worried about having to tell her that she would not be returning to her school in the fall."

"But," Etta chimed in, "she already knew and there's no way she could have."

Mike opened his hands. "She said we shouldn't worry. Imagine, she's telling us not to worry, that everything will turn out okay. We have no idea how it possibly can turn out okay. She's been expelled by the Monsignor. It's baffling. We don't even know the extent of what's possible anymore. It's a very challenging time for us."

Father Desmond leaned forward. "The shawl you gave to Lolly seemed to play a key role in all this. I'm curious, Berry, how did you come to give it so generously to Lolly? Can you tell us anything at all about it?"

Berry Samuelson looked intently at Father Desmond. "I can tell you everything about it."

The others looked on, heightened expectancy showing in their faces.

"The shawl is antique bobbin lace. It was crafted by a maker of fine laces in Florence, Italy, specifically for a Milanese woman going on a pilgrimage to the Shrine of the Most Sorrowful Heart of Mary. Have you ever heard of that shrine, Father?"

Father Desmond tapped his finger against his lip. "In western Turkey?"

She nodded. "Yes."

"I have heard about it," Father Desmond said. "Evidently, decades back, it created quite a stir. A lot was written about it, much of it speculation, criticism or controversy. Things of a certain magnitude tend to be ill received. Over time, interest faded, possibly because of its somewhat remote location, and the probability that it was more myth than truth." Father Desmond turned to the others. "It was a marble statue of our Blessed Mother said to have had...of all things...a heartbeat."

"Of all things," Berry Samuelson repeated flatly.

"Are you serious?" Mike asked.

"But how is something like that possible?" Etta looked

from one to the other. "A marble statue? No wonder people found it hard to believe."

A pleasant looking woman in a pink and white pinafore entered with a smile and a carafe of fresh coffee, placed it on the table, then left with their thanks.

"Anything you can share with us, Berry," Mike said, "will be so helpful to our understanding."

Berry gave him a wry smile. "That depends on what it is exactly that you're trying to understand. I can only provide facts. It's important to know that they may or may not supply the kind of understanding you're seeking. As perhaps Father Desmond has explained, the Church investigates many so-called miraculous appearances or events, but rarely encourages one to believe or not. People must decide for themselves."

"And some things simply defy understanding," Father Desmond said.

Berry nodded. "The Shrine was credited with miracles that involved certain healing powers, sometimes for imparting special gifts. Mostly, it was known for reuniting lost or separated loved ones."

Mike and Etta turned as inconspicuously as possible to catch each other's eye.

Berry dropped two cubes of sugar into her coffee and stirred it. "One of the documented incidents happened in 1920. At that time there was much written about the woman I mentioned a moment ago, an Italian woman named Libera Pascone, who visited the shrine on a pilgrimage under the auspices of the Archdiocese of Milan.

For two years, she had grieved the loss of her daughter, Giovanna, who vanished following a bombing raid during the war. Libera was forty at the time—Giovanna was the youngest of her four children. The trip to the shrine was long and quite grueling, as you might imagine, traveling in those days from Milan to Turkey. Days and days of often primitive transportation and surroundings. But she had complete faith."

"What were her accounts of the pilgrimage like?" Etta asked.

"A deep sense of peace and trust. The deepest. And... indeed...she did hear the beating heart of Mary."

Etta put her hand to her mouth, wide-eyed. "Has that ever been verified?"

"That's amazing." Mike said.

"Libera Pascone was wearing the shawl. She draped it about her shoulders and covered her hands with it as she touched the outstretched marble hands of the statue. Mary's hands. From that time, Libera thought of the shawl as a...shall we say...a sacred garment."

"What about her daughter?" Etta asked. "Did she ever find her?"

Berry Samuelson gazed down at her coffee cup. "It was another long and difficult journey back home, but when she arrived, there was a letter waiting for her from a war refugee official, saying that they believed they might have her daughter. The girl was suffering a form of shock trauma, and had not spoken, but another refugee thought she knew the girl. It turned out to be Giovanna."

"Oh, my," Etta said. "Did the girl ever speak again?"

"Oh, yes." Berry Samuelson nodded slowly. "When Libera and Giovanna were re-united, Libera put the shawl around her daughter's shoulders to wear to church. Shortly afterwards, the girl began speaking again as normally as you and I."

"Holy smoke." Mike rubbed the side of his face, then turned to Father Desmond. "No pun intended."

Father Desmond raised his eyebrows and nodded, looking around the table at the other surprised faces. "Is there any documentation you know of? Or witnesses? Were there other incidents?"

"Only one," Berry said. "Libera became afraid. She was

aware of the controversy surrounding the shrine. People can be dangerously superstitious. They often don't trust miracles or the people who experience them, even people in their own families. Violent things can happen. So, Libera chose to keep it secret. Only once did she bring the shawl to a woman in the village whose young son had suffered serious burns and needed to be sent to a special treatment center in Rome. Before the boy was to leave, Libera visited the hospital with the shawl concealed in her purse. With the mother's permission, she carefully draped it over the boy's bandaged hands and arms. No one else was there. Libera felt she had to be very careful. She asked the woman to promise never to tell anyone of the incident. The next day, when the doctors came in, they were astonished. The boy's mother had removed his bandages and there was not the slightest trace of burns. After that, Libera hid the shawl away for many years."

There was a long silence. The afternoon sun, now lower in the sky, sent a dazzling glare across the dining room.

"We'll have to leave soon to get back to Philadelphia for our train," Mike said, "but I have to ask—are you an historian? You know so much."

The woman looked toward the windows, reticent.

"Were you related to this family?" Etta asked.

Father Desmond eyed Berry Samuelson closely. He leaned in with both elbows on the table, and traced the rim of his plate with his finger. "Tell me. Would you be…comfortable enough to confide in us if…if, in fact, you were…a very close relative?"

"Oh, my God," Etta blurted out in a loud whisper. "You're not…?"

"Libera's daughter?" Mike said it with a slight gasp. "Are you Giovanna?"

"No," Lolly said, quietly. She had been watching and listening intently without saying a word. "No," she repeated, "she's not Giovanna." She and Berry Samuelson had locked eyes across the table.

Berry looked at Lolly and smiled. "You're right, Lolly. I'm not Giovanna."

"*Hmm*, I'm not sure what to make of this." Mike said. "How did you come by the shawl? Did Libera give it to you?"

"No, I came by it because…"

"Because you *are* Libera," Lolly said.

"Lolly," Etta chided, embarrassed for her sister. "You know she couldn't possibly be Libera."

Mike straightened himself and looked intently at Berry. "Is what Lolly just said actually the truth?"

"Yes," Berry Samuelson answered. "It is true."

They looked at each other, astonished. Etta laughed, a nervous chuckle. "Well, how could that be…you'd be…"

"Seventy-three," the woman said.

Mike put his hand on the top of his head. "With all due respect, Berry, I don't see how you can expect us to believe…."

"I told you that the shrine has been credited with various… gifts."

Father Desmond sat back and dropped his hands in his lap. "This is certainly more than any of us possibly could have imagined. It's absolutely astounding."

"After my husband died—Mr. Pascone, that is—I immigrated to the United States with my children. To the Philadelphia area, actually. I was a somewhat educated woman, fluent in English, so when I saw an ad for a private secretary, I applied and got the job…working here for Ryder Samuelson. He was the last of the Samuelsons, a fine and wonderful man who had never married. He was kind enough to set us up with living quarters in one wing of the house on this very estate. He even hired a nanny for the children. We all became quite close. It was Mr. Samuelson who nicknamed me 'Berry.' After a year, we married."

"That's...that's remarkable," Etta said, wide-eyed. "I've never heard anything like it."

"As my children went off to college, we both agreed the estate was simply too extravagant for the two of us. The truth is we had long thought it was too extravagant even for the six of us. We bought a town house in Philadelphia and...well... converted this property to St. Clement. That was nearly thirty years ago."

"What about your children?" Etta asked. "How are they?"

"They are well; successful in their various jobs." Berry picked at the corner of her white linen napkin. "Giovanna returned to Milan after graduating from medical school to work with trauma patients. She is married with two beautiful boys. I'm very proud of her...and all my children, as you certainly are of your lovely Margaret. As for Lolly, well, each time I came here I was taken with her grace and kindness and something more that I still can't quite put my finger on."

Etta gave Mike a side-glance, but said nothing.

Berry was quiet for a moment then looked at Lolly and shrugged. "Who can say what happens or why? When something feels good and right, shouldn't we respond to it in kind?"

"We were knocked for a loop with all that's happened with Mar, and now this. Your story. It's incredible," Mike said.

"Now that we've met you, Berry," Etta said, touching the woman's hand, "I hope we can keep in touch with you. Perhaps one day you can meet Margaret."

"Most definitely," the woman said. "I would like nothing better. Now...if you'll allow me...I'll have Carson, my chauffeur, take you back to Philadelphia. I won't hear 'no.'"

"Many thanks," Father Desmond said. "I do have one final question, Berry. I'm curious. Have you any sense of what the future may hold for Margaret or for the shawl itself?"

Berry Pascone Samuelson looked from one to the other with a wry smile. "You will need to discover that for yourselves."

CHAPTER TWENTY-SIX

Mike and Etta picked up Margaret a little after nine, and on the slow walk home, dazzled her with Berry Pascone Samuelson's incredible tale. "Holy cow," was all she could say.

At a little before ten, they put the key in the door, just as the phone started ringing. Mike quickly glanced at his watch. "Who could that be?"

"I hope nothing's wrong," Etta said. It never used to be this way. Now, every time the phone rang or the doorbell buzzed or an unfamiliar looking envelope came in the mail the immediate reaction was anxiety, not knowing what new odd circumstance could befall them. She went to the stove to put on the kettle for tea.

Margaret had gone into the other room to hang up their jackets, then returned to the kitchen as curious as her aunt.

"Hey, Bill," Mike said to the voice at the other end, then listened intently. "Yes, things went well today, thanks. I'll tell you when I see you. I have to say you're making me a little nervous. It's nearly ten—is anything wrong?"

Etta and Margaret stood together watching Mike, a worried look on their faces.

"You can't be serious." Mike finally said. "Are you kidding me?" He began pacing as far as the phone cord could reach. "That's unbelievable."

Etta fiddled nervously with the belt of her dress. Margaret took her aunt's hand and both of them followed Mike's face as he slowly moved back and forth across the kitchen.

"But how?" Mike asked Bill Fulton. "And why?" He pulled a kitchen chair closer to the phone and plopped down, at the same time giving Etta and Margaret a look of incredulity. "I just can't believe it," he said into the phone. "What on earth brought this about?"

"What is it?" Etta cried out in a whisper, her hand at her throat.

"Holy cow and mackerel," Mike said, looking up at them wide-eyed, after hanging up.

Etta took a step closer with the caution of one who might fear being hit by an oncoming bus. "Just say is it good news or bad?"

"Well, all I can say is it certainly is the kind of news I never expected to hear in a hundred years." He drew a deep breath. "Wallace Loughlin walked into Bill Fulton's office this morning and handed in his resignation. He's moving back to Cleveland."

"What?" Etta set herself down. "Why on earth...I can't believe it. What made him do that?"

Margaret smiled and put her arm around Etta's shoulder.

"He really didn't give Bill any explanation, except that it was a personal matter. Bill says Loughlin was different."

"Different how?" Etta asked.

"He actually apologized to Bill for being so arrogant and for slacking off so much. Told Bill he was sorry for not showing his appreciation for the opportunity he'd had with the paper. Said he'd been through a hard time. Bill was as shocked as we are right now, I can tell you."

"It's unbelievable."

"If you think that's unbelievable, wait till you hear this. After Loughlin left, Bill had kind of a hunch about the briefcase. So he walked over to my desk and, hold on to your hat, there was my briefcase...right back under the desk, just where I left it. And, far as Bill could tell, everything's in it, my journal and all my other papers."

"Yay!" Etta and Margaret hugged each other and screeched for joy.

Mike laughed. "Well, we sure can't make sense of any of it, but it looks like we're back in business."

CHAPTER TWENTY-SEVEN

The crack of the bat brought the Yankee Stadium crowd of thirty thousand to its feet, and Hank Bauer circled the bases to cross home plate and light up the scoreboard.

Bill Fulton playfully nudged Johnny Herring with his elbow. "How's that, son?" he shouted. "Your first real live homer."

Johnny Herring had jumped out of his seat along with everyone else, Margaret pulling at his arm with excitement. He looked up at the man with the square chin and wide smile. No one had ever said that to him—no one had ever called him son.

"That was pretty neat," Johnny yelled back against the din of screaming fans, and looked past Bill to see Elaine Fulton, clapping her hands and cheering. She looked his way, smiling. She was pretty. Margaret was on his right, jumping up and down, her brown hair shining in the stadium lights, and on the other side of her, Mike and Etta Ferry, cheering on New York. It was a day of days. "I never saw anything like this," he shouted up at Bill. "I only heard games on the radio. I didn't even know a ballpark was this big."

Bill patted the boy's shoulder. "Let's think of this as the first of many games you'll get to see." He looked over at Elaine. "Isn't that right, Mrs. Fulton?"

"You bet," she shouted back, then looked directly at the boy. "It's an awful lot of fun for us too, Johnny. We used to come often, but haven't been here in…well…a long time. I'm glad we're back. And I'm glad we got to come with you."

Johnny knew more about it than what she said. Mr. Ferry had told him how their son had been killed in the war—two parents without their boy. And here, a boy without two parents. Life had a way of being strange and interesting. There was a lot of that going on for him lately. He couldn't help feeling a little sad thinking about his father. Maybe somebody would be able to help him where he was. He would be there for a long time. Johnny wasn't sure if or how he would ever get to see him again. He tried not to think about where he himself would go. They would probably send him to a home. There might come a time when he would have to run away again. He would miss all these people who'd been so nice to him.

A hard linedrive smacked toward the outfield by McDougald brought the crowd to a roar again, but the ball never got past the leap of the third baseman, who pulled it down, one-handed, to retire the side.

"Plucked that one like an apple on a tree," Bill Fulton said, laughing. "We love New York, Johnny, but there's a fellow to watch right there."

Johnny, suddenly serious and attentive, followed Fulton's point down the third base line to the player making his way to the Washington Senators' dugout. "Eddie Yost," Bill said. "You won't find a better third baseman in the game. And I don't mean just this game here; I mean the whole game of baseball."

Johnny took a sip of his Frosty Malt and nudged Margaret with his elbow as the Yankee defense took the field. "Who's your favorite Yankee?"

"I love Rizzuto."

How different it was having Margaret as a friend instead of her being a girl who was always afraid of him. He was mean back then, but now...

"Rizzuto's my favorite too. The Scooter." He looked up at Bill. "What about you, Mr. Fulton—who's your favorite?"

"Hard to say, Johnny. There are an awful lot of good ones out there. I think I'd have to agree The Scooter is a pretty good pick. Not only a great shortstop, but next time he's up at the plate, keep an eye out for him to bunt. Probably the best bunter in the major leagues."

"This is really neat, Mr. Fulton." He had to wonder what it was like to be the son of somebody like Bill Fulton, who actually ran a newspaper and knew everything about baseball too. How does somebody get to know so much about different things?

"Why don't you just call me Bill? And, maybe one day even Uncle Bill."

Johnny's eyes lit up. "Would that be okay? It wouldn't make people mad or anything?"

"It'd be just fine," Bill said. "And, if I have anything to say about it, nobody's ever going to be mad at you again."

Johnny followed Bill Fulton's glance over to Elaine, who winked and nodded her agreement. She had a soft look about her, different from his mom, who wore thick make-up.

Sometimes his mom's lips were smeared red and she smelled of beer. Mrs. Fulton smelled like what he imagined baby powder might smell like, and when she touched his shoulder or his arm, it felt gentle. He wasn't used to that kind of feeling.

After a three-one Yankee win, Bill and Mike led the way through the exiting crush to the subway. Johnny and Margaret followed close behind, their excitement still at a high, each carrying the Yankee pennant Bill had gotten for them as a souvenir. Etta and Elaine walked behind them, arm-in-arm. The evening was clear and cool and the crowd was dwindling quickly as people hailed taxis and scattered to trains and buses.

"Etta, I want to tell you," Elaine said. "Bill's going to talk to Mike about Johnny."

Etta stopped. "Oh, no. Did something happen?"

"Well, something happened all right." She leaned in closer

to Etta. "We've given a lot of thought to Johnny's father being in prison and the situation with Mr. and Mrs. Paladino. And... well...we'd like the boy to come live with us."

"Are you serious?" Etta took both Elaine Fulton's hands in hers. "Would you really let him come?"

"He's a nice boy. He's just had a bad life. We'd like to try to make a home for him. We think it would be good for him and...for Bill and me."

"Oh, Elaine, what a wonderful idea. We would be so happy for you."

"My husband was born to be a dad, Etta, and I can see that side of him resurfacing, the side that went away when we lost Tim. Do you think Johnny would like the idea? And Mike? I think Margaret might—they already seem to be good friends."

Etta and Elaine continued along. "Oh, I know Mike and Mar would love the idea," Etta said. "I have to believe it would be best all-around for everyone."

"I really hope so. I..." Elaine stopped with the sudden pull of Etta's arm. Etta tipped her head back, taking a deep breath, as Elaine gripped her around the waist to keep her from giving way. "Etta!" Elaine called up ahead to Mike, and they all hurried back to Etta's side.

Etta grimaced, with her hand on her stomach, and let out a low groan. A few people turned, but moved along.

"It's okay." Etta said. "I'm...I'm okay." She chuckled, a little breathless. "You warned me, Mike, about having that second hot dog." She took his arm and turned to Margaret, who looked concerned. "I'm fine, Mar, honest." But it wasn't the first time. She was worried.

—◆—

Two days later, the Ferrys' quiet Park Slope neighborhood was jolted awake in the pre-dawn hours by the thunder and scream of fire engines barreling along Prospect Avenue, too close to ignore. They scrambled from bed and ran to the windows to see a scattering of people hurrying down the street, some men in undershirts still buttoning their trousers, a few people in slippers and bathrobes. Dozens of others leaned out their windows, even stood on fire escapes for a better look at the nearby blaze, but all soon retreated to shut out the dark smoke that slowly billowed up to the rooftops.

Mike quickly pulled on his trousers along with a light jacket to cover his pajama top, and snatched his pen and pad.

"I'm coming too," Margaret called out in a creaky voice, groggy from her quick wakening. She grabbed the pair of dungarees off the chair in her room and pulled her jacket from the front closet on the way out the door behind her uncle.

Etta stayed by the window. "The two of you be careful."

Firemen already at the scene wrangled hoses and gear, swamping the sidewalks along with storefronts, while positioning a hook and ladder against a third-floor apartment window. A fireman scrambled up and disappeared into a heavy cloud of smoke, coming back into view moments later, to the cheer of the crowd, with someone draped over his shoulder. The flames were visible now as he made his laborious descent, the stench of burning permeating the air.

"Good God," Mike said, turning to Margaret, who could now see for herself that this was the building where Mr. and Mrs. Wortman lived. Along with everyone else, they looked on in horror, sadness and disbelief at the smoldering rubble that for decades had been the neighborhood's beloved candy store.

CHAPTER TWENTY-EIGHT

Etta leaned with her back against the sink, waiting for the last slice of Wonder bread to pop from the toaster. Arms folded across the bib of her yellow gingham apron, she surveyed the kitchen. Even on such a calamitous morning (perhaps *especially* on such a calamitous morning), it remained so wonderfully, so solidly the heart of their home—the sturdy maple table with its decorative brown metal top inscribed with monochromatic flowers and swirls. The wooden chairs with their carved backs adding a charm carried out in the cabinetry, the white ruffled cotton curtains trimmed in red rickrack that matched the red of the floral tin canister set and the embroidered tea towels hanging from the dowel on the pantry door. She never tired of this place. It was the constant that they all needed now more than ever. Their family life had been lived here at this table, on these chairs—things talked over, tears and laughter, homework and hopes and news of the changing world read over breakfast. Meals and memories, and sometimes heartache.

Margaret came into the kitchen, her damp hair wrapped in a towel after showering, and pulled out a chair. "We should have known you'd have a big breakfast waiting for us, Aunt Etta." She spooned scrambled eggs onto her plate. "I didn't think I'd be able to eat anything at all after what happened, but I'm so hungry."

They had returned home a little after 6:30 that morning, exhausted, their clothes, now strung out on the clothesline, reeking of smoke. No open windows this spring morning—the acrid cloud that had drifted lazily through the neighborhood from the ashen remains of the fire had not yet fully dissipated.

Etta poured Margaret a glass of juice. "Very sad."

"When can we go?" Margaret asked, the minute Mike came into the kitchen. He hadn't bothered with the morning paper after washing up. The story had missed the deadline. They would read about it in the afternoon edition—the young fireman, a hero, bravely rescuing a woman from a burning apartment. It had been many years since Mike covered local news, but he had called in to provide whatever eyewitness details he could. For the first time, he would walk the extra two blocks to Sylvan's Drugs for the papers. The candy store was gone.

"We'll have to call the hospital, Mar, to make sure Mrs. Wortman is still there," Etta said.

Mike buttered a slice of toast. "The medics said she would be all right, just took in a little too much smoke. Poor woman was really shaken up. Wortman was beside himself. It's lucky he was down in the store getting ready to open. Heroic as he was, that young fireman likely would not have been able to get them both out as quickly as he needed to."

Etta brought the Pyrex coffee pot to the table and filled Mike's cup. "Thanks, Et." He took her hand, squeezed it, and winked up at her. "Good thing it's Saturday—we'll have plenty of time—visiting hours don't end till eight which is good because I have some finishing touches to the Central Commerce series. I'm shooting for Monday to have it on Bill's desk."

"After all this, to finally get it into print," Etta said, stroking the back of his head. "So proud of you, Mike." That was something that had never changed. From those earliest days in Syracuse when they'd first met, his rock solid and true ways had inspired the greatest pride and respect. He'd always made her feel that he had perhaps felt that way about her. It was a good feeling that made her realize every day of her life how blessed she was.

"Well, that whole Loughlin resignation thing turned out to be a shocker," he said, stirring his coffee. "Never figured on that one...or ever seeing my briefcase again."

Margaret smiled a little sheepishly without looking up.

"You proud of me too, kiddo?" He didn't seem to know quite what to make of that look.

"Always, Uncle Mike."

He reached over and rubbed Etta's arm. "You okay?"

"Good." She put her hand over his, reassuringly. "I'm good."

"I hope you'll take it easy until you see the doctor on Monday—find out what's causing these spells."

"They're not spells." Etta got up and went to the sink for a glass of water. "Don't go making more out of it than it is. I'm fine; probably just picked up a little bug, that's all. It's poor Mrs. Wortman who's having a time of it."

Margaret rested her chin in her hand. "It's hard to believe the candy store is gone. Just like that. Junie will be so upset. The neighborhood won't be the same. I wonder what Mr. and Mrs. Wortman will do now?"

"No telling." Mike set his fork down and sat back in his chair. "Just another example of how fast things can change. Boy, haven't we all learned that the hard way. That's why it's so important to take care." He turned to Etta. "And right now, that means you, my beautiful stubborn wife. Seems you've been doing a little too much. Not that we don't appreciate the breakfast, but maybe it's time to take it easy, huh? Mar and I can go to the hospital by ourselves. That would be okay, wouldn't it?"

She relished his loving ways, knowing he could always see deep into her. She had to hope he wasn't worrying too much about her. That was the last thing she wanted him to do. He'd been worried enough about Mar.

"Please, Aunt Etta." Margaret gave Etta a pleading look. Etta hadn't felt well again that morning and knew that Margaret was aware of it but hadn't said anything to her uncle. Sweet and puzzling child. "I think you should stay home like Uncle Mike says."

Mike cleared his throat, scolding playfully. "*As* Uncle Mike says."

Margaret rolled her eyes, smiling. "*As* Uncle Mike says, Herr Professor."

Etta took a deep breath and looked at the two people she loved more than anything in the world. "Okay. *As* Herr Professor says, I'll take it easy. I promise. But now let's talk about something pleasant." She poured herself a glass of apple juice. "What about Bill and Elaine taking in Johnny Herring? That was quite a surprise."

"Let's see," Mike said, rubbing his chin. "How many surprises are people allowed in the course of a week because I have a feeling we've exceeded our quota."

"It's exciting news though, right?" Margaret said. "He can have a real family now."

Mike took another strip of bacon. "Johnny couldn't believe it. Bill said the boy teared up. Mrs. Paladino did too, when I went by there yesterday to let her know. She gave me a hug that could bring down a gorilla, she was so relieved. She's genuinely happy for the kid. They're good people, the Paladinos."

"Will Bill and Elaine have any trouble making it official?" This was Etta's main concern. She understood what it might be like to have your heart set on a child, then have it all go wrong. She shivered at the thought.

"Bill has a lot of connections. They'll make it happen, all legal and proper, especially since Herring will be away for a very long time. The boy will have a good home now, that's for sure."

How many things were really for sure? Etta wondered.

A little before noon, Mike and Margaret headed over to Methodist Hospital. Neither Mike nor Etta had said a word about it, but Etta knew he was as grateful as she that they didn't have to return to St. Peter's. They had no way of knowing what Margaret thought of any of it. She was simply eager to see Mr. and Mrs. Wortman.

They had telephoned the hospital and learned that Mrs. Wortman would be staying overnight. Mr. Wortman was there with her and doing well with a bandaged left hand. Etta remained at home and since, out of habit, it was difficult for her to take it easy, she stayed busy with a roast in the oven and the ironing board set up in a corner of the kitchen. She brought out the Victrola along with a few of her favorite Margaret Whiting and Jo Stafford 78s, but soon felt herself fading. Maybe she was not as strong as she thought in dealing with all the topsy-turvy craziness that had taken over their lives.

She had eaten very little for breakfast, hoping to avoid anything that might upset her stomach, but the nausea came back more than once, and lingered a bit longer each time. She was increasingly uneasy about what the doctor might say on Monday. The last thing they needed right now was for life to become even more complicated with some serious medical problem or, God forbid, surgery. She would soon have to admit to Mike that it really was a bit more than she'd been letting on.

CHAPTER TWENTY-NINE

Room 3223 at Methodist Hospital was located at the far end of the long third floor corridor where blue-smocked orderlies and nurses in their crisp white caps moved efficiently about their tasks. Here and there, Mike and Margaret sidestepped a rolling utility cart or a wheelchair standing against one of the unadorned pale green walls. Voices in quiet conversation spilled into the hallway, along with an occasional moan and a variety of slightly pungent medicinal smells.

The door to Mrs. Wortman's room stood ajar, no voices or moans. They gave a light knock and slowly pushed the door open. The woman, eyes closed, lay back at an angle against her pillows, her husband, shoulders slumped, dozing in the chair beside her bed.

They tapped harder, not wanting to be found standing over them if they awakened. But a nurse, apparently having no such concerns, moved swiftly past them and bluntly called Mrs. Wortman's name, at which point both of them stirred and quickly noticed Mike and Margaret standing back by the doorway. As soon as the nurse finished performing a few brief routine checks, Mrs. Wortman extended her hand in beckoning, and Mr. Wortman, his left hand bandaged, went to the door to greet them. "Oh, please, come. Come," he said, with quiet exuberance, leading them to the two chairs that were there. "I've been sitting all day," he said off-handedly, and went to his wife's side. "We're very happy you came." He didn't smile, as if even joyfulness was a serious matter.

"Etta's at home," Mike said, "just a little under the weather, but okay. She sends her regards to you both. This whole thing was shocking for all of us. We're so sorry. What's important right now is how both of you are. That hand of yours doesn't look like much fun."

"I'm sorry to hear Etta's not feeling well," Mrs. Wortman said. "Looks like we're both not having such a good day."

"As for me," Mr. Wortman was quick to say, "look what can happen in the world—and all I have is a bruise. Besides…this hand…" He gave an ironic shrug. "It's the one I use to scoop ice cream, so how serious can it be now?"

Mike and Margaret smiled slightly. "Well, you sound in good spirits," Mike said. "How about you, Mrs. Wortman? How are you feeling?"

"This is all for show," she said with mock indignance. "Doctors. What can I say? Tomorrow I can leave, but Isador will have a bandage to wear for a little while. God bless that young fireman," she said, meekly, wiping a bit of moisture from the corner of her eye. "He's a hero. Imagine." Her voice thickened. She gestured to the newspapers folded on the windowsill. "It's on the front page. He'll get a medal from the Mayor. I just want that they should never mention my name or show my picture. My hair didn't even see a comb. Who had time?"

Mr. Wortman bent over to lean his head against hers. "I don't know what I would have done," he lamented. "I just don't know. My Sarah is my life." He looked upward. "That young man was from God. Without him, I don't know."

"I'm so happy you're both okay," Margaret said. She went to the bedside and placed the vase of yellow daisies and pink mums they had brought on the side table. Then she handed an embroidered handkerchief to Mrs. Wortman. "Aunt Etta thought you might like this. She made it herself. We're really sorry about the candy store. It was so special to everybody. I went there my whole life."

Mrs. Wortman held the handkerchief to her cheek then softly patted her heart. "Tell your aunt for me."

"Well," Mr. Wortman said, "it's true the store was part of all of us, but maybe sometimes we don't know when to stop. Life has to do it for us."

"We talked about Florida," Mrs. Wortman said, smoothing her hair back with her hand as if suddenly realizing she still hadn't paid attention to her appearance. "It could be a good time of life for better weather. Miami." She waved her hand against the air. "Who wants to keep pushing snow?"

"Or chasing the boys with the broom," he said, wryly.

"How did it happen?" Margaret asked. She loved to listen to them; she had never heard them say so much. They had an interesting way of speaking. On the one hand, it sometimes sounded comical. But then, their words had a way of touching her and helped her look past the sadness in their eyes.

Mr. Wortman squeezed his wife's hand. "I was in the store getting ready to open." He looked about as if back in that moment. "I was busy with the usual. Then all of a sudden, not so usual. Smoke. I knew it right away. I looked to see if I had done something, maybe that little griddle. I thought, oy, now I'm beginning to forget to be so careful. Then it was a heavy, terrible smell, and I knew it was no small thing. You can always tell when something is burning that is never supposed to burn."

"That apartment building next door," Mrs. Wortman added, waving her new handkerchief toward the window. "I didn't know at first. Sometimes they make a little fire to burn things in that empty lot. I went to turn off the soup I was making for Isador's lunch. You should know the heat came right through the wall, and the smoke with it. At first I couldn't move. I thought how could this be so. I heard the fire engines." She grew wide-eyed, and put her hand over her chest. "My heart started beating so fast I thought it would just...blow up...like that pea soup I forgot one day in the pressure cooker. I heard of such things. I ran to the door and started calling Isador, but the doorknob was so hot I used the corner of my apron to open it, and as soon as I did I never saw anything like it. I was pushed all the way back to the kitchen table, yelling like a crazy woman, and the smoke came like I don't know what."

"I ran from the store," Mr. Wortman said. "Around the corner...to where the building entrance is for the apartment. And I heard her. People yelled don't go in, don't go in. But my wife...my Sarah...." He stopped and turned toward the window, embarrassed by his emotion. He wiped at the corner of his eye.

Sarah Wortman calmly called her husband's name. "Isador. It's all right. I can leave tomorrow. We'll get a room somewhere." She turned to Mike and Margaret and shrugged. "I talk like we know about getting a room. Not since our honeymoon in Niagara Falls."

"What was it like when the fireman came?" Margaret asked, eager to hear something she couldn't even imagine.

Mr. Wortman turned. "That was a good boy raised by his mama. Now a good young man who saved a life." He turned away again, clearly overcome. His shoulders shuddered.

"Isador, have some water," Mrs. Wortman said. "It's good. It's from lunchtime." But he put up his hand. She looked at them. "He's right, my Isador. That young man. What could make someone run into a fire like that? Look at all you would be willing to risk and for someone you don't even know?" She shook her hands in front of her and went on. "He broke right through the window...like..." she glanced here and there to find her words. "Like in the comic strip. Right through the window. All he needed was the cape. What a crash he made and glass everywhere, and before I could even get over it, he took hold of me and out we went. I lost one of my slippers."

She raised her arm as high as she could. "And you should only see what a street looks like upside down from outside a third floor window...."

Mike and Margaret looked at each other and chuckled at the dry humor of Mrs. Wortman's story. Mr. Wortman turned and gently caressed the top of his wife's head. "My Sarah."

"I hope you don't mind," Mike said, leaning forward in his chair, "but I spoke with our landlord today. The apartment downstairs in our brownstone hasn't been rented. He's saving it for his daughter who's getting married soon. But he would gladly let you have it until then, if you like. It'll give you some time to work things out. And he won't charge you anything. He was one of your good customers."

They looked at each other, wide-eyed. "This is too much." Mr. Wortman clutched his wife's hand.

"Nothing is too much for good people," Mike said. "Remember what you did for us, for Margaret." He nodded his assurance that the offer was, indeed, appropriate.

"Yes, well...what can we say?" Mr. Wortman looked at his wife, who reached over and took Mike's hand. "Yes," she repeated, "what can we say?"

Once they recognized that Mr. and Mrs. Wortman were in better health and now in better spirits than they had expected, they felt comfortable making small talk. Margaret told them about Johnny Herring and how different he was. Mike explained, to their further astonishment, that the boy was going to live with Mike's boss and his wife.

"The newspaper manager." Mr. Wortman tapped his forehead. "And they say nothing is new under the sun."

"Yes," Margaret said. "Can you imagine? We're actually friends now. Isn't that amazing? I think Junie would be his friend too, but she's not allowed to play with me for a while. I don't think she'd be allowed to play with him either."

Mrs. Wortman turned to look directly at the girl, remembering another amazing thing in the store with Viola Steich, then her eyes went to Mike and a look passed between them. "Well," she said, "when amazing things happen, people don't always understand or accept."

Mike's brow twitched. He resisted the impulse to look at Margaret, but was left to wonder if, in fact, the Fultons had also been the beneficiary of the girl's...what was so hard about saying it...gift. He could see that Mrs. Wortman understood as well. She had witnessed it—Etta had told him.

"It's a wonderful thing about Johnny," Mike said, lightly, trying to steer the conversation back to a more comprehensible reality, "to see a kid get a second chance at life."

With that, the mood abruptly changed. Mr. Wortman turned to the window. "Yes," was all he said, his back to them. Mrs. Wortman, who had been somewhat animated since their arrival, went still, her head down, her hands resting in front of her, fingering the lace edge of Etta's handkerchief. After a moment, she called quietly to him. "Isador." He didn't answer. "Please come," she said.

Isador Wortman remained at the window, looking out at the long slants of late afternoon light that sliced moodily across the sycamores.

Mrs. Wortman looked at Mike. "It's been a lot," she said, by way of apology, and the room went still. Mike looked about as if to locate the source of the sudden, deep silence, as if perhaps life itself had momentarily come to a stop.

What happened next was so unexpected that it brought only questioning stares and silence. Margaret's hair. Of the three, only Mr. Wortman had not observed the phenomenon and, with his back to them, could not see it now. Mike and Mrs. Wortman must have sensed that something in Margaret was stirring, but neither of them could possibly anticipate what was to follow.

CHAPTER THIRTY

Margaret rose from her chair and stepped to the foot of Mrs. Wortman's hospital bed, her gaze settled on Mr. Wortman who stood with his back to them at the window. Her face had an open look, her eyes wide with sympathetic concern. And something else. Mike was the first to sense it, but very quickly Mrs. Wortman must have, as well, from the look she gave him. She had seen it before. Her fingers began to move nervously. She shot a look at Mike.

"Well, Mar," Mike said, trying off-handedly to head things off, "I guess we'd better be getting home." He had picked up his hat as Mrs. Wortman, over and over, ran her fingers around the lace edge of her handkerchief. Mike had only heard Etta's accounts, but Mrs. Wortman had witnessed the girl's unusual ability. Whatever they were to call it, she had seen it firsthand that day in the store with Viola Steich—during that mesmerizing, almost otherworldly enchantment. But why here?

"Isador," Mrs. Wortman said in a soft, worried tone, "would you like to bring something from that little coffee shop downstairs." It was clear to Mike that she too was trying to get him out of the room to avoid what might happen. "Some coffee would be nice, yes? If you go now, you might get there before it closes. Maybe Mr. Ferry would like some too." Mr. Wortman remained at the window, without responding.

It occurred to Mike that this odd turn of emotions started with all the talk about Johnny Herring. Mr. Wortman clearly had been overcome by the whole incident, but there must be more to it than that. Something else was going on here. "Thanks, Mrs. Wortman," Mike said. "Etta's waiting at home. I'll have to pass on the coffee."

Margaret tilted her head. "Oh, Uncle Mike, we can stay just a few minutes more, can't we?"

Mike hesitated. She was such a child, and yet, something in her manner was quietly commanding. So this was what Etta meant—the unassuming expectation that came as a question, but, as Mike could clearly see now for himself, was not at all a request. She was not asking. Reluctantly, he nodded and sat back down with some odd realization that it was not for him to stop this from playing out. And in the next moment Margaret's hair fluttered lightly about her head, the soft brown curls briefly lifting in wisps. Everything else was still and silent, as when something of consequence is pondered. Even in the outside corridor, a calmness settled. Time seemed slower. Mrs. Wortman blinked resignedly and watched, as if with some small sense of knowing, though she herself must have understood that there was no way of knowing what exactly was going on.

"Why don't you tell us, Mr. Wortman?" Margaret finally asked.

Mrs. Wortman looked up, puzzled, perhaps wondering what more her husband could be expected to tell about the fire. Hadn't they explained it all? Margaret's question surprised Mike as well. Maybe he'd been overthinking it. Maybe this was just a child's curiosity gone too far. He had better rein her in.

"Margaret." Mike's tone was deliberate now. "Mr. Wortman's had a long day, let's just go ahead and leave now. I'm sure Mrs. Wortman needs the rest too."

Margaret's steady gaze did not leave Mr. Wortman as he turned slowly and answered with a tired sigh. "There's really nothing more to tell." He had a sluggish look about him, his thinning gray hair as disheveled as his rumpled white shirt, a sympathetic figure with his bandaged hand and sagging shoulders. It had not been just a long, tiring day for him, Mike thought, but perhaps many long, tiring years.

"Tell us." Margaret's voice was mellow. "About David."

Mrs. Wortman, clearly stunned, lifted her head off the pillow, and with a look of panic extended her hand toward her husband. "Isador," she lamented, then clutched the handkerchief to her lips.

Sarah Wortman had told her husband about Margaret's mystical encounter with Viola Steich, but Isador Wortman had discounted it, explaining to his wife how such things can appear to happen through a mere misconception of the circumstances—an illusion of sorts was how he described it. She had grown frustrated and impatient with him for not accepting what she had seen for herself to be true and real. Now, clearly frightened by this shockingly unexpected moment and the prospect of what might follow, she reached out to him. She could already see the anguish in his eyes, as he scanned the room, forehead crimped, rummaging through all the painful years gone by, remembering.

"Tell me," Margaret repeated softly.

"What can you know of our David?" he asked, his voice weak with quiet challenge, his head moving from one side to the other as if to shake off some burdensome thing. He looked at his wife with sad and heavy eyes, then at Mike. "What can she know, this beautiful girl?" He gazed at the ceiling in thought. "What can she know of our David?"

Mike turned from one to the other. "Who is David?" He sat back down, bewildered.

"Our David." Mrs. Wortman pressed the handkerchief to her eyes. "Our beloved David."

Mike knew enough to realize that whatever it was that Margaret was about to do, there was no stopping her. "*I promise*," he recalled. "*I promise*," was what Dr. Vianney had heard her say. It was Margaret's mission from The Lady. Apparently, she intended to keep that promise to whatever extent was necessary with whatever mysterious knowing came upon her.

"He was such a boy, our David," Mr. Wortman said.

"Isador," Mrs. Wortman extended her hand again. "Please. Come."

He walked to the bed, daze-like, and she took his hand, but he was somewhere else. He gazed off, squinting, as if to bring into focus that precise faraway place and time he had finally located. "Such a chilly night. October fourth." He poked his thumb into his chest. "It's branded right here that date. I had to hurry and lock up the store quickly after Sarah called. Very quickly I had to do it. There might be so little time. She was with him at the hospital. At St. Peter's. That's where they rushed him. He had asthma, our David. So young. We were living only a block or so from Prospect Park in those days. He loved the hills, but they were hard for him. His breathing couldn't take it. He had to stop all the time. And then at home, that one terrible night, for no reason, he couldn't get his breath, like if you were far under water struggling to reach the surface." He moved to turn back again toward the window, but Mrs. Wortman held on to his hand and pressed it to her cheek, gently forcing him to stay with them.

"I had to get to the hospital," he continued. "There was no time to lose. I went on the avenue to get a cab, but I saw something. It was dark and something was at the curb. It was windy and late, after nine. No one was there. No one at all, but something at the curb was moving. And then I saw it was a woman. I heard her moan. I was already so frightened and anxious about our David, and about my Sarah, alone there, worrying to death about the boy. And out of nowhere was this woman." He motioned slowly to the floor. "I went over to her. Then I could see. She was with child and calling for help. I was in a panic. Who was there but me? No one could turn their back. I had to open up the store to call for help. I had to. But I had to get to St. Peter's…to David and Sarah. Yet, how could I leave this woman? I…I ran back inside and called the ambulance. Then, I ran back out and put my coat under her head. I couldn't lift her. She was barely able to speak. She was as frantic as I. She told me it was time and she was on her way to the hospital but missed her connection with the second bus. I didn't even know where she started out from. Her husband was away in the Navy. I wanted to run back inside and call Sarah at the hospital, but I couldn't leave this woman alone again out on the cold dark sidewalk. I never knew such desperation. Such desperation." He turned here and there slowly, and gently broke loose of his wife's hand, returning to the window. For a silent moment, he looked out at the approaching nightfall, his hand gripping the frame. "What could I do? What could I do? I might have to help with that baby. If the ambulance didn't come fast, I, Isador Wortman, would have to help with that baby, while my own son…." He leaned forward, pressing his bandaged hand against his forehead.

Mike was astounded, listening to the man's story, watching as he returned to the terrible faraway memory that still burned as hot as the flames he had escaped that morning. Oh, how Mike knew that feeling. St. Peter's. Waiting. A life, more precious than your own, hanging there by a thread in those endless, terrifying moments.

For a while, nothing more was said. Then, Mr. Wortman shrugged, as if having touched, at last, upon his own resignation. "I rode in the ambulance. At least it was going to the same hospital I was going to. Someone had to stay with her." He chuckled wryly. "And I didn't have to deliver the baby, after all. It was a boy. Imagine. On this of all nights, a boy she had. A boy arrived in the world." He signed deeply. "And a boy left."

"Isador," Mrs. Wortman's voice was thick with sorrow.

"Come sit by me." And finally, he did.

"I'm so sorry," Mike said, not as yet processing the fact that Margaret had knowledge of all this.

"My Sarah and I sat Shiva all that next week. We sat Shiva together, with me knowing how I had let her down, let her down. All alone." He hung his head and shook it back and forth slowly.

"Isador, Isador. I was not alone. I was with our son in the very last moment of his life as I was at the very first moment nine years before. Both of those moments precious to me, Isador. Please, we said a long time ago, *no more.*"

"We said it, but we have lived it every day of our lives since then, haven't we, Sarah? All these years, you wished you could have swept our David off the Coca-Cola chest along with the other boys. Boys he would have had as friends. Boys being the boys God meant them to be, alive with mischief and playfulness. I know what you carry with you, Sarah." He stroked her head.

"I never had any idea about your loss…your son," Mike said. "I don't think anyone ever knew." He looked at Margaret. She'd been standing still as a statue, her pale, soft hands— child's hands—lightly gripping the top of the bed's metal footboard. Why had she led them down this path? On this of all days? Dear God, hadn't they suffered enough with the loss of their home, their store, their livelihood? Why was he so incapable of comprehending any of this? She had to know that talking about their son this way, bringing back all the pain, would be a terrible anguish. Find the good? What good could possibly come of this?

Margaret glanced Mike's way, expectantly, and a look passed between them. Something ticked in him—a flash of odd reasoning not yet clear. He straightened slowly. He realized he wanted to say something, but couldn't yet formulate the thought. Margaret wanted him to say something. She was waiting, counting on him. He looked down, searching. Finally...

"I'm sorry that all this talk about the young fireman has brought back thoughts of the man your David could have become." He leaned forward resting his arms on his knees and clasped his hands. "Mrs. Wortman, you wondered how that fireman was willing to risk everything to go back into that flaming building to get to you—someone he didn't even know. That's what makes him a hero in people's eyes, isn't it? Well, if that's the case, Mr. Wortman, why are you any less a hero? Look what you were brave enough to risk to save that woman's life, a woman you did not know, and the life of her unborn child. You made the greatest of all sacrifices. I've covered human interest stories for a long time...all through the war, as a matter of fact. I know a selfless, heroic act when I see it, and what you did, Mr. Wortman, was the most selfless, heroic thing a person can do."

Mr. and Mrs. Wortman turned to him, the anguish easing in their eyes, as perhaps they realized some measure of truth in what he said and took small comfort in his words.

"I...I never thought such about myself," Mr. Wortman said, blotting his eyes with his hand. He looked at his wife.

"He makes sense, Isador," she said, brighter now. "He's a smart man. He makes sense."

Margaret had stood quietly, watching the emotions play out, the corners of her mouth lifting into a serene smile. "Uncle Mike is right, Mr. Wortman—you were a hero and eventually good will always come from something done for good. Don't you think so too?"

Mr. Wortman raised his hands and let them drop to his sides, resignedly. "Young people are the dreamers of the world. All these years, Margaret, and I should still wonder what good will come of losing my boy, my David. I hope ..."

There was a tap on the door. A dark-haired young man poked

his head in with shy hesitation. "Excuse me," he said, stepping into the room. It took them only a moment to recognize the young fireman who had saved Sarah Wortman's life.

Chapter Thirty-One

When the young man entered, Mike immediately got to his feet. Margaret joined him, slipping her arm through his.

Mrs. Wortman pointed to him with a wave of her hand. "Oh, my hero," was all she seemed able to say, excitedly fingering the neckline of her hospital gown.

"I'm Andrew Stankiewicz." He was tall with black hair and muscular shoulders that were apparent in his crisp, white long-sleeved shirt. "May I come in?"

Mr. Wortman, walked around the bed less wearily now and reached out his hand to the young man. "Come. Come. Please. I'm honored. You saved my Sarah. If not for you, who could say?"

"The honor is mine," the young man said. "I'm glad I was able to get here before the end of visiting hours. I just got off work a little while ago and had to go home and change."

"We're doing very well, thanks to you, Fireman Stankiewicz," Mrs. Wortman said.

"Please call me Andrew."

"These are our dear friends, Mr. Ferry and his niece Margaret."

Andrew Stankiewicz nodded hello and narrowed his eyes thoughtfully when he looked at Margaret. "You look familiar?" His eyes went to Mike, then back to the girl. "I feel I've seen you someplace."

Mike thought it no wonder that a story about the miraculous

healing of a girl struck by a car would possibly still be resonating somewhere in the mind of a young man charged daily with saving lives, but he let it pass.

"My uncle writes feature stories for the *Tribune*," Margaret said. "Maybe you've seen his picture. He sometimes gets awards."

"I have read your articles," Stankiewicz said, enthusiastically. "Pleased to meet you, sir." He turned to Mrs. Wortman. "It's good to see you're doing a lot better than this morning."

"Only thanks to you," she said. "I don't know how you learn to have such courage and then so strong to go with it."

"They give us a lot of training," he said, dipping his head self-consciously. "There are a couple of people here with me."

Mr. Wortman raised his eyebrows, amused. "Maybe the Fire Chief? He'll give you a medal right here. We should have the Brownie camera with us, Sarah."

Mike gave Margaret a quick glance, as he felt her press his arm, her eyes shining with expectation—yet another moment of frustration as he tried to decipher these signals that something surely was going on, though he no longer seemed capable of putting two and two together with this child.

Fireman Stankiewicz opened the door to a petite, dark-haired woman who appeared to be in her early forties, followed by a naval officer. "Hello." She gave a polite nod to everyone. "We're so glad you're both okay," she said, looking at Mr. and Mrs. Wortman. Her eyes welled.

"Now, I've seen everything," Mr. Wortman said, tapping the top of his head. "They send the Navy for a simple house fire?"

"What's so simple, Isador?" Mrs. Wortman said. "The house is gone, remember."

The woman settled her gaze on Mr. Wortman "It's been a very long time, Mr. Wortman. I doubt that you remember me."

Sarah and Isador Wortman glanced at each other. "Forgive an aging man, but I should know you?"

"I'm sorry to say we were never officially introduced," she said. "We didn't even know your name until I saw the story in today's paper. I'm very sorry about the fire."

"Were you a customer?" Mrs. Wortman asked. "Isador is usually very good remembering people."

"No, not a customer. In fact, when we met, I didn't realize you owned that store. I wasn't even sure what neighborhood I was in. I ... I was alone on a dark, cold night and ...very pregnant."

In the blink of an eye, Mr. and Mrs. Wortman, threw their hands to their mouths, while Margaret looked up at her uncle with a satisfied smile.

"You ... you're ..." Mr. Wortman pointed, stammering. "That woman. You're that woman."

"Yes," she said, "that woman. That very, very grateful woman who has never once forgotten your kindness." She turned to the man in the naval uniform. "This is my husband. He was a young ensign at the time. You may not remember that he was away at sea. I was all alone and terrified. You were...you were my guardian angel, Mr. Wortman." She put her fingers to her lips, clearly choked up.

The woman's husband gently clasped Mr. Wortman's shoulder and shook his hand. "We have never forgotten your kindness, Mr. Wortman. I'm so grateful that I'm stationed in Brooklyn, right here at Floyd Bennett Field, so I could come today to meet you and thank you in person. We've wondered about you all these years."

"Prayed for you every single day," the woman said. "You saved my life and the life of our child."

Mrs. Wortman pressed the handkerchief to her eyes and looked at Margaret. "I think your aunt knew very well I would need a hanky today. Tell her I could have used two more."

"And this," the woman said, placing her hand on the young fireman's arm. "This is the child I gave birth to that night."

No one could have been more astonished than Mike Ferry, as the news swept through the hospital room like the tail of a comet.

CHAPTER THIRTY-TWO

"And you knew all about this the whole time, Mar?" Etta had brought a small tray into the living room on that evening when they returned from the hospital, a cup of broth for Mike and Margaret, while supper was finishing on the stove.

"Oh, no, Aunt Etta, not the whole time. And not all of it." She took a sip. "Remember, I told you I only get bits and pieces."

Mike leaned forward. "Did you know about the fire? I mean, that it was going to happen?"

Margaret laughed. "No. How would I know something like that?"

Mike looked up at the ceiling and shook his head. "Well, you seem to know everything else."

"So, you didn't ... cause the fire?" Etta asked, tension showing in her furrowed brow.

Margaret shook her head emphatically. "Aunt Etta, that would be crazy."

Etta sat up taller. "Well, you have to admit, you do make things...happen."

Margaret hesitated, giving it some thought. "It depends on what you mean. I can't really make things up. Mostly, I end up just knowing about things that are already there somewhere ... kind of like a secret."

Etta and Mike would later agree with each other that the word secret seemed to explode like the backdraft of a furnace, but that in the moment they had done their best not to let on for fear that Margaret would quickly pick up on it. There was a secret, after all.

"You knew about Mr. and Mrs. Wortman and their son David and the pregnant woman? The fireman? You knew all that?"

"A little at a time. Let me think." She looked across the room, squinting. "I knew there was a reason we had to go to the hospital to see Mr. and Mrs. Wortman, and not just because they were hurt. Then when we were there, it came to me that Mr. Wortman had something important to tell."

"Did you know that the boy who was born that night was the same person who rescued Mrs. Wortman?" Mike asked.

"Eventually I did. It came on me like a surprise, and I was so happy. That's kind of how it feels when it happens—like a warm and happy surprise." She nodded enthusiastically over another small sip of broth. "That's when I know what it is I have to do."

Etta wondered if the surprises would always be happy ones. "So, then," she pressed, "what do you think it is that you have to do?"

"Well." She took a moment to formulate her thoughts. "I guess when you think about it, I do what Aunt Lolly always says we should do—I find the good. I think that must be what my promise is for."

Etta and Mike looked at each other. They were quiet for a moment before Etta asked about Viola Steich. "Didn't you cause her to change?"

"Mrs. Steich already had kindness in her. Nearly everybody does, Aunt Etta. She had lost track of it, that's all. A lot of people do that. I just helped Mrs. Steich find it again."

"You certainly did that, didn't you?" Etta said. "She can't say enough about what a nice boy Johnny Herring is."

"Funny, isn't it? Margaret agreed. She took another sip.

"This soup is so good. I can't wait for supper. I got so hungry at the hospital."

"But how did you know to use the salt and sugar the way you did when you talked to Mrs. Steich?" Etta asked.

Margaret crinkled her forehead. "I'm not sure. It just came to me. Just like with Mr. Loughlin."

"Wait." Mike snapped to his feet. "Wait a minute here. Wallace Loughlin? You talked to Wallace Loughlin?"

Etta looked at Mike, puzzled. "I didn't know you'd seen him that day in the City."

"Oh, Uncle Mike didn't see him. Just me."

"But you were with us the whole time. This is crazy. How did you even know who Wallace Loughlin was? You never saw him."

Margaret extended her hands in front of her as if to clearly illustrate her account. "Remember when I asked if I could go into Rexall's for gum, and you said yes?"

Mike gave her a sly side-glance. "Yes."

"Well, I had just seen Wallace Loughlin go into that store."

"But how could you possibly know it was him?"

Margaret shrugged. "I looked at that man and I just knew it was him. I have to do these things by myself, that's why I couldn't tell you, Uncle Mike. There was something I had to do."

"And what exactly was that?" Etta asked, trying to remain the calm voice.

"Well, I walked in and told him some very good news about something that happened back in Cleveland, and..."

"Cleveland?" Mike's voice had gone up an octave. "How on earth could you ..."

"Mike," Etta said, quietly. "Isn't that the point of all this— how Mar knows what she knows?" She turned to Margaret. "Go on, Mar."

"Well, that's where he's from and I had to tell him what

happened back home … with Isabelle and…that's all I can say about it."

"That's all you can say about it. That and the fact that you told him to resign from his job and return my briefcase?" Mike struggled to restore his calm.

"Oh, no, he did those things on his own. He's actually a good person. Sometimes things happen that cause a person to be mean, when they're really not. They just get kind of off track."

"Lord have mercy," Mike whispered, and sat back down heavily in his chair.

"What kinds of things did you tell him, Mar?" Etta asked, taking hold of Mike's hand.

"Oh, that's only for Mr. Loughlin to know." She shrugged. "Anyway, he didn't want to talk to me at first. I knew he would be a little bit of a challenge—can you imagine him paying attention to an eleven-year-old, even though I'm almost twelve? But he finally believed what I told him because it was all true, and it would end up making him and Isabelle happy. It's a good thing he finally listened to me because the store manager was beginning to keep an eye on us." Margaret looked from Etta to Mike. "Are you mad at me?"

Etta went and sat beside her on the couch and put her arm around her. "Oh, Mar, how could we be mad at you? It's not your fault that your uncle and I get anxious about all these things that happen. As you already know, it's been a bit hard to get used to."

"Your aunt is right, Mar." He rubbed his chin then leaned forward, elbows resting on his knees, hands clasped. "Is there any way you can, you know…resist…these impulses to talk to someone the way you did with Mr. Loughlin and Viola Stcich? What if you didn't? What if you just waited, held off a little. Maybe the feeling or thought would pass."

"I did make a promise, Uncle Mike."

Etta winced and rubbed her stomach, her shoulders tipping forward.

Mike moved quickly to her side and put his arm around her. "Here, put your feet up, Et." He eased her back on the couch and put a pillow under her head. "Is it bad?"

"No. I'm okay…just a little off kilter, I guess."

"You'll be okay once you see the doctor on Monday."

"Yes, I…I'm sure I will."

He stroked her head. "Try to rest for a little while. Probably just stress."

Margaret went into the other room and returned with the shawl to cover her aunt.

"Oh, I don't think you should cover me with your beautiful shawl, Mar," Etta said. "It's too special."

"But that's exactly why I like to cover you with it, Aunt Etta. It's just as special as you are."

Etta closed her eyes as Mike turned off the lamp. "We'll come get you when supper's on the table."

Mike turned on his side and moved closer to Etta, resting his hand gently on her shoulder. She was staring straight up at the ceiling, and in the narrow slices of moonlight coming through the blind slats, he could see the worry in her eyes.

"How are you feeling?"

"I'm fine right now, Mike. It's the other thing that's worrying me." She turned her face to his. "We have to tell her. I know we said we'd wait till she's older, but I think we need to tell her… and soon."

He took a deep breath. "I know you're right. With everything that's going on with her, we can't trust that waiting is the best idea anymore."

"Especially when she seems to know so many things," Etta said. "What if she were suddenly to know this too?

Mike rolled back, putting his hand behind his head. "It's been on my mind a lot. I guess what worries me is what she'll think of us for keeping it from her all these years. But what choice did we have? Haven't we always wanted what was best for her? Shouldn't it count that we did it with the best intentions?"

"You and I see it that way, but is that something Mar will be able to accept and not... hate us for?"

"Just hearing you say that sends a shiver down my spine." They were silent for a few moments. "I think for now the best thing is for us to find out what's making you sick. Your whole system might be in overload with all that's happened. But it'll all work out, Et. It's got to." He turned and pulled her close, tucking her snugly into their familiar spoon.

CHAPTER THIRTY-THREE

Before leaving for work on Monday morning, Mike leaned over and kissed Margaret on the top of her head. "Try your best not to...you know..." He raised his hands to his head and wiggled his fingers in a fluttering gesture. "I mean...don't go out of your way to do anything."

"I know," she said, chuckling.

"That means staying away from Monsignor, right?"

"Right." She got to her feet and put her arms around him. "I promise to do my best, Uncle Mike."

He gave her a sly grin. "And that means no Russian immigrants either."

"And no Russian immigrants either," she repeated, laughing.

Margaret tried. She really did. Since her recent return to school, she had spoken to Sister Bernadine only once, briefly, and that was because she happened to run into her in the hallway. She missed her a lot; she had not been to Sister's office at all. She had not even seen Monsignor Carnavan. So that was a good thing. Uncle Mike would have been happy. But then, quite unexpectedly, everything changed.

It happened right after she and Junie had finished eating their lunch in the school cafeteria. It was such a beautiful day that they decided to sneak across the street to the churchyard. They knew they were not supposed to play together—Mrs. Giordano was still extremely wary. The story may have died down elsewhere, but not closest to home where people from the neighborhood who knew them or knew of them still sometimes eyed them with either wonder or suspicion.

"Nobody said anything about being together at lunchtime, right Mar?" Junie said, laughing, and off they went for the remainder of their hour to sit on the low concrete wall around the churchyard fountain. Junie had Jacks in her purse, hoping to see how many she could scoop up without bouncing the ball into the water. It was the warmest part of the day and they squinted in the glare of the sun until reaching the soothing shade of the sycamores.

"Where are we going to go for sodas and candy from now on?" Junie asked, running a small twig along the wrought iron fence pickets. "Panyi's doesn't have the kind of candy I really like. Don't you think it's so sad? And what about Mrs. Wortman being carried out the window by a fireman. Who could be that strong? And where are they going to live?"

"Uncle Mike arranged for them to have the apartment downstairs from us until they decide what to do." Margaret knew more than she would ever say to Junie.

"Really? Imagine having Mr. and Mrs. Wortman right downstairs. Maybe they'll have lots of candy down there, but I bet they'll be the crankiest neighbors anyone ever had."

"Sometimes there's a reason for people being cranky," Margaret said. "Besides, they're really very nice."

"If you say so."

They walked along slowly and in silence for a few moments. Then Junie asked, "Have you been doing any more crazy things?"

"Don't be silly. I don't do crazy things. Sometimes people just see things the way they want to see them or the way they're not used to seeing them, that's all."

"My mother says you have scary powers. Mrs. Salamone told her someone saw you bring a black cat back to life. You never told me about that. I think it's neat. Why don't you do something so I can see for myself?"

"Oh, Junie, that's what's crazy—the way you talk. How could I bring a dead cat back to life?" Margaret picked at the boxwoods lining the walkway that circled behind the church and rectory, and held a pinched leaf to her nose to enjoy the sweet, milky scent.

Junie kicked at a pebble, then stopped and faced her friend. "What flavor ice cream am I thinking about?"

"I haven't the slightest idea."

"They say your hair goes a little crazy."

"Why is it that you and your mother listen to people who see everything as being crazy? An awful lot of people pray for a miracle, but when one happens, nobody believes it. They just make up terrible stories about it."

"So it's not true?" Junie asked. "Your hair doesn't do anything?"

Margaret, thoughtful, ignored the question. Sometimes it was hard getting through to Junie. She decided to change the subject. "Did you ever get the feeling that sometimes people who do mean things are really good underneath?"

"You must be talking about that awful brat Johnny Herring?"

"That's the thing—he's not an awful brat. He's nice."

"Now I know you're crazy. How can somebody be good who tried to kill you?"

"Oh, stop. He didn't try to kill me. Everybody should know that by now. People don't want to listen. It was all an accident." Margaret hesitated. She was beginning to think about just how much she should share with Junie. Maybe it was Junie saying weird things that made Mrs. Giordano so suspicious. "He came with us to the Yankee game a few nights ago. We all had a good time. It's not his fault that his mother left him and his father beat him all the time. They didn't even give him anything to eat. How would you feel if it was you?" Margaret pinched another boxwood leaf. "Besides, my Aunt Lolly always says to look for the good."

"Well...but..." Junie said with a quirky smile, "Lolly isn't really...you know...not really...normal."

Margaret stopped. She looked at Junie, but could not be angry with her. Junie was childish. "You're right, Junie. Aunt Lolly isn't normal. She has so much more beauty and kindness and...and wisdom than what you call normal people have."

"Well, I'm definitely not telling my mother that somebody she says is a little crazy—you—is hanging out with somebody she says is bad—Johnny Herring. She'll never let us play together again."

They heard voices and stood still, listening.

Junie sucked in a quick breath. "Monsignor," she cried out in a loud whisper. They crept a few steps farther to peek around the curve of the walkway and saw the priest standing by the fountain with his back to them. He was speaking with one of the Russian women. Junie grabbed Margaret's arm and started to pull her back. They looked at each other and Junie jerked her head to signal Margaret to go back with her. The Russian woman sounded as if she were near tears.

"Sons hard to go to Vincent." The woman struggled to make herself clear. "Sons go hard by bus. Money too many. Too long bus time."

Margaret put her finger to her lips for Junie to be still.

"I cannot help you, Mrs. Yenkov," Monsignor told the woman. "It is going to be better for your children at St. Vincent."

"Children hard for too far Vincent. All children hard. Why no kindness for us?"

He shook his head. "I've told you. I cannot help you. It has nothing to do with kindness. I must go now."

"Please," she said, mournfully, dabbing her eyes with a handkerchief.

"There is no use," he repeated and turned toward the

rectory. The woman took a few steps to follow, but he waved her away, repeating, "There is no use, Mrs. Yenkov. Decisions have been made and we must adhere to them."

The two girls stood silent, Junie still clutching Margaret's arm, as Monsignor made his way to the rectory still unaware of their presence. Margaret's hair lifted and Junie pulled her hand away. She stared wide-eyed and speechless, then took a step back and ran off as Margaret proceeded in the direction of the rectory.

———•————

"I must tell you again," Monsignor said, turning, "I cannot..." But it was not the Russian woman; it was Margaret Ferry. "What...?"

"Good afternoon, Monsignor."

"What are you doing here? You should be in school."

The Russian woman continued to watch them from across the churchyard.

"It's okay. It's lunchtime, Monsignor. And I have a very important question to ask you."

At that moment, the girl's hair fluttered again as if in a breeze. Monsignor Carnavan looked about, noticing that not a single leaf was moving. All was still. His face flushed. "I...I don't have time for you or your questions. Go on back to your classroom. You have no place here." He turned and continued toward the rectory. Margaret followed.

"I think it will only take a minute, Monsignor."

"I don't have a minute where you're concerned," he said with a wave of his hand as he reached the side door. It was locked. He went through his pockets to find the key. "I told you to go back to your classroom." He jiggled the door handle hard, but it wouldn't budge.

Margaret stepped forward. "Let me see if I can help," she said, and effortlessly turned the handle and opened the door.

Monsignor Carnavan stepped back, staring at the girl, as Mrs. Finnerty, the housekeeper, came to the door, apparently startled at how extremely agitated the Monsignor looked. She turned to Margaret with surprise and delight. "You're...you're the girl."

Monsignor plowed past the two of them. "Tell Mrs. Hughes to get Michael Ferry on the telephone," he barked, and headed toward his office. "I want to speak to Michael Ferry. You want to talk?" he shouted back at Margaret. "Good, we'll talk. But you're not going to like a single thing your uncle and I will have to say." His voice was loud and hard. "We're going to deal with all of this once and for all. Your uncle can pick you up and I promise you, young lady, you will not return to this school after today. I had been kind enough to give you until the end of the school year, but your incorrigible behavior has forced me to do otherwise."

Margaret paused in the entry hall and turned to the housekeeper, a slight, timid woman with kind eyes and a sweet though diffident smile. The woman gave a subtle nod, as if some knowing had passed between them. "The secretary is at lunch," she whispered, a spark of gleefulness on her face, and retreated to the kitchen. There would be no call to Michael Ferry this day.

Monsignor's office was as dark as Margaret expected, but prettier than she had imagined. She looked about at the shelves filled to the ceiling with books, and took a seat in the deep leather chair facing the oversized desk. "I like your office, Monsignor. This is my first time in the rectory. I never saw so many books in one place, outside of the public library, I mean. Do you have *The Lives of the Saints?*"

Without looking up, Monsignor Carnavan pulled open a side drawer, fumbled to remove a file folder, and slammed the drawer shut. "You may be interested to know that I am filling out the paperwork for your immediate expulsion from this school." He uncapped his black fountain pen and began to write.

"I especially like the dark wood," she said. Her hair had settled itself, and she sat with her ankles crossed and her hands resting in her lap. "But here's what I'd like to ask, Monsignor."

He kept to his task without responding.

"See, my Uncle Mike always tells me…"

"I have no interest whatever in what your uncle or anyone else tells you."

"He always tells me not to hold on to things that make me unhappy or angry. It's the same thing we learn in school—that it's important to forgive. So, I keep wondering, Monsignor…" She leaned forward. "I keep wondering…isn't it a little silly for you to go on not liking poor people just because you were so poor? Aren't you ever going to forgive your mother and father?"

Monsignor Carnavan raised his head slowly, a look of disbelief on his face.

"You send all of these poor Russians away," she went on, "but…"

"Just what manner of demon are you?" His voice was a growling whisper as he got to his feet. She kept his gaze.

"You send them all away, but it's as if…well…as if you keep sending your mother away or your father. And that can't be a good thing, Monsignor. Can it?"

Monsignor Carnavan, red-faced and frantic, dropped the pen onto the desk blotter and bellowed, "Where is my call to Michael Ferry?" There was no answer. He barreled out from behind the desk and stomped to the door of his office. "Mrs. Hughes," he yelled.

"I think you must have been a very sad and angry little boy, and now that you're a very sad and angry grown man, you hurt a lot of people the way you were hurt, but it never gets rid of your sadness or your anger does it, Monsignor?"

"Mrs. Finnerty," he called. "Mrs. Hughes. Doesn't anyone...?" He trailed off, putting one arm up to brace himself against the doorjamb. He turned slowly to face her.

"Your father did the best he could cleaning stables," she went on. "Your mother kept the bathrooms at the school you attended spotless."

"You horrible child. You..."

"It's too bad other children made you feel so ashamed—kids can be very cruel, can't they, Monsignor? But then, people grow up. That boy Dennis has managed the same grocery store for nineteen years. You remember George, don't you? He became a top insurance salesman, and that other boy Buddy—the one who was especially mean to you—is really good at repairing typewriters. I can't imagine their parents being more proud of them than your parents were of you. I don't believe they would have been surprised by your great success in the church. They prayed for you night and day, Monsignor. Night and day. Imagine."

He stared at her in silence, dumbfounded, and made his way to his chair where he sat heavily, staring into space.

"I have to go back to school now," she said with calm abandon. "Lunchtime will be over soon, and I don't want Sister Eutrice to wonder what happened to me."

Monsignor Carnavan rested his elbow on the desk, his forehead cupped in his hand. Margaret leaned over and placed the pinched boxwood leaf in front of him. "Do you remember how sweet the boxwoods smell? The world needs sweetness, doesn't it?" She curtsied and left the room.

CHAPTER THIRTY-FOUR

He had lost all track of time, sitting dazed in an unrelenting whorl of resentment and humiliation. And…what? Something else. Something strangely undefined and unsettling. His energy nearly drained, he planted his hands on the edge of his desk, and pushed himself up from his chair, unaccustomed as he was to what he could only judge to have been outrageous impertinence. What eleven-year-old would have the audacity to even think of speaking to a clergyman in that manner? Let alone a Monsignor. And to speak to him so blatantly of his own mother and father. How utterly wretched. Wretched. Margaret Ferry's uncle must hear of this. He must. He should. But what exactly would he, Monsignor Francis X. Carnavan, say? Would he reveal what it was that she had told him? Perhaps leave that part out. In the end, though, could he even muster the spirit to object to such pure knowing? What exactly had happened here? The truth is he could hardly fathom it. No, he could not fathom it at all.

He walked sluggishly to the window and looked out before grabbing a handful of the heavy maroon drapes and yanking them back, unprepared for the blast of piercing sunlight that was so rare to the room. For a moment, he shielded his eyes. Then he took hold of the window latch as if to rip it off by its screws and gave the wooden frame one swift blow with his fist until it loosened enough to be thrown open. Warm, sweet air wafted in. Didn't anyone ever open a window? He banged it again for good measure, his mind still buzzing with what he was unable to grasp or reason, incapable of comprehending the notion that he had been violated to the core.

Mrs. Finnerty hurried to the doorway with timid concern, one corner of her apron wadded up in her hand. "Is everything all right, Monsignor?"

He was so deep in thought that the interruption startled him. He turned quickly, nearly losing his balance. "Did I call for you?" he snapped.

"No sir, but I heard…"

"Perhaps you hear too much. Go back to your duties." He took off his black clergyman's suit jacket and tossed it over the corner of the desk. Then he collapsed again into his chair, noticing the boxwood leaf lying there on the blotter where the girl had left it. He eyed it for a long moment before picking it up and rolling it between his fingers, releasing its sweet milky aroma. An insignificant little cutting he knew so well from childhood, from the long, low narrow hedges that lined the walkways where his father had kept the grounds and stables. Daniel Xavier Carnavan had pruned and swept and shoveled tirelessly, day upon day, with so little by way of recompense or respect, a state of affairs that hounded his son at school and on the playground. A proud, decent and endlessly patient man, he would pat his son's shoulder in bleak encouragement, the stink of manure permanently infused in the wool of his coat, the same coat that he had been married in. His devoted wife, Mary Lafferty Carnavan, frail and gaunt, would stroke the boy's head when she returned home far into the evening hours, her hands reeking of disinfectant, her eyes sagging with a weariness beyond her years. Their pain and misery had never left him; his most faithful vow was to never forget.

He dropped the boxwood leaf to the floor and ground it

in with his foot. Then he leaned back in his chair, covering his eyes with his hands, squeezing his watery eyes with his fingers. *Only God could know how this child had gotten it all so right.*

CHAPTER THIRTY-FIVE

When Mike arrived home from work, the house was unusually quiet. He had telephoned Etta several times from work to find out what the doctor said, but there had been no answer. "Et? Mar?" He made his way to the living room. "Hey, anybody home? What's going on around here?"

He found Etta standing at the living room window, looking out.

"Etta, hey," he said, softly. "I called you from the office to find out what Maggio said. Where's Mar?" She was wearing a white-collared navy blue dress he hadn't seen on her for a long time. A favorite of his.

As she walked toward him, he could see she had been crying.

"Oh, Et. Et, tell me." He reached for her. "It'll be okay, no matter what. We'll get through it. You'll see."

She shook her head, taking both his hands in hers. "I'm fine, Mike. Just fine." Her voice choked.

"Thank God." He held her close. A moment later, he stepped back. "Oh, wait a minute. I get it. Bill Fulton called you, didn't he?" His shoulders slumped a little. "I always thought that lug could keep a secret. I wanted to give you the news myself." He reached into the back pocket of his trousers for his handkerchief and softly blotted her eyes. Then he put his arms around her and kissed her on the forehead. "Bill said he was a little surprised himself that the paper acted so quickly— the series starts running a week from Sunday, sooner than we thought. The big guys upstairs loved it enough to give me the promotion right off, official the fifteenth. But he told you all that, didn't he? That mug." He gestured toward the dining room. "Mar isn't going to jump out of the closet holding a balloon or anything, is she?"

She shook her head. "I dropped her off at the Paladinos' after school. She wanted to see Johnny. Bill and Elaine are picking him up tomorrow. Wait till she hears your wonderful news." She looked down and her shoulders trembled. He lifted her chin and saw that the tears had come back. "She'll be as surprised as I just was."

Mike stared at her for a moment. "Wait. Bill didn't call you?" He took hold of her hand and led her to sit on the couch. "Oh, God, Et. It *is* the doctor, isn't it?"

She nodded, tears streaming down her face. "I wanted to tell you before we said anything to Mar."

He held her close. "I don't care what it is. And you don't have to be afraid to say it. It doesn't matter. I swear to you, Et, we'll get through it. I'll do whatever it takes. I'll get the best doctors in the world. I'll quit the paper. If we have to, we'll pack up and move to another climate..."

"I'm going to have a baby."

Mike Ferry jumped to his feet and stood back, looking with astonishment at his beautiful wife of seventeen years.

"We..." she said, all smiles and tears, "we are going to have a baby."

CHAPTER THIRTY-SIX

As much as Mike and Etta would have preferred to contain their amazing news at least for the time being, they quickly realized it was too rich a blessing to keep to themselves, and word traveled fast. Most people were as shocked as they were elated. Jo and Rae nearly brought down the phone lines with their screeching. Bill and Elaine Fulton had stopped by when they picked up Johnny Herring and took everyone out for a celebratory dinner at Barsotti's. Mr. and Mrs. Wortman came up each day from their temporary living quarters, cheerfully bringing meals of hot soup, and beef with buttered noodles, and Mrs. Paladino made a specialty bread from Sicily—an old family recipe that her mother always prepared for such occasions. Viola Steich brought two pairs of knitted booties, one blue pair and one pink pair, since the baby's gender was not known. Mike and Etta decided to tell Lolly in person when she visited that coming weekend. It was most certainly an odd and astonishing time.

Margaret was ecstatic about having a little brother or sister. She had been dying to tell Sister Bernadine all week, but Sister had an unusual number of meetings, including a rare trip to the diocesan office across Brooklyn. It wasn't until Friday afternoon, while on an errand for Sister Eutrice, that Margaret caught sight of her turning a far corner in the hallway.

"Sister," she called out, racing down the hall, breathless, her black and white oxfords clacking on the shiny linoleum.

Sister turned, as much for the pounding of footsteps as for Margaret's excited voice.

"I know I'm not supposed to be bothering you—Monsignor wouldn't like it—and I really have to go back to class, but I just had to tell you something."

"It's all right, Margaret. Slow down before you burst, and tell me what it is that's making you jump out of your skin."

"I'm sorry, Sister." Margaret nodded. "Sorry." She took a deep breath. "I just had to tell you. Aunt Etta is going to have a baby."

"Oh, Margaret," Sister said, taking hold of the girl's hands, "what wonderful news. Absolutely wonderful. I'm so happy for all of you. I wish you and your family every blessing."

Sister's hands felt smooth and strong, like Sister herself. Margaret couldn't remember a time when she had actually held them. She could feel the soft bulge of veins, the firmness of her grip. Flesh and bone. It made Margaret feel even closer to her favorite nun. "Thank you, Sister." She straightened herself. "I better go before we both get in trouble again with Monsignor."

Sister Bernadine hesitated, without letting go of Margaret's hands. "Come with me to my office. There's something I want to talk to you about. I'll explain to Sister Eutrice later."

Margaret held still, her eyes narrowing as she looked up into Sister's eyes, curious. Was she in trouble again, but for what this time? Well, she could imagine a number of things. At the same time, some thought was trying to become clear in her mind, but she couldn't make out what it was, kind of like trying to read the label on that olive jar Aunt Etta was soaking in the dishpan that morning. A blurry thought.

Sister smiled reassuringly. "You're not in any trouble, Margaret." She put her arm around Margaret's waist and walked with her down the hall.

The priest sitting behind the desk stood quickly when the

two entered Sister's office. Margaret thought he looked familiar, but couldn't place him, and couldn't imagine what he was doing there. She had never seen anyone else sitting in Sister's chair.

"Thank you, Sister, for the use of your office," he said cheerfully, as he came around to greet them. He was a thin man with slightly reddish hair and a quick, easy smile that came as much from his eyes as from his lips.

"Margaret," Sister said, pleasantly, "I believe you may know Father Raymond."

Yes, that was it. She had seen him once at the Passion play at St. Vincent's. She curtsied as the priest took her hand. "I remember you, Father Raymond," she said, smiling.

"And I certainly know who you are, Margaret Ferry," he said, enthusiastically. "You are one special young lady, and quite the talk over at our diocesan office yesterday."

Margaret had barely a second to imagine what all the talk was about before Sister spoke up.

"Margaret just told me that she's going to be a big sister to a very lucky little boy or girl." Sister appeared much happier than she had been in a long time. Margaret was glad she'd had good news for her.

"Oh, what a wonderful blessing," Father said.

Margaret didn't know what to make of it. She was curious as to what Monsignor might have told them about their conversation. It couldn't have been very good. She could almost be sure of that. Not that it would bother her. Things didn't trouble her the way they once did. Well, at least Father Raymond was smiling, but what was he doing in Sister's office to begin with?

"Margaret," Sister said, "I feel Father Raymond and I can share some news with you in confidence." She went to her chair, sat tall, and clasped her hands in front of her on the desk. "Please," she said, gesturing for both Margaret and Father Raymond to sit.

All Margaret could think about was what might happen if Monsignor Carnavan came plowing in the way he did. Would he be as furious with Father Raymond as he was with Sister? Does one priest ever get mad at another? Maybe Father Raymond didn't know how Monsignor behaved around her, that he had ordered her and Sister out of the school. It could all be very embarrassing for him and for Sister.

"Father Raymond is our new pastor."

The words hit like the gong of a giant bell, and for a moment, Margaret could only stare at Sister in disbelief, before turning to Father Raymond, who simply nodded and raised both eyebrows in gleeful agreement.

"We know this is quite a surprise, Margaret," Sister went on. "We're all still trying to get used to everything."

"*Everything?*"

Father leaned over and put a hand on Margaret's shoulder. "Well, for one thing, your Russian friends will be returning. Sister told me how important this is to you. It's important to the rest of us, as well."

"Stanny and Mikhail," Margaret blurted out with excitement. "They're coming back? Peter too?"

"Peter too, and many others."

Margaret turned sharply toward the corner cabinet and saw a box sitting on the small table where she had always done her work. "Those are all the files."

Sister nodded. "Yes, and it most certainly is going to surprise you to know that this was all Monsignor's idea. Everything about Monsignor would surprise you, Margaret. It's a miracle." As soon as she said it, she eyed Margaret and locked on, suddenly aware that this likely involved the girl in some way. "Did you…know anything about this, Margaret?"

Margaret shook her head. "No, Sister. I had no idea Monsignor was leaving."

"Father Gregory from St. Catherine's was due to go on a

special mercy mission out of the country," Father Raymond explained. "But Monsignor…"

Margaret's blurry thought was coming into focus. Her hair lifted slightly in a feathery swirl.

Father Raymond straightened, wide-eyed. He looked at Sister, whose raised eyebrows appeared to signal that this, indeed, was the oddity he had been told about. "Monsignor," he continued, clearing his throat, "requested to take Father Gregory's place. It was a surprise to us all. It didn't seem the type of assignment Monsignor would volunteer for."

"Not at all. And he was really quite humble and unexpectedly soft-spoken," Sister Bernadine agreed. "But he was adamant about how important it was for him to go and be of service."

Margaret, glanced to the side, as if distracted. "India."

"How did you…?" Father Raymond caught himself and looked to Sister, who drilled him with her gaze. "Yes, that's right," he said.

"He'll be working at a special hospital for poor orphans," Sister added.

"In Calcutta," Margaret said, which again gave them pause.

"With the Sisters of Loreto, actually." Father said. "They're quite a hardworking, dedicated group. Monsignor told us he thinks it will be good for him and for the Church to work there for a few years with the holy woman who started it."

"Yes," Margaret said, as if with silent deliberation. "The Albanian nun."

CHAPTER THIRTY-SEVEN

Friday night supper at the Ferrys' was a buzz of spirited conversation as Margaret shared her incredible news of all the changes at St. Aloysius. She had hardly been able to contain herself. Afterwards, they went into the living room waiting for "Wuthering Heights" to come on the TV at 8:00.

"Calcutta." Mike said. "That's pretty amazing. Can't imagine what brought that on."

"Can't you really?" Etta said, her gaze steadied on the cup of tea she held in her lap.

Mike stopped and looked at Etta, as if to collect his thoughts, then at Margaret. He leaned forward. "Did you...did you, by chance, talk with Monsignor, Mar?"

"Yes." Margaret said with bright-eyed innocence. "Only I don't think you can say it was by chance."

"You promised to stay away from him."

"And I meant to, Uncle Mike, honest. But Junie and I saw him in the churchyard with one of the Russian women. He wasn't being very kind."

"Here we go," Mike said, throwing his hands in the air. "The Russians again. I told you about that too. And just as a side note, have you and Junie forgotten that Mrs. Giordano does not want you two playing together? What goes on in that head of yours?"

"Mike," Etta cut in. "I...uh...think we have to remember... things are not as they once were."

Mike didn't answer, perhaps accepting the truth of Etta's statement—what went on in that head of hers was not at all the same as what used to go on there.

"Here's what happened, Uncle Mike," Margaret said, taking a sip of the cream soda she had brought in from the kitchen. "We walked over to the churchyard because it was such a beautiful afternoon. Junie wanted to play Jacks, but we really didn't go over there to play. Anyhow, when we got there, we saw Monsignor and one of the mothers. She was so upset."

"So you and Junie just butted right in to Monsignor's conversation."

"Oh, not Junie. She got scared and ran back to school. Junie gets scared a lot. And I think she saw...you know..." She broke off, wiggling her fingers above her head.

"Oh, terrific," Mike said. "That's really terrific. Junie tells her mother she saw your hair flying all over the place, and now Mrs. Giordano has no doubt at all that you're like one of those Salem witches they used to burn at the stake."

"I had an important question to ask him, but he wouldn't listen. So, I followed him."

"Good God, Margaret." Mike got to his feet. "You followed him into the rectory?"

"I had no choice, Uncle Mike. Honest. I had to speak with him."

Mike ran his fingers through his hair. "Couldn't you have come to us? I would have gone with you. Just what was so important you had to ask him right then?"

"I can't tell you. It's only for Monsignor. Just like when I had to speak to Mr. Loughlin, remember?"

"Oh, I remember, all right. And whatever the heck it was this time, you got a Monsignor of the church, our pastor, to pack up and head to India." He looked at Etta. "What do we do with this?"

"Okay, okay," Etta said quietly, putting up her hand. "Let's everyone stop." She took a deep breath. "There's just no point. We go through this every time and every time there's some unbelievable turn of events that ends up being good for someone, and Mar is just fine through all of it, right? And it never appears to us that she has been harmed in any way? Do we think this thing with Monsignor Carnavan is the last of it? No. Any more than Wallace Loughlin was the last of it, or Viola Steich or Bill and Elaine's decision to take in Johnny. There's just no point, Mike."

Mike dropped back into his chair and for a few moments no one spoke. Margaret sat up straight, her ankles crossed, her hands resting in her lap, waiting.

"What can I say?" he said at last. The frustration in his voice had eased. He motioned for Margaret to come to him. "I know you must do what you have somehow become destined to do, Mar. I'm sorry."

Margaret went over and sat on the arm of his chair. "I'm sorry too, Uncle Mike. I don't mean to make you scared or unhappy. When my hair moves, I know there's something very, very important I have to do."

He looked up into her eyes. She was not a little girl anymore. What he had thought of as childish immaturity must be the innocent expectancy of youth coupled with a true and loving heart. He gave a slow nod. Then he put his hand on her knee. "Please don't ever apologize, Mar, for this very special gift you've been given. I should know better by now. Et's doing a better job than I am."

"We're all doing our best," Etta said, with a sympathetic smile. "Besides, Mar, you said Monsignor told everyone he really wanted to go to India to work in that special mission. That's a good thing, right?"

Mike laughed. "Well, he's out of our hair and that's definitely a good thing. I wish him well."

"And...funny thing...," Etta said, running her hands across

her lap to smooth the fabric of her dress, "we've actually got some news of our own, Mar."

Margaret's eyes widened. "What kind of news?"

"We think it's very good news," Etta said. "And we're hoping that if you keep an open mind, you'll think so too."

Margaret crinkled her brow and looked curiously from one to the other.

"We've talked about it in the past," Mike said, "but now something has come up that requires us to make a decision. About moving."

There was a time when Etta and Mike would have expected Margaret to be devastated by such news, but since this whole phenomenon had occurred, disappointing news seemed to be far less unsettling to her. Still…

"Are we going to leave Brooklyn?" Margaret had gone back to sit on the couch, listening intently, her eyes trained on her uncle.

"Well, we'd have to," Mike said. "I have an opportunity at work that can make a big difference for all of us."

"What is it?" Margaret asked, looking a bit forlorn. "Will we go far? We would miss Brooklyn a lot."

"Yes, that's true, although maybe moving away will be good for everyone," Mike said, "and Long Island isn't that far away." He leaned forward, resting his forearms on his knees. "I got a call from a fledgling newspaper called *Newsday*. They've offered me a job as Managing Editor. It's one of the top management positions at the paper, the kind of challenge I've been ready for, for a long time. And it doesn't hurt that it comes with a heck of an increase in pay."

Margaret looked wide-eyed, first at Etta, then at Mike. "Wow, that's wonderful news. Things can really change in a hurry—first the candy store, now us. But at least ours sounds like mostly good news." She tilted her head. "Mostly."

"Mostly," Mike agreed. "It's true we'll have to leave Brooklyn, but not forever."

"We'll always come back to see all the friends we have," Etta added.

"And," Mike continued, "we'll be able to buy a house with a yard and trees. Long Island has a lot of rural areas, dirt roads and all. You'd like that. It's not built up. You can have a dog, and a bike if you want. Maybe even a couple of rabbits." He laughed. "Besides, we're going to need a bit more room when the baby comes."

Margaret looked down, her shoulders sagging a bit. "Things will be so different without Junie and Sister Bernadine. And Peter and Stanny." Her eyes glistened. "I'll really miss St. Aloysius, especially now that I know they'll be coming back. Mikhail too."

"I know," Etta reached over and took Margaret's hand. "But look at it this way. You'll be leaving St. Aloysius anyway when you go to high school, so you wouldn't be seeing Sister any less by us moving. Right? And, now and then, we can take a ride in on weekends and visit everyone. As for Junie, I have a feeling Mrs. Giordano is not going to let her go to the same school as you anyway."

Margaret gazed toward the window. "We'll never go to Germaine's again, will we? My favorite store in the world. We won't be able to go anymore for Santa and all our beach stuff for Coney Island. Everything will be different."

"Not everything," Mike said. "The important things never really change. We're still a family. We'll still come back and see the people we care about. We can still visit Germaine's at Christmas. And you'll be amazed how many new things you'll discover. In fact, Bill and Elaine are thinking of moving to Long Island too. Their neighborhood is changing and they want the best place to raise Johnny."

"Elaine knows about this lovely town called Massapequa Park," Etta said. "There's a pretty good chance you and Johnny might end up in the same high school."

"Really?" Margaret said, lifting her head.

Etta looked at Mike. "And there might be one other really nice thing that we are positive you will like."

Margaret looked at them expectantly.

"We're going to ask Aunt Lolly to come live with us.

Margaret shrieked and jumped to her feet. "Oh, Aunt Etta. Aunt Etta." She ran to the window and back. "Uncle Mike."

"We're planning to talk to Lolly about it while she's here over the weekend," Etta said.

Margaret knelt down in front of her uncle's chair. "Do you think she'll say yes? I hope so."

Mike rested his hands gently on Margaret's shoulders. "We hope so too. But, mostly, we just want to make sure that you're happy, Mar."

"Oh, I am. I am." She looked from one to the other. "I'm happy, Uncle Mike. I love you and Aunt Etta. I love Brooklyn and school and our whole family. Sister Bernadine. It's true I wasn't happy about all our Russian friends going away or how Monsignor was treating people. And sometimes I'm not very happy about how silly Junie can be. But mostly everything here is the best in the world that a girl can have and I know it's always going to be the best place wherever both of you are… and now even Aunt Lolly. Holy cow."

"You're a very special girl, Mar." Mike touched her cheek. "Long before the accident and the promise you made and all of these crazy amazing things, which we still can't comprehend… you've always been extra special to your aunt and me."

Etta leaned forward to brush a curl from Margaret's cheek. "We would always hope you know how much we love you. Everything we have done, we have done with love."

CHAPTER THIRTY-EIGHT

Mike and Etta lay there in the dark, she nestled in the curve of his arm, his lips touching the softness of her brow, for a long time saying nothing, except with the closeness of their bodies. Her arm rested across his chest. She could feel them breathing in rhythm. Perhaps the precious little one inside her could too. They had gone to bed by 9:30, hoping for a good night's sleep before the busy weekend with Lolly's visit, yet here they lay still and sleepless.

"I wish I were sure about what to do," Etta said softly. "I'm not feeling very confident about how to go about this. I'm worried." She could feel him nod.

"Are you having second thoughts?"

Etta drew a deep breath. "Not so much telling Lolly about the baby—she'll be as surprised as everyone else. I'm pretty sure she'll be delighted. And I have to believe she'll love the idea of coming to live with us…"

"Once we figure out where Andrew Grassley fits in her life."

"True." She took a deep breath. "There's so much going on right now, Mike. So many uncertainties. I guess that's why I've been thinking that maybe we should put off…the other. It's… it's just too much, don't you think?"

"I'm not comfortable either way, but I think you're probably right, Et. And the fact is—it's been months since all these… odd…things have been going on with Mar, and she still hasn't picked up on…you know…on anything. We might be worried for no reason. We could tell her everything when we're settled in after the move, couldn't we?"

"Okay," Etta said, "then as far as tomorrow is concerned, please just get Mar out of the way for a while so I can have a few minutes alone with Lolly. I want to make sure the news of the baby doesn't overwhelm her."

"I'll handle it," Mike whispered. "It may not be easy—you know how Mar clings to her. I'll make up some reason for the two of us to go downstairs to see Mr. and Mrs. Wortman. Mar likes going down. Maybe there's something we can take to them."

"Take the fresh kielbasa I got at Pacha's today. I think they'll enjoy it." There was a long pause. "Are you sure we're doing the right thing?"

"I'm not sure of anything anymore." He stroked her arm. "It could be risky to wait. Everything has changed. It's so unpredictable. If we don't deal with it now, there could be consequences beyond what we might be capable of fixing. On the other hand, with everything else going on, this may end up being the worst possible time."

"We've gotten through all the rest that we've been challenged with; we'll get through this."

He pressed her to him and for a few moments there was only silence. "But it has been a good life all in all, hasn't it, Et?"

"All in all, through thick and thin, Mike…the best." Then she slowly lifted her face to have her lips meet his.

CHAPTER THIRTY-NINE

Lolly arrived on Saturday, and immediately held Margaret out at arm's length with a deft and approving eye. "You are still our Margaret...all right." Although Etta had updated her sister by telephone nearly every day in those first weeks following the accident, and even had Margaret speak with her, this was the first time Lolly had seen the girl. She cupped Margaret's face in her hands. "Angel."

Margaret threw her arms around Lolly. "I'm so happy you're here for the weekend. I miss you."

"Hug me all you like," Lolly laughed, "I'm in wash and wear." She moved away in a slightly awkward half twirl, the skirt of her new gingham shirtwaist dress swinging about her. "Three hours on the train and...hardly a wrinkle." She was all in blue and prettier than Margaret could ever remember, full of high spirits and exuberant stories about the often odd goings on at St. Clement—just the day before, a cow had wandered onto the property from a nearby farm and followed Lolly through the front door of the main building, sending everyone scrambling. Lolly used rice pudding to lead the animal back out without incident, although no one had ever heard of a cow liking rice pudding.

"We have a new chef," Lolly said, expecting that to explain everything.

"Only you, Loll," Mike said, shaking his head.

She had brought gifts—for Margaret the latest *Brenda Starr* and *Archie* comic books, along with a navy and white purse, and for Mike the new *Life* magazine with Dodgers catcher Roy Campanella on the cover, plus two Sundays worth of the *Philadelphia Enquirer*, a four-pound gift that hogged much of her suitcase. Etta's delicately wrapped gift—a mother-of-pearl hair comb—took very little space.

"Oh, Lolly, it's beautiful," Etta said. "You didn't have to." She slipped the comb into her hair which was gathered at the back of her head in a chignon.

"If I could say the word spec…tacu…lar, that's how I would say you look." They all laughed.

"I have missed you. I love being here, and I did have a very good trip." She rubbed the side of her head thoughtfully. "I think Helen Twelve…trees was on the train."

"Who?" Margaret crinkled her brow. "Is that a real person?"

"Oh, yes. An old-time movie actress," Etta said. "Then we'll need a special prayer at dinner for Helen Twelvetrees."

"Thank you, Etta," Lolly's tone momentarily sobered. "It's nice to remember the ones who might other…wise be forgotten. She has very sad eyes, but she has always been such a chari…table woman. I think people have forgotten her with… out ever knowing of her great kindness."

"But if she was so famous, they would know, wouldn't they?" Margaret said.

Lolly quieted her voice to a near whisper. "Oh, even the people who think they know us best, don't always."

"So," Mike said, clapping his hands together, "how is this fellow who has pinned his ribbon on your heart?"

Lolly squeezed up her shoulders and flashed a shy grin. "We go for a walk on the grounds every day. The grass and flowers smell so sweet. Andrew is respon…sible for them, you know. He does such a good job. And he's also very kind. Everyone says so. Plus, isn't he handsome? Didn't you think so when he picked you up that day?"

"Better than Errol Flynn," Mike said. "Does he have a sword?"

Lolly poked him in the arm. "No sword, but he does like Frost as much as I do. And Sandburg…those *little cat feet*." She threw her hand to her mouth and squeezed her eyes shut, embarrassed. "Not Andrew. Andrew doesn't have little cat feet." The sudden outburst of hilarity swept the room and the lightheartedness continued into lunch. Margaret felt dazzled by the joy that Lolly brought to every moment. There were more quirky stories about St. Clement and about things she and Andrew had done, tales as eccentric as Lolly herself, like the day she strolled nonchalantly out of the woods with a tiny bear cub at her side without realizing the mama bear was gaining on them. Luckily, Andrew was nearby clearing brush and managed to frighten the bears off with noise from the chain saw, after which he threw Lolly over his shoulder and carried her back to the main building with a brief admonition and a playful whack on the behind.

"But now, Mar," Lolly said when the bouts of laughter had finally subsided, "there are much more important…things to talk about, like what all these many weeks have been like for you. Talking with you and Et on the phone has been nice, but I'd like some of the in-person details. I never ac…tually met a miracle child before."

Margaret put down her fork and looked up, her eyes still glazed from laughter. "Gosh, Aunt Lolly, I don't feel like a miracle child. I don't even know how to explain any of it." She paused pensively. "Sometimes I just know things about people, even people I never met before."

Lolly looked over at Etta with a sober glance, then back at Margaret. "Yes, I heard. But what is it like when you rea…lize you know it?"

"Well, that reporter on the street? I just looked at him and I knew that he was so unhappy about not finding the man who saved his life during the war. Then there was a thing that happened with this gossipy woman in the neighborhood, then a fireman, and...well, there's more, but it comes to me like... like the correct answer on a test. You just know it's right and true." She shrugged and wiggled her fingers near her ears. "And my hair kind of floats around. Junie's mother won't let us play together anymore."

Lolly reached over and touched Margaret's arm. "Some people are just too narrow for the bright things of life. Something extra...ordinary and wonderful happened to you."

Margaret knew that Lolly would never say something was crazy that turned out to be good. It just wasn't her way. She was a gentle soul, and funny and odd in the most beautiful way, from her slightly crooked smile and the way she walked, to her unique experiences. But she also had a certain calm knowing that all couldn't possibly turn out any other way but right.

"We won't lie." Mike ran his hand down the side of his face. "There's been a worrisome side to all this, Loll. A bit of a roller coaster of blessing mixed with fear, I guess you'd say...all these encounters of Mar's. Talking to strangers, challenging people. She can tell you later about her little chat with Monsignor Carnavan."

"Oh, Mar," Lolly said with a wry side-glance. "Not the Monsignor."

The kitchen was washed in a buttery light and since the heat of summer was still some weeks away, the air billowing through the curtains was refreshing with an added sweetness wafting up from Mrs. Wortman's kitchen.

Lolly drew a deep breath. "*Mmm*, smells like...I think maybe Nessel...rode pie."

"What kind of pie?" Margaret could always count on Lolly to come up with something that she had never heard before, especially if it involved a funny name—Helen Twelvetrees, Nesselrode pie. "Did you make that up?"

"Nesselrode," Lolly said again slowly. "Right, Etta? Maybe?"

"Could be." Etta passed the bowl of macaroni salad. "It's hard to say what Mrs. Wortman might be coming up with next. She's a wonderful cook. And, yes, Mar," Etta said, this time with a chuckle, "it's a real word and a real pie."

"We have a neighbor downstairs now," Margaret explained, enthusiastically. "Well, for a while anyway. Remember the cranky candy store people, Mr. and Mrs. Wortman? Well, they're really very nice. Their place burned down and Mrs. Wortman had to be carried out of the third floor window by a fireman, who…"

"Mar, slow down," Etta put a gentle touch on her arm. "You're going to exhaust us all."

Margaret went on, her exuberance momentarily in check, and told about Mr. and Mrs. Wortman, and their son, David, and the whole fire rescue hospital visit.

Lolly put her fingers against her cheek and shook her head. "What an amazing story, Mar. We never do know all about people, do we? I mean, what their true life is like that people don't get to see."

"Uncle Mike says he's going to talk to them and to fireman Stankiewicz's family to see if they would let him write one of those human interest stories for the paper."

"Oh," Lolly said, giving Mike a serious look, "I know you would make it the most beautiful story, finding all the good in it. Uplifting for all."

"Thanks, Loll."

"And there's more," Margaret said, going on to tell about Monsignor's unexpected departure and the return of the Russian families, along with Johnny Herring being adopted by Mr. and Mrs. Fulton.

When Etta was able to get a word in, she mentioned that Mike's bank exposé series was to start running the following week. "And I'm also proud to say the paper offered him a promotion. Long overdue, I'd say."

Lolly looked from one to the other. "Such good news all around. Isn't it a good time, after all?" She looked down, her hands folded in her lap. "We have to wonder, don't we, about what Mrs. Samuelson told us. You know…about the shawl."

"Yes, and there's even more to it." Mike put his napkin to his mouth, then set it aside. "Etta and I want to run something by you, Loll."

Margaret straightened up, her eyes bright with expectation, anticipating Lolly's reaction.

"I've been offered a terrific position with a new paper out on the Island. It's a great opportunity, but it means we'll have to leave Brooklyn."

"Oh." Lolly gave Margaret a worrisome look.

"We know it's a big move," Mike went on, "but we've already told Mar we can come back to visit friends. We won't be that far away. There's a town called Massapequa Park. It's on the South Shore and a lot of the area is still pretty rural."

"Tell her the rest, Uncle Mike."

"We'd like you to come live with us."

Lolly threw her hand to her cheeks, and turned to Etta, then to Margaret who was popping up and down in her seat.

"Do you think you would like that, Lolly?" Etta said.

"I don't know what to say. It's such a kind and loving surprise. Makes me want to cry." She turned to Mike. "You deserve all good things for your great talent and hard work. You do. Oh, I don't know how to thank you."

"Just say yes."

Margaret was ecstatic. It was the most wonderful, special moment with her favorite people. She would remember it forever.

"Well," Lolly said, "I guess I should tell you some special news of my own."

CHAPTER FORTY

Lolly looked down in a momentary clutch of bashfulness. "I was going to wait until we had dessert. It seems like the kind of news that goes with something sweet." She looked around the table at the expectant faces. "Andrew has asked me to marry him."

The excitement was instant and breathtaking. Mike slapped the table with his hand, while Margaret jumped to her feet and threw her arms around Lolly's shoulders. "Oh, Aunt Lolly, this is the best news ever."

Etta reached over and squeezed Lolly's hand, smiling. "You said yes."

Lolly nodded. "I said yes. Twice I think. I guess even a sideways kind of a woman in her mid…thirties can be swept off her feet."

"But a very special woman," Etta said.

"Well, it looks like we're all broken out in good news." Mike lifted his glass of cream soda. "To you, Lolly. Congratulations and all good wishes. Looks like you're about to make a great guy a wonderful wife."

Lolly smiled and shook her head. "Amazing and glori… ously unexpected. So very many blessings."

Margaret sat back down and pulled her chair closer to Lolly, her chin resting in her hand. "Tell us everything. When is the wedding? I hope it's soon."

"Not too soon," Lolly said, almost apologetically. "The

end of October. We want an autumn wedding. We both love autumn. All the colors and the chill and the scent of pine coming from the woods. I have always thought autumn is the most…poetic season—everything is changing. It's coming to an end, but in the most beautiful way possible because… something new will follow not so long after?"

"Well, it's always been a favorite of mine," Mike said. "Football season."

"Have you and Andrew decided where you'll live?" Etta asked.

"Oh, yes. I don't know if you had a chance to see Andrew's cottage by the lake. That's where we'll live. Right there at St. Clement…by that beautiful lake. There are swans there in autumn, you know."

"Oh, Lolly, you'll let us help, won't you?" Etta asked.

"I can help pick out your wedding gown," Margaret jumped in. "And flowers. Lots of flowers with ribbons and bows."

Mike looked at his watch. "I've got to go downstairs for a few minutes. You said you picked up some kielbasa for Mr. and Mrs. Wortman and I want to make sure we get it to them in case they'd like it for supper." He got up from the table. "Mar, why don't you come along with me? They always like it when you drop in. You can all do wedding plans when we come back up. In fact, you'll have all day tomorrow."

Margaret gave them a frown in protest, but Etta had already taken the brown butcher-wrapped package from the refrigerator. She handed it to Margaret. "Here you are. Give Mr. and Mrs. Wortman my regards."

An hour later, Margaret trailed her uncle through the door with a gingerly grip on the warm Nesselrode pie that Mrs. Wortman had insisted they take. "You were right, Aunt Lolly. Look."

Lolly hurried across the kitchen with a quivering smile, her eyes pooled with tears, and took Mike's hands. Even with a condition that might have made others appear awkward, there was a grace to Lolly's uneven gate, an almost rhythmic bobbing, unusual but appealing all the same, like Clark Gable's large ears or Humphrey Bogart's lisp. "Oh, Mike, I'm so happy for you and Etta. A baby. No one is more deserving."

"Well," Mike said, clearly pleased to finally be able to talk about it with Lolly, "I guess Et told you we had no idea. We were a little worried there for a while. She hadn't felt well, but honestly, in a hundred years we never imagined."

"But all is well now." Lolly turned to Margaret, still tearful. "And a little brother or sister for you, the most wonder…ful big sister a little boy or girl could ask for."

"I was on pins and needles waiting for Aunt Etta to tell you." Margaret couldn't imagine what had bothered Aunt Etta so much about telling Lolly she was going to have a baby. It made Lolly cry, but those were happy tears. Now they could have Mrs. Wortman's pie and plan Lolly's wedding. "And maybe next year you'll have a baby of your own."

She looped her arm through Lolly's. "I have an idea. Let's go down to the drug store and get a bridal magazine. You could have one of those long, long trains out to here." She made a slow sweeping move with her arm. "And then they put a bustle on the back. And a tiara with another long veil. Kind of like the Queen just wore."

Lolly laughed. "I promise you, Margaret Ferry, when I become Queen, I'll do just that." She tilted her head, consolingly. "But for now, I think a simple dress will do…a soft kind of cream color. And a nice hat to match. A hat with a short veil in front." She traced the outline of her face with a circling motion. "Like that. Just simple." She looked at Margaret, then at Etta. "Right?"

Etta smiled. "Sounds perfect. Don't you think so, Mar?"

"I guess so," Mar said, dejected. She thought for a moment, then brightened. "Okay then, what about the flowers? A big pretty bouquet goes with a dress and hat. You have to have a bouquet." She looked expectantly from one to the other.

Lolly gave an approving nod, and patted Margaret's arm. "Oh, yes, Mar, I think you'll help me pick out a…beautiful bouquet. What kind of flowers do you think would be nice? It'll be October remember?"

"Mums?"

"Mums would be nice," Lolly said. "And maybe clematis or dahlias."

"And baby's breath." Margaret was excited. "All those little dots of white make it look even prettier."

"Okay, you two," Etta scolded playfully, "I've got to finish making supper so we won't miss our evening walk—it'll be too beautiful a night. You can go on about it then." She gestured to the wire basket at the end of the counter. "Mar, you can start peeling some potatoes." Etta continued snipping the ends off the string beans. "Lolly, why don't you sit right down here and tell us all about D…" She stopped herself and shot Lolly an anxious look. "I mean Andrew."

Lolly looked up wide-eyed and there was a momentary silence. "You were about to call him Drew, weren't you?" She chuckled, fingering the embroidery on the tablecloth. "How did you know? People call him that all the time."

"Pretty neat, Aunt Etta."

"A lucky guess," Etta said, ticking her head to the side with a shrug, and went back to snapping green beans.

Chapter Forty-One

The long unbroken stretch of Fifth Avenue between 25th and 36th Streets was bordered on one side by the black wrought iron fence that formed the west perimeter of the lush and historic 438-acre Greenwood Cemetery, and on the other by a curbside flank of sycamores that completed the pastoral setting for an evening stroll. To the average outsider, acres of headstones, crypts and funereal monuments might have seemed an unlikely backdrop for an evening's recreation along a promenade, but not so for residents of the Park Slope neighborhoods loyal to the tradition. It was a scene populated by families with and without baby carriages, elderly couples ambling in lock-step arm-in-arm, and occasional teens on skates or bicycles milking the day of its last drop of light. There were those who walked alone, some with canes or accompanied by a dog nearly every child stopped to pet. On this evening, there was an elderly woman in a black headscarf, motioning in the air and muttering to herself, as she hurried past the young couples on a date, full of each other, unaware. The air was filled with the murmur of quiet conversation, laughter and chatter, and sometimes a pleasing silence, all of it mixing with the unobtrusive *whir* of passing cars. Now and then, the savory aromas from Gina's Pizzeria and Benny's Steakhouse wafted in on a breeze from one of the side streets across the avenue, enticing a few pedestrians to abandon their walk, which more than once had been the case for the Ferrys. But not tonight.

"What did you think of Mr. Icchio's crepe myrtle, Aunt Lolly? Did you ever see one before? He said they doen't even grow in this part of the country."

"Just beautiful. And imagine having one right here in Brooklyn."

"The flowers are too fragile for a wedding bouquet though, aren't they?"

"I think we'll need a sturd…ier flower, like the mums you said. And dahlias with the baby's breath. Such a good idea, Mar."

"Are you sure you don't want a gown with a train?"

"You know I've always liked simple things. Simple is okay, isn't it?"

Etta, walking side-by-side with Mike, called softly from behind, "Mar, don't be nagging Lolly about a gown."

Lolly gave Margaret a reassuring pat on the hand. "It's okay. I love your wonderful enthusi…asm."

"Margaret is nothing if not enthusiastic," Mike said.

"That's my girl." Lolly took Margaret's hand in hers. Her touch was warm and Margaret was surprised by the sensation it gave her, serene and uplifting. She swooned, but Mike saw it in time and caught her.

"Hey, kiddo. You all right?" He kept his arm around her and cupped her face in his hands. "Look at me."

Margaret looked up with a tenuous smile, her eyes glassy. "I'm fine, Uncle Mike. There's nothing wrong."

"We've been gone a long while," Etta said. "Probably best to head back anyway."

It was the evening Etta had predicted—too beautiful to miss, a lovely walk along the avenue, sweetened by the occasional sprigs of forsythia, viburnum and lilac poking here and there through the iron pickets or arched above the rails. Chatter and laughter, skates and bikes and babies, even Mrs. Schiano padding by at a pace that was likely more suited to Stoogie, who'd led the way on his leash.

How quickly things changed.

"I think maybe I'd better hail a taxi," Mike said.

"Uncle Mike, I'm fine. Honest," Mar drowsily protested, even as her shoulders slumped. "I just feel a little tired all of a sudden."

It took only ten minutes for the cab to drop them back at the brownstone.

"It's our fault, Mar," Etta said, placing the back of her hand against the girl's forehead. "We just get walking and walking and time disappears—it's nearly ten o'clock. Well, at least there's no fever."

"Why should I have a fever? I'm...I'm just sleepy."

Lolly gave her a gentle hug. "Then a good night's sleep is just what you need, and maybe some warm milk."

"That's a good idea, Mar," Mike said, stroking the top of her head. "A little warm milk."

"I think...I think..." She yawned, barely able to get the words out, "I just want to go to bed, Uncle Mike."

"Is it my imagination," Etta said with an anxious edge to her voice, "or did Mar's hair lift a little as she went to her room?"

"I thought so too, but..." He ran his hand down the side of his face and across his chin. "Maybe it was just a fluke—we're all tired." He was sitting on the couch in the living room with his arm around Etta's shoulder. "Even your sister looked exhausted when she turned in."

"It's just that I've never seen Mar like this, not even before the accident—to lose all her energy so quickly, just like that. She was absolutely drained." She turned to him with a worried look. "Is it possible that she's...I don't know...regressing in some way?"

"Et, we can't over think every single thing. Mar is healthy.

And you know how she gets when Lolly comes—she just wears herself out." He leaned in and kissed her cheek. "Come on, finish your tea and let's get to bed ourselves."

"I wonder..."

"I think we've done enough wondering." He pressed her to him. "In your condition you ought to be in bed right now too."

"Doctor Maggio said walking is good."

"Yes," Mike nodded, "walking not worrying."

"We'll check on Mar first."

"Don't we always? You'll see in the morning, she'll be just fine."

They entered Margaret's room and, as usual, moved quietly to the bed. In the small spill of light that followed them in from the hall, they could see that she was asleep, her face peaceful, her breathing normal. They looked at each other and silently gestured their agreement that everything was okay. They loved looking at her, this sweet, special girl, this blessing assigned to them at birth. Etta made the sign of the cross as they turned to leave, and Mike gave a light reassuring squeeze to her arm. Then, Margaret's voice stopped them cold. "Is it you?" they heard her whisper.

They remained silent, turning slowly to see that the girl was sitting up. As they cautiously approached the bed, they noticed that her eyes were still closed. They didn't move and, a moment later, she lay back down as before.

Out in the hall, Mike and Etta looked at each other, wondering.

CHAPTER FORTY-TWO

Mike and Etta fell fast asleep despite their efforts to figure out one more thing, one more question, one more possibility—they could make no more of that day.

"Everything is going to be okay, Et." Mike's words trailed off.

"I pray you're right." She was so tired she could only think the words.

———◄•►———

Margaret lay back down to a troubled sleep. Her brow pinched, her lips tightened into a line, she turned to one side then the other. In her dreams she was frantic, searching room after room in some unfamiliar house. Room after room. Searching for what? No, not what. Who? Who was it? Who was it she had to find? She was sure she would know, sure that it would all be clear once she found the right room. That's all she had to do—find the right room.

———◄•►———

"Two roads diverged in a yellow wood…" Lolly whispered at the open window, only slightly comforted by Frost's words and the cool air of the May night. Her hands clasped in a prayerful grip, she mindlessly rubbed her thumbs round and round over each other, as if to massage away her growing anxiety. Three a.m. Her thoughts were like the night itself—fast moving clouds, one moment inky darkness, the next moonbeams and the welcome rustle of young trees. "...and sorry I couldn't take them both and be one traveler, long I stood, and looked down one as far as I could..." Her thoughts were unsettling. *What if?* She could tell Etta had been on edge all day, and not because of the baby. Everyone but Mar knew it. Mike was always good at pleasantries, feigned or otherwise. He had been their rock. But even he was surely aware with all that had happened, all the mystery and uncertainty, all that was possible. He knew. The time was getting close now. The time when...

She turned slowly to find Margaret standing in the doorway, a look of innocent expectancy on her face. Curious. Waiting. She held the shawl, neatly folded, in her hands. And for a long moment they could only take each other in as if, in a way, for the first time...a very long-awaited time.

Lolly ticked her head to the side, her smile reluctant and contrite, her brow lifted as if in apology. Her eyes welled— she sensed that the time had come. Margaret went to her, letting the delicate vintage lace unfurl, and draped it with great care around Lolly's shoulders. Then she held her close and whispered, "Mother."

CHAPTER FORTY-THREE

They had met again on a February evening at a little get-together at her friend Sissy's place. Just fellow teachers—girls only—until Sissy's brother George stopped back at the house to get a warmer jacket. He had a couple of friends with him, nice young men. One of them was Dan Ferry. She had seen him several times over the years. He was Etta's brother-in-law, for a while away at school getting his business degree, then for a longer time, working as a corporate marketing apprentice in Chicago. On this particular evening, he was celebrating his permanent homecoming with a night out on the town. She'd heard he was back, and had been invited to Etta and Mike's for a welcome home dinner, but a teacher's conference had kept her from attending.

She was sitting in a chair by the window. They noticed each other at once and he went over to her. Artie Shaw's *Frenesi* was playing on the radio. "Missed you the other night, Lolly. Sorry you weren't there." She would never forget how his warm, dark eyes made her heart leap. The next day, he asked her to a movie, *Northwest Passage* with Spencer Tracy. Afterwards, they went on to Buckram's Ice Cream Parlour for hamburgers and ice cream sodas. In the weeks that followed, they went dancing, bowling and ice skating. Dan was athletic and gentle. She fit so well in his arms, where everything in the world seemed right. They were married the following year—their first dance together, Bing Crosby's "Only Forever."

She was young—a woman, a bride, and so quickly a mother-to-be. She wished there was a way to tell him in person, but the letter would have to do. She would have to take it easy, the doctor had told her—the letter wouldn't mention that part; why worry him on the other side of the world. No, she would only tell him the best part—in a little over seven months she was going to have their baby.

She would do as Doctor Scala said: avoid exhaustion, no strenuous activity, bed rest as often as possible. She would not have to give up her teaching job right away unless it became too stressful—the children could be rambunctious at times, but mostly a joy. "Yes, Doctor," Lorelei Ferry had said, gladly, and meant it.

Dan had been gone only a month—once President Roosevelt instituted the draft, he figured he'd better choose the branch of service he preferred, and enlisted in the navy. They hadn't counted on him going so far away, but it would only be for two years, and Mike had reassured her they might let him have leave when the baby was due, even though Hawaii was a long way from Syracuse. She was comforted by that and by the care and helpfulness of family, especially Mike and her sisters, as well as her co-workers at the school. She was happy, and well. Only Dan's being here could have made it perfect.

——◆——

She had returned to their little apartment near Lake Skaneateles after noon Mass, around two in the afternoon. She hadn't even thought of walking home in the below-freezing weather. There was still snow on the ground, but the bus let her off just down the street, and even at seven months pregnant, as long as the sidewalks were clear, it was still a somewhat easy walk to the front door. She would have to begin curtailing her activities and spend more time at home taking it easy—doctor's orders. She had left her teaching job in her fifth month, and were it not for the fact of such a wonderful reason for doing so, she would have been crushed.

The apartment was warm and she was happy to be back home. She made herself a cup of tea, turned on the radio and was pleased to hear *Frenesi*, now a favorite of hers and Dan's. It felt good to put her feet up. She tossed the small plaid coverlet over her legs and put her head back. One song after another that they both loved so well, songs that brought back sweet memories—"Green Eyes, Blue Champagne..."

It was dark when she opened her eyes, unaware of how long she had slept or what the racket was that had awakened her. The music was gone and in its place a raucous overplay of loud and frantic voices—bulletins, urgency. What was going on? She was startled to hear the doorbell, and with a half-drowsy and cumbersome effort, she lifted herself from the chair to answer the door. It was Mike and Etta, cheerless and accommodating. Etta took her hand as they entered.

"Is something wrong?"

"Lolly," Mike said, then glanced over at the radio, "are you aware of what's happened?"

"I had music on. I fell asleep. What...?" And then the first of it—the first she'd heard of the terrifying and fateful words: *Pearl Harbor...Japanese...bombs*. She threw her hands to her mouth and began to go limp before Mike led her to the chair. Etta brought a glass of water from the kitchen. "Lolly, we don't know anything yet. Really. It...it might be okay. Maybe Dan's area was not involved at all."

But Dan's area was involved. They were all involved, by the thousands—over 2,300 dead; over 1,200 wounded.

She went to stay with Mike and Etta, rarely coming out of the bedroom, refusing to eat or to see anyone except them, her eyes red-rimmed from tears and the cold that had gripped her, likely from her rundown state. Then the officers from the Navy Department arrived with the telegram and made it official: Petty Officer 3rd Class, Daniel Brian Ferry, was killed at Pearl Harbor on Sunday, the seventh day of December, 1941. He'd been topside aboard one of the first destroyers that were hit. He died instantly.

Doctor Scala was worried. "I'm recommending that we admit her. She's going to need an intravenous line or suffer serious consequences for herself and the baby."

For the sake of Dan's child, Lolly agreed. Mike, putting aside his own grief at the loss of his brother, intended to drive her, but Doctor Scala insisted on sending an ambulance so the medics could attend to her on the way. It was en route to the hospital that Lolly suffered a massive stroke. The birth had to be induced, and that very January night in 1942, Margaret Ferry came into the world. It was the name that Lolly had suggested and Dan had loved.

By March, Lolly was still unable to walk on her own and her speech was halting at best. Her face was contorted and the use of her arms and hands diminished—she had difficulty feeding herself. In fact, there was no ordinary task that she could accomplish on her own. Perhaps worst of all, she could not hold her baby, could not feed her baby, could not clearly speak her baby's name. At times, the new mother cried for hours. Mike and Etta had to take Margaret home with them, but with special permission, brought the baby back to the hospital several times a week to be placed carefully and with Etta's close watchfulness in her mother's lap.

In April, it was decided that since the hospital could not deliver the long-term care and rehabilitation that Lolly required, she would have to be sent to a special facility. A co-worker at the Syracuse newspaper where Mike worked recommended St. Clement, where her own sister had spent several years before moving to a place with more independent living capability.

Lolly was depressed, realizing the distance this would place between her and her daughter, but by now, she also realized that the typical mother-daughter interaction was out of the question.

By full agreement—scrupulous about being certain of Lolly's intention and what she was able to arduously communicate—Mike and Etta took custody of Margaret. It was Lolly who initiated the tale that the baby's mother had died in childbirth at the news of the father's death. It was Mike who initiated the idea of relocating to a place where people would not know the truth of the situation.

CHAPTER FORTY-FOUR

It took until five in the morning for Lolly to tell her daughter of their sad and remarkable history. Margaret, quite stunned at first, listened intently with a deep sense of inner peace at having finally found the precious treasure that had been lost for such a long, long time. She hardly knew what to say. Lolly asked for Margaret's forgiveness, but to Margaret's thinking there was nothing to forgive. *Look for the good*, Lolly always said, and this was no less a time for doing just that. For Margaret's entire life, Lolly had been that rare someone beyond all others, someone who touched her in ways no one else could. Theirs had always been a bond without logic, sweet and inexplicable. She felt a kind of joy she had never experienced, a sense of wholeness to finally know her real mother. The photograph in the drawer of her nightstand all these years, the one of her mother and father at Lake Skaneateles on their wedding day— the woman with her face half-obscured by the brim of her hat—that was Lolly. However astonishing it all was, Margaret was happy to know that Lolly was the beautiful, special woman her father had loved.

And yet, in the midst of it all, even with this extraordinary blessing, Margaret could not deny—nor could she ever deny— that Aunt Etta and Uncle Mike were her parents and would be so until the day she died.

CHAPTER FORTY-FIVE

Massapequa Park—January 1955

"The deep blue one with the rhinestones, Aunt Etta. Oh, my gosh, it's so beautiful." Margaret leaned forward in the pink cushioned chair outside the dressing room at Sylvette's Fashions, her face cupped in her hands. "Wait until Uncle Mike sees it."

Etta held the two gowns on their hangers out in front of her. "You're sure? Prettier than the pink?"

"Prettier than all of them you tried on."

Etta looked at the sales woman, who smiled and nodded her agreement.

"Will you be able to have the alterations done by next week?" Etta asked.

"Definitely," the woman said, as Etta returned to the dressing room. "All it really needs is the hem and a small tuck at the shoulders."

A short time later, Margaret and Etta buttoned their woolen coats, pulled on their gloves and headed along Clark Boulevard, with a quick glance up at the four-sided town clock that stood across the street.

"Well, that didn't take us very long," Etta said. "It's just a little after one. Uncle Mike will be happy. I hope he likes the dress."

"Oh, Aunt Etta, he'll love it. It's even prettier than the one you wore to Lolly's wedding."

"Speaking of Lolly, she telephoned last night after you were in bed, all excited. She and Andrew will be able to come the weekend of Uncle Mike's party. They can't go to the awards dinner, but they'll be with us for the party afterwards."

"I'm so glad," Margaret said. "I miss her. Feels like forever since the last time she was here. And I really like Andrew. Don't you feel so happy for them?"

"More than you know, Mar." For a long moment, there was only silence.

"I think I understand, Aunt Etta."

Etta gave her a knowing smile, her cheeks red as apples as they walked arm-in-arm, tucked in close against the frigid January air. "Yes, I believe you do, Mar."

They held their collars tight as they went, once again realizing that it was just as cold here on Long Island as in their beloved Brooklyn. Still, so many things were different—lawns and woods, fields and parks (though none as large and majestic as Prospect Park with its zoo and its high rolling hills), clusters of quaint shops instead of blocks and blocks of stores, far less traffic and, in many places, far fewer sidewalks, all of which had its own charm. Instead of numbered streets and avenues, many of the streets here had the names of states and cities— Chicago, Cleveland, Connecticut, and so on. There were no subways, but it was not a very long walk to the railroad station in town. Margaret would have enjoyed meeting Uncle Mike at the train the way she had in Brooklyn, but he now drove to work. Many new things and many new ways.

It was partly the newness of it all that had helped her adjust. She was fascinated by the different places that were now part of their everyday life: Croon's Lake, Sunrise Highway, Merrick Road. Amityville, where she and Johnny Herring attended school, and where he had taken her to their first school dance. Even though the two of them had to take a school bus, they now had their own bikes and no end to the rural side roads to explore, but they would have to wait again for summer.

Her first summer had been a pleasant surprise. The long evening walks she used to take with Etta and Mike along the avenue outside Greenwood Cemetery or down by Red Hook Park now took place on a few of their newly discovered tree-lined country lanes, where the night air carried a hint of sea breeze off the Atlantic. They now had to drive to the places where they wanted to walk. They had to drive most places—to St. Rose of Lima, the beautiful new Catholic Church on Merrick Road, and to Bohack's grocery store for the week's food shopping.

At the same time, there was comfort in the familiar—once in town, they could walk to DiMonda's Italian Bakery or to Musicaro's (where the pizza was as good as Barsotti's), places that felt like their old neighborhood because so many people had emigrated from Brooklyn. The 5 &10 was not nearly as big as Germaine's but it was a wonderful place with a tank by the front door that held fish and turtles. She had found so many little things to buy there at Christmas. There was even a candy store, Fay's, and next to that a deli. And a Rexall drug store.

"Woo, it's cold," Etta said. "We'll have to be sure that Uncle Mike warms up the car."

It wasn't a bad thing that driving was now a part of their lives—they had decided to make the most of it. Farther out on the Island, they had discovered the potato farms, beet farms and strawberry farms. During the summer, Uncle Mike drove with the windows rolled down on those balmy evenings when the humid air was cool and refreshing against their faces. They agreed that the musky scent of the cabbage fields mixed with the occasional skunk was not so unpleasant after all. When the wind blew in the right direction, they might even pick up a whiff of the petting zoo or the duck farm past Amagansett on the way to Montauk. But now it was winter again.

Their second.

"Will Uncle Mike let me wear a little tangerine lipstick soon?"

"Now you know he's not going to do that, Mar. I don't like the idea either. Not until you're fifteen. You're still too young. It should be enough for now that you're allowed to wear pale pink nail polish…and shave your legs. You've been doing that since you turned twelve."

"But I'm thirteen now, Aunt Etta. I'm a teenager."

"Your uncle and I think you're pretty enough just the way you are. Besides, you don't want to grow up too fast. Right?"

"I guess," she said, half-heartedly. "I wish I was going to the Waldorf-Astoria with you and Uncle Mike. What do you think it'll be like?"

"Oh, it's a beautiful place. Quite elegant. Uncle Mike and I went there for our wedding anniversary many years ago. They serve things like capon and Cornish hens and baked Alaska."

"If it's as cold as it is now, you could probably bring some home—the ice cream wouldn't even melt." They laughed.

"It'll be nice by the fireplace tonight," Etta said.

A fireplace. Something else that was new to them, along with an upstairs and downstairs, a front lawn and a backyard, an attic and a basement, just as they had once talked about. They had planted an apple tree with the help of Mr. Santo, who owned the local nursery. "The secret," Mr. Santo had said, "is to plant a one-dollar tree in a ten-dollar hole." They had also put in a bed of hydrangeas and rhododendron, all of it gone to wood for the season, but they expected the tulips to begin to show themselves with the first robin. There was something almost sacred about the whole process. Margaret liked the smell and feel of the rich Long Island loam pressing through her fingers, along with the idea of planting something in the earth that could be there for the rest of their lives.

When they reached the coffee shop, they had to pull hard

on the heavy glass door to open it against the wind, laughing and out of breath as they entered. The aromas of fresh-brewed coffee, sweet rolls and cinnamon pastry greeted them along with pleasant chatter. The place was busy but they immediately spotted Mike at a table in the corner, his heavy jacket on the chair beside him, and on his knee, little Danny popping up and down with delight.

"Well, it's about time, isn't it, Danny?" Mike said good-naturedly. "Tell them. Tell Mommy and Sis how we even had a nap."

"Hi, you cutie pie," Etta said, leaning down to kiss his round pink cheek.

"And where is our other little angel?" Mar peeked into the stroller. "Brian's still asleep?"

"You should have been here twenty minutes ago," Mike said, "when everybody in the place was fussing over the two of them. You'd think they'd never seen twins before. It just wore Brian out." He reached for the little white bakery bag next to him on the table and looked up at Margaret. "Guess," he said. "And it was the very last one, by the way."

"The chocolate cinnamon twist?" She peeled off her gloves and opened the bag before she even settled into a chair. "Thank you, Uncle Mike. I think dress shopping makes me hungry for sweets."

He handed Danny to Etta while he went to the counter to get a cup of hot coffee for her and hot chocolate for Margaret, along with some pastries to take home. The baby cooed, happy to see them both, but soon grew sleepy-eyed as Etta rocked him, and before long was fast asleep beside his brother in the stroller.

"So, tell me, how did you two make out?"

"Uncle Mike, you will not believe the gown that Aunt Etta got. She will definitely be the most beautiful woman there."

Mike brushed his finger against Etta's chin. "Your aunt

could show up in a gunny sack and still be the most beautiful woman there." He gave her a sheepish grin. "But exactly how much has all this beauty cost me?"

"We did very well," Etta said. "But I had every intention of going overboard. How often does a husband win the Pulitzer Prize?"

A young woman who had been seated at the next table came over to them. "Excuse me," she said, looking at Mike, then to the others. "I'm sorry to bother you, but I couldn't help overhearing what you said. Are you, by chance, the man who wrote that series about the candy store people?"

Mike hesitated, surprised. "Yes, I am," he said, a bit self-consciously.

"I thought I recognized you from the paper," the woman said. "What an honor to meet you, sir." She appeared to be about thirty with a friendly, though slightly shy way about her. "Your story touched my whole family. My husband is a fireman over in Farmingdale. My parents owned a small grocery store there even before I was born, so we could only imagine what it was like for those people to lose their business that way and then...well...finding out about everything. It was amazing."

"Thank you very much," Mike said.

The woman looked at Etta and Margaret, who greeted her warmly. "I've always wanted to be a writer myself. I studied journalism for a while before our first child came along, but to tell the truth, I don't have anything really interesting to write about."

"Oh, I'm sure you do," Mike said. "Sometimes new writers think they have to find something sensational. Don't overlook the ordinary. There are stories everywhere."

"I will definitely keep that in mind," she said. "Thank you so much. And have a nice day." She returned to her table and pulled on her coat, preparing to leave.

Etta gave Mike a look, and he quickly noticed that Margaret's hair was lifting ever so slightly. They said nothing.

"Excuse me," Margaret called to the woman, her hair settling down.

The woman turned.

"Remember the time your mother rescued your neighbor's bulldog from that man who tried to steal him?" Margaret said. "That would make an interesting story."

The woman moved closer to their table, her brow furrowed. "How on earth could you possibly know about that?"

Etta looked at Mike over her coffee cup, and their eyes met in amiable resignation. Having gotten nothing more than a shrug from Margaret, the woman left, clearly bewildered but energized.

A few minutes later, as they put on their coats and bundled up the babies in the stroller, Mike picked up the small white bakery bag off the table and handed it to Margaret. "Don't forget the pastries," he said, and left ahead of them to warm up the car.

THE FLOWER COTTAGE

A PREVIEW

CHAPTER ONE

Long Island—New York, 1955

Abigail Sweet watched the cortege make its way to the exit of St. Charles like a long curl of ribbon drifting amid the flanks of sycamore. The last of the mourners but hardly the last of the mourning, she thought. She turned her glance back to the gravesite that she and Ben had picked out only a few years earlier. Now, here they were; one of them anyway, and much too soon. "Oh, Ben. Ben," she longed to cry out, but remained silent. Everything was different and she was too outside of herself to make sense of it.

She could still hear the last desperate words they had whispered to each other over and over like a mantra, "Breathe. Breathe with me, breathe," one speaking, one repeating until words and breath were exhausted. How quickly a life can be over. How easily a marriage of twenty years can come to an end. The doctors were kind; she knew they had done all that was possible.

Funny, the things you remember from the darkest moments—a water stain on a ceiling tile, the clack of someone's hurried footsteps in a hospital corridor, the near silent brush of the last rose tossed onto a casket. Amid the worst of it, the light-hearted chatter had gone on at the nurses' station outside the ICU as did the sober muttering among police and staff dealing with a wounded robbery suspect. Ordinary things don't stop just because an ordinary life is about to.

The thoughts that tumble recklessly through the mind, regrettable things, disappointments, unfulfilled dreams and plans. Maybe it's best that way to balance the memories of love and joy and beauty that would make the devastation impossible to withstand. "Oh, Ben, my darling, forgive me for the times I surely must have made you crazy, let you down. You never said so, but I must have. 'What now?' you would ask, but only lightheartedly, never in anger. You were endlessly patient with my whimsy, and so supportive, you precious man. Precious husband. My love. Look how the tables have turned, dearest— I'm the one asking 'what now?'"

Abigail Sweet wondered if it were possible to make amends, to finally do what Ben had always hoped for her. "Can't I still be the girl who made you feel pleased and proud?" She watched the afternoon shadows peel away the sunlight from the freshly mounded grave and pondered the far from ordinary existence that she was now so clearly destined to embrace.

CHAPTER TWO

One Year Later

"I don't understand. How can you do this?" Kate got to her feet, astonished, waiting for an answer from the man who until a moment ago was her boss.

Professor Edward Darian leaned forward, hands clasped in front of him on his desk. "I'm so sorry, Kate. This is all about budgets and funding. There were expenditures we had to curb, and although it often doesn't seem to make sense, you know it's true that faculty is the first place they look for cuts."

"Well, doesn't my performance count for anything? If I may humbly say, I think the awards I've received testify to my excellence as an instructor. So do the dozen grants I've been awarded on behalf of the school." She felt as though she'd been run through with a long dull knife, leaving a hole from which her energy, heart and spirit were flooding out like a punctured water balloon. She was, after all, suddenly and inexplicably out of work. Out of work. Sole provider with a mortgage and an ugly black smudge on her previously pristine curriculum vitae. "Edward, I'm a year away from tenure."

"I know, Kate, but my hands are tied."

"Did you even speak up for me, for all my hard work, my loyalty?"

"The Board was...is...very sorry about it, but adamant."

"How did the others take it...," she asked flatly, "being

terminated, I mean?"

"Others?" Darian moved in his chair. "Oh…well, you know…no one is ever happy when something like this occurs."

"Was Lonny…Professor Kagan…as shocked as I am?"

"Professor Kagan?" He had lost eye contact, rolling a rubber band back and forth around his thumb and index finger. "Well…," he stammered again.

Kate eyed him with suspicion. "Wasn't Lonny Kagan let go?"

Darian rose and went to the window, making a sweeping gesture to the vista of rolling hills and stately turn-of-the-century buildings. "The cuts were, you know, across the entire campus. Professor Kagan wasn't in the mix at this time."

"Not in the mix?" Kate leaned forward, her fists resting on Darian's desk. "Assistant Professor Kagan, who's been here a little over a year and hasn't gotten through a semester without a crisis? Assistant Professor Kagan who would have already been thrown out on his ear from any other institution? That Professor Kagan?"

Darian lifted his shoulders in a slow begging shrug, and said nothing.

"Who then?"

He hesitated, cleared his throat and almost inaudibly said, "Grounds. Building Maintenance. That Korean woman in the cafeteria."

"Are you kidding me?" She pressed her lips tight together, and nodded. She felt her nostrils flair. "I see."

"I'm not sure you do, Kate. You are one of the finest professors Milston College has ever had. Awards, yes. Grants, yes. The highest student satisfaction rating. But the fact is that…well, for one thing you've been slow to publish, and…"

"Slow to publish? Tell me you're not serious. Who was it who did all the research and crafted that article for you on Max Perkins and Marjorie Kinnan Rawlings? And the one on

Hemingway and Scott Fitzgerald? For which, if I may be so bold as to mention, you received endless accolades and the Fittingham award. How can you do this to me, Edward?"

"You must know, Kate, how endlessly appreciative I am of all your efforts here. Truly. But all that aside...

"Oh, yes, let's definitely push all of my efforts aside."

"What I'm trying to say is...and I know this is hard to hear...but the fact is you're a bit low key."

She folded her arms and didn't respond.

"Lonny is out there. He's managed to get himself on the program at conferences. He makes a speech here and there. He has a local media presence, such as it is. But he's on the right track. It's what the school needs."

"Oh, and don't forget the uncle on the board."

"Kate, you know how it is. Everywhere Lonny goes he's got Milston's name on his lips, telling Milston's story. He's good for enrollment and donor money."

She turned toward the door, then stopped. "*Hmm*, maybe I should just go out the window along with our principles."

"Kate. Wait." Darian came around the desk. "Wait. Please know how much we all admire the work you've done here over these last four years. How well liked and respected you are. This was, to say the least, a very difficult decision." He picked up a white business envelope from his desk. "There's two months severance, and one heck of a letter of recommendation. Why not treat this as if you were taking the summer off to scout a new position for the fall semester?"

He said it so offhandedly that, at first, she could only stare, drilling him with her eyes. Shiny black hair, threaded with silver, prominent brow—a decent looking man. Odd that the word *decent* would come to mind. How different people can look when you hone in on the survival tactics that ultimately belie their integrity. They'd always had a respectably close and comfortable relationship that included many a long talk about life and learning over lunch at the local diner. Who is this man, after all, that she had shared her French fries with? "Try this chicken salad; it's the best," he might say. "Are you going to eat that pickle?" How easy it is to be cozy or lofty when there's nothing at stake. On occasion and off the record, they had discussed Lonny. He was a risk. She could have gone on about him now—young, incapable Lonny, whose chief asset was his charm in getting someone to bail him out of his crises and save his neck. Lonny, who twice entered the women's dorm at night and on more than one occasion was told by the Korean woman in her typically diplomatic manner to please not come into the cafeteria after hours on his way to a party to remove snacks and beverages. The woman had been kind enough not to report him, but she was given a warning when Lonny had a note put in her file suggesting that she was pilfering food. Even school officials knew it to be a lie. Interesting that she, too, had just been terminated. They knew what Lonny Kagan was. No need for Kate to badmouth him. Nor did she wish to. It wasn't her way. He was Milston's problem and they would likely suffer soon enough for it. She took the envelope without uttering a word and left.

———◆———

Stunned as she was, she drove ten blocks past her turnoff and finally pulled into the farthest parking spot at the 7-Eleven to cry as she hadn't cried in years. There had been many days of tears when her grandfather passed away six weeks earlier. That wonderful man who had helped raise her. His passing at 89 had not been a devastating shock, but a sad and lonely loss, a prayerful end of a special life that had spiraled into erratic behavior and life-threatening falls at the senior care facility. Today was different. No solid ground underfoot, as if her whole life were swirling around the drain. *How on earth could this have happened?*

CPSIA information can be obtained
at www.ICGtesting.com
Printed in the USA
FFOW03n1139031117
41875FF